ANXIETY ATTACK

A Kate Huntington Mystery

Kassandra Lamb

ANXIETY ATTACK
A Kate Huntington Mystery

Published in the United States of America by *misterio press*,
a Florida limited liability company
www.misteriopress.com

~~~~~~~~~~~~

Edited by Marcy Kennedy

Cover and interior design by Melinda VanLone,
Book Cover Corner

ISBN 13: 978-0-9974674-3-7 (misterio press LLC)

ISBN 10: 0-9974674-3-6

PROLOGUE

He plugged in the password he wasn't supposed to have. A bead of sweat dripped from his nose onto the keyboard. His heart rate, already racing, kicked up another notch.

Not worth it. Never again!

He willed his hand steady on the mouse as he copied another file.

Just get it done.

Click, *copy file*, click, *paste,* click.

This was taking too long. The night guard would be making his rounds soon. Would the bluish glow from the monitor show around the door?

Hurry!

Click, *copy file*, click, *paste,* click.

A subtle shift in the air.

No. It's your imagination.

Click, *copy file*, click, *paste,* click.

The slight whoosh of a door opening.

He froze. That *hadn't* been his imagination. He whirled around.

No one was there.

But the door he'd propped slightly ajar when he'd entered the room was now halfway open—the automatic closure mechanism slowly pulling it shut behind whoever had just entered the lab.

He struggled to hear past the pounding of blood in his ears.

Hitting the power button on the computer, he yanked out the flash drive. Then fumbled it. A metallic sound as it hit the workbench.

He should try to find it, but someone was in the room with him, hiding in the darkness. Panic overpowered all else.

He bolted for the door, grabbing its edge as it was about to close.

CHAPTER ONE

The police radio chattered with unintelligible codes. Kate shoved a dark curl out of her eyes and stifled a yawn.

From the driver's seat, Officer Peters glanced her way. A corner of his mouth quirked. "Don't know who said it first, but it's true. Police work is mostly boredom, punctuated by moments of sheer terror."

She flashed him a smile. "Sorry. It's been a long day."

What have I gotten myself into?

"All available units," the radio squawked. "Shots fired. Armstrong building."

The officer sat up straighter.

Kate couldn't make out the address the dispatcher rattled off. All she caught was "…third floor."

Armstrong building. Why does that sound familiar?

"Unit 12 responding." Officer Peters hit the siren and lights. The cruiser surged forward.

Kate's heart went into overdrive.

At nine o'clock on a cold and rainy Sunday evening, the business district of Towson was relatively quiet. The few cars on the roads quickly got out of the way. Kate suspected it wasn't nearly as easy to get to a crime scene during a weekday, when these streets would be teeming with cars and pedestrians and delivery trucks.

They careened around a corner onto York Road. Her heart rate kicked up another notch. "Remember to call me once you have the scene secured," she yelled over the wail of the siren.

Officer Peters nodded slightly without taking his eyes off the slick road in front of him.

He pulled into the parking lot of a high-rise office building. Braking to an abrupt stop, he killed the siren and unhooked his seatbelt. The actions seemed to happen all at once.

Impressive, Kate thought.

"Stay in the car until I call," he said.

The order was unnecessary. She had no desire to end up in the middle of a gunfight.

He was out of the car and running toward the building, one hand on his holster, the other keying the radio on his shoulder. No doubt checking on backup.

She transferred her phone to her left hand and made a note on the pad in her lap. Going into an ongoing crime scene by oneself would definitely heighten the stress level of the officer.

She'd no sooner finished the note than two more cruisers screamed into the lot. Their sirens ceased with a dying screech, and two officers—one female, one male—bolted from their cars.

Peters had reached the front of the building. He grabbed the handle of one of the big glass doors and pulled it open.

That was odd. Wouldn't an office building be locked up tight at night?

The other officers were hard on Peters's heels as he bolted into the building.

Kate scratched out the note she'd just made.

Temporarily, her moments of sheer terror were over. She sat in the cruiser, its motor humming, blue lights reflecting off the wet pavement in front of it.

Minutes ticked by.

Mist swirled around the car, adding to the eeriness of the night. The yellowish glow of the streetlights surrounding the parking lot created mini rainbows.

Kate studied her reflection in the side window—her pale face, the dark mop of curls, sprinkled with gray and frizzy from the dampness, crow's feet around blue eyes dull with fatigue. What she would give for a good night's sleep.

She willed her face muscles to relax, smoothing out the worry lines on her forehead.

Butterflies danced in her stomach. What was going on in there? Her phone chirped in her hand. She jumped.

"Hello?"

"We have a gunshot victim up here," Officer Peters said. "Ambulance is on the way. Come inside and hold the elevator on the ground floor for the EMTs."

"Sure, okay." She fumbled with her seatbelt release, got out of the car.

Another siren in the distance, a different pattern to the sound. The ambulance.

She jogged to the building and entered the lobby. Stopping for a few seconds for her eyes to adjust to the darkness, she willed her heart to slow its pounding. It didn't listen.

She located the elevator in the shadows of the lobby and punched the up button. The wail of the ambulance's siren was growing louder.

A ding and the doors opened, the light inside the elevator blinding. She stepped in and squinted to find the open-door button.

Her finger was numb from keeping it on the button by the time the EMTs were maneuvering their gurney and equipment into the cramped space.

"Okay," one of them said.

A frisson of panic ran through her. *Which floor?*

The older of the EMTs reached past her and punched the button for three.

"Sorry," she mumbled. "I couldn't remember."

"Ride along?" the EMT asked.

"Yeah." She considered explaining further but suddenly felt exhausted.

The elevator dinged and the doors slid open. The EMTs hustled across a carpeted space to double glass doors.

A security guard held one of the doors open for them. Kate

grabbed the other one and shoved.

The EMTs hurried past her. The guard gestured toward a lighted hallway. It was one of many, like spokes in a semi-circle off the oversized reception area, but it was the only one that was well lit. The others had dim lighting along the floor on each side.

Kate started to follow the EMTs, her heart in her throat. She'd seen the aftermath of crime before, but she wasn't sure she was up for this tonight.

The guard held up a hand.

She stopped. "I'm with Officer Peters, doing a ride-along for the governor's task force on PTSD in police officers."

"Sorry, ma'am. This is a restricted area."

"But I need to observe the officers in action. I won't do anything to contaminate the crime scene."

"That's not my worry, ma'am. We have top secret projects here."

Movement in the corner of her eye. She turned her head.

A stocky man pushed through the glass doors. He wore a brown business suit and carried himself like a police officer. Stopping in front of the guard, he pulled back his suit jacket to expose a detective's shield attached to his belt. He was only a few inches taller than Kate's five-seven but his broad stance conveyed authority.

"Detective Russell." He looked from the guard to Kate and back again. "What's going on?" He glanced past her to the lit hallway.

The guard opened his mouth but Kate jumped in. "I'm with Officer Peters. I need to be at the crime scene."

Detective Russell raised an eyebrow. "You a witness?"

"Yes." It wasn't a total lie. She'd witnessed the call.

He took her by the elbow. "Come with me."

The guard seemed to hesitate, then stepped aside.

They walked briskly down the hallway. Rounding a corner, they entered a long room. Its walls were flanked by metal work-benches, with computer monitors scattered along them, all dark.

Officer Peters stood at parade rest just inside the room, holding a small book.

The detective let go of her arm, held out his hand to indicate she should stay back and again flipped his jacket aside to show his badge. "Russell."

Peters wrote in the book, checked his watch. Wrote the time. "What's the deal?" Russell said.

Kate took a step to the right to see past the detective and Officer Peters, who was giving his report in a low drone.

She froze, her heart skittering around in her chest.

She blinked and stared in horror at the man lying on the floor, the EMTs working with quick, efficient movements to stop the blood oozing from his side. A scream erupted from her throat.

Officer Peters pivoted toward her. "Mrs. Huntington, please. Go out in the hall."

His words barely registered in her brain, which was still trying to process what her eyes were seeing. "My God, Manny!" Her hands flew to her mouth to stifle another scream.

"You know him?" Detective Russell said.

She nodded, willing herself not to faint. "Y-yes," she stuttered. "He's M-manny. Manuel Ortiz. He works for my husband."

~~~~~~~~~~

A sharp January wind rattled Kate's office window.

Her client jerked in his chair.

Kate didn't react. She was used to this man's hypersensitivity to loud noises.

Hal Murdock ducked his head. Dark hair, slightly too long, flopped down over his forehead. It reminded Kate of her husband's unruly hair, only Skip's was lighter, a medium brown.

She gritted her teeth behind neutral lips. She was having trouble focusing. The events of the previous evening were more than distracting. And she hadn't slept well when she'd finally gotten home.

I'm a great one to be on the governor's PTSD task force. She couldn't even control her own traumatic stress responses.

She tried again to zero in on the client's words.

"I'm sorry." He pushed the hair back with a slender hand that shook slightly. "I lost my nerve."

A lump grew in her throat. He now had her full attention. She felt so bad for this young man who struggled so with the simplest of human interactions.

"I couldn't do it, Kate." A pink tinge colored Hal's cheeks, made pale by too much time spent inside, in front of a computer monitor.

"Okay," she said. "Let's see if we can break it down a little further. Instead of introducing yourself, just ask her to recommend a dish on the carryout menu."

Hal had been trying for weeks to date a young woman he admired, who frequented the same Chinese carryout place he often stopped at on his way home from work. He was a good-looking man, slender and tall, with a boyish face, but he suffered from avoidant personality disorder, the most extreme version of social anxiety there was. The very thought of asking a woman out sent him into a full-blown anxiety attack.

"Maybe. Yeah, I can try to do that." His words implied more confidence than his tone.

He looked up at her. "I'm thirty-two." His voice was desperate. "What if I never…" He ducked his head again and stared off to his left, at the subtle pattern in her office carpet.

She knew what he meant. He desperately wanted to marry, to create the happy family he'd never had. It was a common goal for survivors of highly dysfunctional families.

And his was definitely that. His father had beaten his mother every Friday, after he had spent most of his paycheck at the local bar on his way home. His mother had stayed "for the sake of her kids," but Kate couldn't help wondering how much the woman's own insecurities had to do with it.

Kate couldn't fault her for staying. She knew how abusers manipulated their victims, tearing them down, convincing them that they couldn't survive on their own, doling out minimal housekeeping money so there was never enough to finance an escape.

Hal's older brother had survived their childhood better. He was married with kids and seemed to be okay. The key word was *seemed.*

But Hal had been born with a different genetic makeup. His predisposition toward shyness had combined with the abusive environment to produce an incredible level of social anxiety. It was amazing that he managed to work. Some people with avoidant personality disorder became shut-ins, living on disability payments.

Kate spent the last few minutes of the session helping Hal devise a game plan for his seemingly spontaneous conversation with the woman at the Chinese carryout place.

She worried what would happen if this woman suddenly stopped craving Chinese food. No doubt Hal would assume it was because she didn't like him, and it would set him back weeks, maybe months, in his therapy.

Her shoulders drooped with the weight of concern. She sighed. *I'm beyond burned out.*

~~~~~~~~

Skip Canfield stood in the middle of the hospital corridor, his jaw clenched. He ought to move somewhere out of the flow of traffic. Visitors eyed him—tall, broad-shouldered, tense—and edged nervously past him. Nurses gave him sympathetic glances.

He was trying to wrap his mind around the fact that one of his best operatives, a man who had worked for him for years, was still unconscious, in critical condition.

Skip swallowed down the bile in the back of his throat.

Manny didn't have any family. His life was his job—that and the AA program that only he, Rose and Kate knew about.

Skip rubbed his aching chest. Should he call Kate?

She would most likely be with a client, but he knew she was worried sick about Manny. He opted to text her.

At hospital. Manny still unconscious. Serious condition. How u doing?

No response. She must be in session.

Sitting down on a chair in the ICU waiting room, he tried to gather his thoughts. He needed to decide what to do about this case.

He'd been hesitant about taking it in the first place. But he'd been going over the books that day, and things hadn't been looking all that great.

He and his partner, Rose, had an agreement. She handled the personnel—the hiring and firing and scheduling of their investigators—and he did the bookkeeping and recruiting of new clients. He particularly hated scheduling, and up until recently, he'd felt he had the easier end of the deal.

Until six months ago, when the numbers hadn't quite balanced. He'd pulled the calculator closer and punched in the figures again. Same result, a net deficit of ten dollars and ninety cents.

In the total scheme of things, it wasn't a big deal. *Eleven dollars, whoop-di-do.* They had plenty of cash reserves.

But it had bothered the hell out of him. They'd had a surplus each month for the last several years–*adding* to those cash reserves, not depleting them.

He'd been leaning away from taking the industrial espionage case until then. It wasn't really their forte. But he'd let money worries override his instincts.

Granted the monthly billings for that case had kept them above the red ink line for the last six months. But now they were hip deep in a swamp full of alligators, and Manny was fighting for his life.

~~~~~~~~~

At the end of the hour, Kate shook Hal's hand and gave it a squeeze.

"Wait." He pulled his hand free and reached into his pocket. "I almost forgot. I got this for you." The small plastic box resting on his palm looked like a cell phone, only half the size. "It's called a parental tracker."

He stepped over beside her. "Look, you punch in a kid's cell phone number here." He hit an icon in an upper corner of the screen and a box and tiny keyboard appeared. He poked at a few keys and numbers appeared in the box. Then he erased them.

"It will give you the phone numbers of calls to and from that phone," his voice rose, excited, "and it hooks into the phone's GPS and tells you where the kid is."

Her first thought was this contraption would be a stalker's dream come true. *When did I start seeing evil everywhere?*

He tried to hand it to her.

When she didn't take it, he looked confused. "You said you'd gotten your daughter her first cell phone, but were worried she might misuse it."

It had been casual chitchat the previous week, to put Hal at ease as she'd ushered him into her office at the beginning of a session. Something to say in response to his mumbled, "How are you?"

She'd been trying to model normal social interactions, and now it had backfired. Ethically, she couldn't accept the gift.

"Not worried she'd misuse it really," she said, stalling for time, "but that she'd get on the Internet with it, and maybe some predator would contact her."

He made eye contact, a rare occurrence. "Kate, it wasn't expensive. I got it online from this website for techie gadgets." He thrust it toward her. "It'll give you some peace of mind."

Rather impressed by his astute assessment of why she was hesitating, she opted to take the gizmo rather than make a fuss, which might add to Hal's sense of social awkwardness. But she had no intentions of using it to spy on Edie.

She thanked him and reminded him of his appointment time for the following week.

Once Hal was out of her office, she slumped into her desk chair, free to ruminate again about Manny.

Her cell phone pinged when she turned it on. The text message from Skip was not particularly reassuring, but still that small connection to her husband helped to relax her tense body.

Dear God, please let Manny be okay.

She was gathering her things to head out for lunch, when noises that were not part of the normal hubbub of downtown Towson penetrated her awareness. She moved to the window to see what all the car door slamming and raised voices were about.

Her eyes scanned the steel and glass high-rises on the horizon. Then her gaze dropped to the older, two and three-story storefronts on York Road.

"Get in the car." A loud voice, directly below her window.

She leaned forward and looked straight down. And sucked in her breath at the scene on the sidewalk in front of her building.

A handcuffed Hal Murdock was struggling with two men in business suits.

CHAPTER TWO

Kate bolted from her office and down the fire stairs. Out on the sidewalk, two men were trying to shove Hal into the back of their car.

A strobing blue light on top of its dash identified the two men as plainclothes detectives.

Hal was passively resisting, literally digging in his heels, refusing to lift a foot to climb in. "You've got the wrong guy. I never heard of this dude."

"Yeah, that's what they all say," the detective who had him by the arms responded. The man had his back to Kate but he looked vaguely familiar.

The other man tried to block her approach. She veered around him.

"What's going on here?" It came out sharper than she'd intended, the tone she used with the kids when they were acting up.

Hal's cheeks turned beet red.

Kate realized too late that her tone might be a trigger for him. "Why are you arresting this man?" she asked, as much to clarify for Hal who she was mad at as to get the information.

"Police business, ma'am," Detective Number 2 said, holding an arm out between her and the car. "Please move back."

"They think I killed some guy," Hal said.

Kate's heart stuttered in her chest.

"*Attempted* murder," Detective Number 1 said. "He's still hanging on." He forcibly shifted Hal sideways, put a hand on his head and shoved him down and into the backseat.

"You have a lawyer?" Kate called over the man's shoulder to Hal.

Detective Number 2 stepped right in front of her face and puffed out his chest. "Back up, lady."

The maneuver would have been more intimidating if Kate hadn't seen it used before on more than one occasion, by Skip's people when they were providing bodyguard services.

"I know a good one." She raised her voice to be heard past the wall of the policeman's chest. "I'll see if he's available."

Hal mumbled a response that she couldn't make out.

The first detective, having finally managed to get all of Hal into the unmarked car, turned to his partner. His eyes flicked Kate's way and he did a double-take.

With a jolt, she recognized him. Detective Russell from last night. She stepped back, but he grabbed her arm.

"Wait just a minute, lady. You're that shrink that was doing the ride-along last night."

Confusion and tension made Kate's stomach roll. Why was this man suddenly everywhere she turned?

A glimmer of awareness blossomed in her brain. "Dear God, you think Hal shot Manny?"

"I don't know the dude," Hal yelled through the closed window of the car. "Never heard of him!"

The detective opened the passenger-side front door and stuck his head partway in. "How about Luis Gomez?"

Hal's face paled and his chin dropped.

"That's what I thought," the detective said with a small smirk.

It was a good thing Kate's clenched stomach had no interest in food right now, because it was looking like most of her lunch hour would be taken up by this husky man sitting in her client chair.

"Again," Detective Russell said, "how do you know Harold Murdock?"

Kate sighed. "Look around you. What kind of office is this?"

He stared at her without blinking. Those brown eyes had been softer, almost kindly as he'd taken her statement the night before. Now they were hard as marbles. His hair was clipped short, dark with a smattering of gray.

"Detective, I cannot *legally* even admit that I know Mr. Murdock, but of course that ship has already sailed. I can tell you nothing about him nor my relationship with him."

"Okay, I get it that he's a client, but there's got to be some explanation for the fact that you also know the victim, *and* just happened to be riding along with the cop who was first on the scene."

"I told you. My husband runs a private investigations agency. Manny works for him. They were investigating something at Strategic Electronics."

"But how's that connect to you and Mr. Murdock?"

Kate stifled another sigh. "Sometimes things *are* a coincidence."

Russell snorted.

"I know, cops are allergic to coincidences," she said.

Russell squinted at her. "Where'd you hear that line?"

Kate aborted an eye roll a third of the way into it. "Dolph Randolph works for my husband." Dolph was a retired Baltimore County homicide detective, and a family friend. The "allergic to coincidences" line had been coined by him.

The detective's eyes were still slits. "Who don't you know in this town, lady?"

"Lots of people, but I've worked and lived here for twenty-three years." Heat was growing in her chest and face.

Great time for a hot flash.

This cop would probably think she was pissed, which she was, but not to the point of turning red.

He ran her through the entire battery of questions he'd asked the night before. She tried not to appear as weary as she was while she answered them.

Then he said, "Did you know Murdock worked for Strategic Electronics?"

"No, I knew he worked for an electronics company, and they did a lot of contract work for the government. That's all he'd ever said about it."

"Somebody's been selling the details of one of Strategic's top secret projects to their competitor. That's what your husband's been investigating."

Kate wondered why he was volunteering this information. Cops were usually pretty tight-lipped. Then again, maybe he assumed she was already aware of the details of Skip's case.

"I knew my husband was working on an industrial espionage case, and he mentioned something about the Armstrong building a couple of times."

"What else did he mention about the case?"

"Not much. We're both bound by confidentiality constraints in our jobs."

"So what the devil do you talk about over dinner?"

"Our kids, the rest of our lives." Her tone was getting a bit sharp. She reined in her temper and reached for a tissue from the box on her desk. He watched her intently as she patted beads of sweat from her forehead and upper lip.

"What aren't you telling me, Mrs. Huntington?"

"Honestly, Detective, I don't know a thing that would help with your investigation."

"Humph, you seem awful nervous for an honest, law-abiding citizen."

Okay, that does it.

She stood up behind her desk. "What I am, sir, is a middle-aged woman having a hot flash who happens to be mildly annoyed that you've used up her lunch hour."

She looked at her watch, more for effect. She'd already checked the time on the wall clock across her office. "I have exactly five minutes left to wolf down a protein bar, so if you will excuse me."

Detective Russell lifted his bulk from his chair. "Thank you for your time, ma'am," he said in a flat voice. He didn't offer a hand to shake, and neither did she.

After he had left, Kate gobbled down the protein bar—it was a little stale from having lived in her desk drawer for weeks—as she held her phone to her ear. Hopefully, Rob Franklin was in and available to help Hal.

"Franklin."

"Thank God." Kate filled him in as quickly as she could, aware that her next client was probably in the waiting room by now.

"Wait," Rob said, "so how do you know this guy, and why are you so sure he's innocent?"

"Can't tell you, and because he couldn't hurt a fly."

"Ah. So he's a client, but how the heck did he end up getting involved in this situation with Manny?"

"As I told the detective, coincidences do happen. Gotta go. Can you take on his case?"

"I'll go talk to him."

She knew that's the most he would promise until *he* believed Hal was innocent. Rob was a general-practitioner-type lawyer, and he only handled criminal cases when he cared about the accused. She also knew he was only agreeing to see Hal because she was the one who was asking.

"Thanks a million," she said. "I owe you one."

Rob chuckled. "We'll see how much you owe me after I talk to the guy." He disconnected.

Kate was already running late but she took an extra second to text Skip.

Any change?

No. Probably be late tonight. Eat wo me.

Worry clogged her throat.

She pulled herself together and opened the door to the waiting room. Time to focus on her next client.

~~~~~~~~

Skip rushed home, barely making it for the kids' story time. He went into Billy's room first. His son had recently offered token protests to being read to, claiming he was too old for that baby stuff. So Skip had switched to super hero comic books.

He stretched out beside his son on the twin bed, feet dangling off the end. They took turns reading each frame.

A similar strategy had worked with Edie eighteen months ago, when she'd begun to resist story time. Although his daughter's tastes in literature did not include super heroes.

And recently, her "story time" had evolved again, into a short father-daughter rehash of her day.

Kate hadn't said much when he'd told her about this shift. But it had to sting some, since her own relationship with Edie had been strained lately.

After this evening's chat with their daughter, he found Kate in their usual spot on the living room sofa. Her face looked pinched and tired. Settling beside her, he laid an arm across the back of the sofa. "Sorry you got stuck with single-parent duty tonight."

She shrugged. "It wasn't a big deal. They kind of take care of themselves these days."

"Billy did all his homework without stalling?"

She chuckled softly. "Well, no."

Skip sniffed the air. "Smells like pizza for dinner."

"There are a few slices left. You want me to heat them up for you?"

"Nah, I grabbed something in the hospital cafeteria when I stopped by to check on Manny again."

"Any change?"

He shook his head. "I did finally get a few answers. His sponsor was there. Apparently Manny had made him his medical surrogate. He's got a head injury as well as the gunshot wound. The doctor has him in one of those intentional comas. I'm blanking on the term for it."

"Medically-induced," Kate said.

"Yeah. Apparently there was some swelling in his brain, but the doctor told his sponsor that he's guardedly optimistic." Skip dropped his hand onto her shoulder and gave it a squeeze.

"Did you hear anything from the police today?" Kate asked.

"No. I–"

"It was in the Baltimore Sun." She pointed to the newspaper, folded over on the coffee table. "Manny's name is given as the shooting victim, but they refer to him as a Strategic employee."

Skip's muscles tensed. *Great, just what we don't need.* "No mention of industrial espionage or that he's a private investigator?"

She shook her head.

He relaxed again. He would read the article tomorrow, but tonight he just plain wasn't up for it. "I'm considering bailing on this case. I shouldn't have taken it in the first place. And now that it looks like the spy has been caught…"

Putting another person undercover, to make sure all the holes were plugged, would be a logistics nightmare. They'd lucked out that Manny had an Associate of Arts degree in electronics. He'd known enough about the subject to do a decent job of faking it. But it had taken six weeks to push his security clearance through the government bureaucracy, and several more weeks for Manny to get into the good graces of the other employees.

And if anyone else was in on the espionage, they'd be highly suspicious of a new person coming on board now. No, it was too risky.

While he had been ruminating about industrial spies and counterspies, Kate had turned in the half circle of his arm to face him. "I need to tell you something that's confidential."

Aw, crap! He hated hearing those words. They almost always preceded some request that got his agency and/or his family into some mess related to one of Kate's clients.

Kate's face was pale as she looked up at him. Her sky blue eyes had faded to the dull gray they became when she was stressed.

"The man they arrested today… that they suspect of shooting Manny. He's one of my clients."

He tensed. He definitely hadn't wanted to hear *those* words.

"Would it be a conflict of interest for you to help Rob find out who really shot Manny?"

He pulled back a little and shook his head. "Oh, darlin', there are so many things wrong with that question. Yes, it would be a conflict of interest, and no, I'm not willing to help the man accused of shooting my operative and my friend, and three, how the heck did Rob get involved?"

Kate folded her arms across her chest—never a good sign. "Well, you don't have to get obnoxious about it."

His own temper flared a little, but he tamped it down, realizing both their fuses were shorter than usual. "I'm not trying to be obnoxious, but... Look, it's been a long day." He stopped to soften his tone even more. "Can you just tell me how Rob got involved?"

"I called him on Hal's behalf. The man was arrested outside my office building. I don't know how they even knew he was there."

"They probably had a BOLO out on his car."

She nodded, her body relaxing some. "I'm really worried about him. He's got... Uh, he's not going to fare very well in jail."

"Look, I know you can't tell me anything specific, but does whatever disorder he have make him prone to violence?"

"No, anything but. He's a gentle soul." She turned her head to the side, biting her lower lip. "Can you recommend another P.I. agency?"

"Sure, but let me give it some thought. I'm brain dead at this point." He pushed himself to a stand and reached for her hand.

She let him pull her upright and lead her toward the bedroom.

They seemed to have reached a truce, for now. But he made a mental note to be extra gentle in bed tonight.

It was not a hard vow to keep, as it turned out. He was asleep as soon as his head hit the pillow.

~~~~~~~~~

On the way to work the next morning, Kate's phone rang through the Bluetooth of her car.

"So in two sentences or less," Rob's voice, a little gruff,

reverberated inside the car, "why do you think this guy is innocent?"

"Well, good morning to you, too, Mr. Sunshine."

"Sorry, I'm swamped this week. Not sure I'll be able to go to lunch tomorrow. I'll text you later."

Kate smiled. The old technophobe had finally figured out how to send and receive texts, most of the time. If his thick fingers hit the wrong button, he usually had no clue how to get back to the screen he'd been on.

"To answer your question," she said, "because I know him and he is not capable of attacking someone. I'm not sure he'd even defend himself all that well if *he* were attacked."

"Okay, I'm going to take his case, but he'd better be innocent."

Kate fervently but silently agreed. Then chastised herself for her lack of faith in Hal. "Thanks. See ya tomorrow, hopefully."

"Hopefully." He disconnected.

She groaned when she saw who was waiting outside the outer door of her office suite. Nudging past the detective, she stuck her key in the lock. "I have a client in twenty minutes and I need to do some things before she arrives. I don't have time for you."

She knew she sounded rude but, bottom line, she didn't like this guy.

Detective Russell held up his hands, palms out. "Hey, sorry we got off on the wrong foot yesterday."

Wrong foot was an understatement. "Come in, but I only have a few minutes."

She dumped her briefcase in her office, then went about her opening routine—plugging in the hot water for tea, starting the coffee machine, checking paper supplies in the tiny powder room off the waiting area.

Russell stood in the middle of the room, asking questions in a neutral voice as she flitted past him. "Did you see anyone or anything on the parking lot besides the police officers?"

"You already asked me that. No." She instantly regretted her churlish tone. The man was only doing his job.

Why the change in attitude?

Had he realized her position on the PTSD task force gave her an inside track to the Baltimore County police chief, not to mention the governor of the State of Maryland? Of course, she wouldn't use those connections to complain about him. But she was glad he was being a bit more pleasant.

"Any vehicles?" he asked.

She stifled a sigh. "As I said before, I only saw three cars, two nondescript sedans in the middle of the lot and the old pick-up nearer the door." They had turned out to be the guards and the janitor's vehicles. "Why are we going back over this?"

"No shifting of shadows, no sense of movement anywhere?"

"No."

"Are you very sure of that, Mrs. Huntington?"

The stress of trying to get the office ready and also answer his questions got the better of her. She rounded on him. "Are you accusing me of lying?"

His hands came up again in the apologetic gesture. "No, just double checking."

She felt a little queasy as a thought occurred to her. "What do you think I should have seen?"

"A witness places your man, Murdock, in the lobby, a few seconds before you and Officer Peters came roaring up to the building."

Kate tensed. "What witness?" Why was he telling her all this? Was he trying to undermine her trust in Hal? Could he be afraid she'd use her connections to try to interfere with the investigation itself?

She'd never do that. But some people would, so she could understand such a concern.

Russell hadn't answered her.

"That lobby was dark," she said. "It was all I could do to find the elevator."

"Hmm, Murdock may have hid somewhere until you went inside, then took off. Could he see you in the cruiser?"

"Probably, a silhouette at least. I wasn't trying to hide my presence."

The detective nodded. "I won't take up any more of your time then, Mrs. Huntington. Call me if you think of anything else."

Once he was gone, Kate hurried through the rest of her morning set-up, then went into her office and closed the door. She grabbed the receiver of her desk phone and started to punch in Rob's number, then thought better of it.

At lunchtime, she would go see Hal Murdock in jail. She'd get his side of the story before telling Rob that she might have dragged him into a case he couldn't win.

CHAPTER THREE

Kate sat at a metal table, on an uncomfortable chair that was bolted to the floor. She wished they'd let her bring her pad in with her.

She didn't trust her memory. Sleep was an elusive thing these days, thanks to the night sweats. And last night, a nightmare about Manny's shooting hadn't helped matters.

The guard brought Hal Murdock into the room. The bright orange jumpsuit did nothing to enhance his pale complexion.

"Thanks for coming, Kate." He ducked his head as he sat down across from her.

She nodded, then waited for the guard to leave the room. "I had to tell them I was your counselor in order to get in to see you. I hope that's okay."

"Sure. Uh… I was going to ask if you'd come to my hearing anyway. It's Thursday."

What hearing? "Didn't they set bail yet?"

"Yeah, yesterday, before I met with Mr. Franklin. But it's really high. The prosecutor claimed I have no strong ties to the community because I'm single and don't have kids." His cheeks shaded to a pale pink. "So Mr. Franklin got a preliminary hearing for me, to talk to the judge about the bail mostly, I think. Mom's working on getting the papers together to use our house as collateral. We're both on the deed."

Aha. That's why Russell didn't care if she knew about the witness who'd seen Hal. No doubt, the prosecutor planned to use his or her testimony at the hearing to help substantiate probable cause.

"Why do you want me there? It's unlikely they'll let me testify."

Hal ducked his head again and his blush deepened. "I... I maybe can stay, you know, okay enough to talk, if you're there."

Kate's chest ached. Being in jail had to be torture for this shy man. And standing before a judge is terrifying for anyone. For Hal, it was hell on earth.

"I'll see what I can work out." She'd try to get Maria to babysit. She didn't like leaving the kids alone, even though, at ten and twelve years old, *they* thought they were old enough to take care of themselves.

Hal nodded, his gaze still on the table.

"I'm sure I can make it happen," she said with more enthusiasm.

"I'll pay for your time, of course." He still wasn't making eye contact.

"We'll deal with that after this mess is cleared up. But Hal..." She leaned forward, trying to force him to look at her.

It kind of worked. He raised his gaze, but with his head still partially down.

"I need to ask you about something. The detective let slip that they have a witness who saw you in the lobby that night."

His head jerked up, his cheeks pale again. "No!"

Her stomach clenched. "No, you weren't there, or no, no one saw you?"

His eyes had gone wide. Suddenly he crossed his arms on the table in front of him and dropped his head into the crook of one elbow.

For a second, she thought he might be crying.

Then a fist thudded on the table with a dull clang. "Damn, damn, damn." A strangled whisper.

This wasn't looking good. She checked her watch. She had twenty minutes before she'd have to leave to get back to her office. And the guard might call an end to the visit before then.

"You'd better tell me quickly. What's going on?"

"Okay, see there's eight of us in our department, me and six other techs and the new guy, Luis. I mean this Manuel Ortiz guy, who got shot... And our supervisor. We all work for another guy, Fred Latey. Fred called me into his office awhile back and said he thought somebody was leaking info to one of our competitors and he asked me to keep an eye on the others, and report to him anything that seemed suspicious."

"How long ago is awhile back?"

"About six months ago. It kinda bothered me at the time, 'cause I found it hard to believe, and I didn't like the idea of spying on my coworkers. So I pretty much put it outta my mind." He ran a hand through his hair. "Then I overheard a phone conversation–not all of it. See, we have these partitions between our work stations."

Kate vaguely recalled seeing frosted glass barriers between the computers on the metal workbench in that room Sunday night.

"So I couldn't be sure who it was," Hal said. "And the guy was whispering, but I caught a few words. It sounded like he was gonna come in that night after hours—which we're not supposed to do without approval—and do something. He didn't seem to want to do it, but whoever was on the phone with him was pushing."

Kate's heart accelerated. Did her client have the solution to Skip's case, and to who shot Manny? But who would believe him? They'd just think he was trying to throw suspicion off of himself.

And maybe he is.

Hal looked straight at her and swallowed hard. "I didn't know what to do. Most of these guys and me, we've worked together for years. And whoever it was, he sounded so scared. I didn't want to tell Fred, and maybe what I'd heard... well, maybe I'd misunderstood." He ducked his head slightly.

Kate got his self-doubt. It went hand in hand with the social anxiety. Hal tended to mistrust his interpretation of other people's words and actions, even though she'd found him to be fairly astute.

"Wait." Again, she brought up the mental image of the lab at

Strategic Electronics. "Couldn't you get up and walk down the room and see who was on the phone?"

"I did that, but whoever it was, they must've hung up. There were four guys at their stations, all of them working on their computers. So I figured I'd come by the building around the time this guy had said he would be there. I parked my car on the street, so he wouldn't see it in the lot. When I got to the front door, it was open, which was totally weird. It's always locked at night. I went in and headed for the elevator, but then I got cold feet. And I wasn't even sure where this guy was gonna be. Maybe not even in our area, or he could've written down the info whenever he wanted and carried it out in his pocket. Although there's the risk you'll be the one chosen to be frisked."

"They frisk you when you leave?"

He nodded. "They pick people randomly, every second to fourth one. Sometimes you have to turn out your pockets, and the ladies' purses are always searched."

"Isn't that rather extreme?"

Hal shrugged. "Not really. We deal with some pretty secret stuff. They hired a security firm, about six months ago, and that guy recommended the tighter security."

With a jolt, Kate realized he meant Skip's agency, and "that guy" was probably Skip himself.

This situation was weirdly disorienting.

Hal had fallen silent.

Kate gave him a moment to gather himself, but a quick glance at her watch said they were running out of time. "So what did you do?"

"I was standing there in the lobby, trying to decide what to do, when I heard footsteps running down the fire stairs. And a voice, real scared, yelling, 'Send the police. I hear shots. Send the police.' So I got the hell out of there and ran around the side of the building."

"And hid there until the officers and I were all inside the building," Kate said.

"Yeah. I knew if I ran across the lot to the street, somebody might see me. So I stayed put until I thought it was clear."

"Wait, aren't there security cameras in the lobby?"

"Just a couple of them. I know their blind spots, and I stayed in the shadows, along the walls."

That gave her pause. How did he know the cameras had blind spots, and how would he figure out where they were? Had he slunk around in that dark lobby before?

He must have read the doubt on her face. "A friend of mine works for the security company that has the building's contract."

Hal did have a few friends, but he'd never mentioned this one before. "Not the same company that Strategic uses?"

"No. Our security is in-house. My buddy… I went to his work to meet him for lunch one time, and he was showing me the monitoring screens for those cameras and complaining that the building management was too cheap to put in enough to cover the whole space."

"And how do you know this guy?"

"He and I went to the same technical school. We had a lot of classes together."

That made sense. People with social anxiety could and did make friends. It just took a lot longer for them to trust enough to get past their nervousness. And Hal tended to be a bit more comfortable with men whom he viewed as peers, social status and age-wise.

"Okay, you need to tell all this to Rob, uh, Mr. Franklin."

Hal's eyes went wide again.

"You have to. I can't tell him because of client confidentiality, but I *am* going to tell him what the detective said. Then Mr. Franklin is going to demand you tell him what happened, and he may be annoyed enough he won't want to defend you anymore."

She softened her voice. "If you voluntarily tell him, he'll take it better."

Hal nodded and opened his mouth.

The guard opened the door. "You all done?"

She suspected he was being polite for her sake, by couching it as a question. But his tone said it was a statement. Their time was up.

The guard led Hal away.

Once in her car, Kate pulled a pad and pen from her briefcase and jotted down some notes. Should she tell Skip what Hal had said? *Could* she tell him, considering confidentiality issues?

~~~~~~~~~

"*Mother*, I do *not* need a babysitter." Edie stood in the middle of the kitchen, blue eyes blazing, the beginnings of a figure showing under her sweater and jeans.

A mere four months ago, she had used Mom and Mommy interchangeably. Now it was Mom or an exasperated *Mother*.

"You don't want to see Maria on Thursday?" Kate asked, keeping her voice innocent.

Indecision flitted across Edie's face. "No, yeah, of course I want to see Maria. But I do *not* need a babysitter."

Kate suppressed a grin. "Well then, think of it as a visit, and it would be incredibly impolite if you weren't here to greet her when she arrives."

Edie turned and huffed out of the kitchen, her dark, curly ponytail bouncing behind her.

Kate shook her head. She suspected the subject of that curly hair would come up again soon. Edie insisted on pulling it back year round, since they wouldn't let her get it straightened.

Kate had gone through a similar phase of hating her curls. Her mother had also resisted her lobbying to get them straightened.

Should I let Edie do it?

She fixed herself a cup of tea and sat down at the table. Toby, their golden retriever-something else mutt, sidled over and put his head in her lap. She stroked his soft ears.

Why *was* she resistant to letting Edie straighten her hair? Was she giving the same answer as her own mother's as a knee-jerk response? Maybe they should let Edie experiment with different looks, as long as she didn't do anything too drastic.

Kate let out a sigh. Only a few months ago, parenting had seemed so much easier. She'd talk to her hairdresser and find out what was involved in straightening hair.

Billy blasted into the room. "Hey Mom, I got my homework done already. Can I go over to Jimmy's house?"

She held out a hand, the gesture saying, *Show me your homework journal.*

Billy had recently been diagnosed with a mild case of Attention Deficit Hyperactivity Disorder, Inattentive type. He had a tendency to think he was done with his homework when he wasn't.

The ten year old deflated, then turned and left the room.

Kate knew he might or might not be back. He wasn't stupid. He would double-check his homework journal himself.

The journal was a big help. Billy's teacher checked and initialed it at the end of the school day, to make sure the boy had written the assignments down correctly. Then it was checked and initialed by Kate or Skip after the homework was done.

Billy's ADHD was one of the reasons they weren't willing to let the kids be on their own after school. Impulsivity tended to go hand in hand with the disorder. The boy needed a bit more maturity under his belt before he could be trusted to make good choices on his own. And he didn't take direction well from his sister.

Footsteps clattered on the stairs. Kate grinned. Billy bolted into the room and shoved the tattered spiral notebook at her. "Done!"

"Okay, be home by six for dinner."

He was around the corner before she'd finished her sentence. The front door slammed.

She chuckled, then sobered as she got up to stare into the freezer. The greatest downside to Maria's marriage and defection from her position as their housekeeper and nanny was that Kate now had to produce meals when Skip worked late, and she was a dreadful cook.

Reality hit her in the gut, followed by a wave of guilt. She'd been so busy, she hadn't thought about Manny all day. Why hadn't Skip called with an update?

She pulled out her phone and texted Skip. *How is Manny doing?* She held her breath.

After a few seconds came the answer. *At hospital. No change. Coming home.*

She flopped down into a chair at the table. *Thank you, God.*

Her chest tightened as she processed her reaction. She was grateful for *no change*, for the continuation of an induced coma.

Toby whimpered and put his head in her lap again.

~~~~~~~~~

Rob wiggled his bulk across the bench of their favorite booth. The new black vinyl squeaked in protest. "Is it me, or are these not as comfortable as Mac's old booths?"

"They're not as comfortable," Kate said. The manager of Mac's Place had talked the owner, Kate's old childhood friend, into remodeling the restaurant. The Irish pub appearance had been replaced with clean, chic lines and lots of chrome and black.

From an objective viewpoint, it looked good and the place did a booming business, but Kate wasn't sure she'd ever get used to it. She missed the old brown Naugahyde booths and the heavy wooden pedestal tables. As children, she and her siblings and Mac had played hide and seek, ducking under and behind those tables, on Sunday afternoons when his parents, devout Catholics, had closed the restaurant.

Now tall pub-style tables, also in chrome and black, were scattered around the black and white checkerboard tile floor.

"I already ordered our usual," she said to Rob.

"Good girl. I might have to bug out early." He grabbed the glass of water in front of him and took a healthy swig.

Kate winced. She wasn't sure he'd be calling her *good girl* when she'd finished telling him what she knew. She opted to get it over with. "About my client–"

"You were right," Rob interrupted. "He's a gentle soul, but I may have to put him on the stand so a jury can see that."

"He'll dissolve into a puddle of sweat," she said.

Rob's broad face sagged a little. He ran a hand over his thatch of silver hair. "I'll need your help prepping him, if it comes to that."

"Well, before we work on that strategy, I need to tell you something I found out." She sucked in a big breath and plunged in.

He sat in stony silence as she told him about the witness who could place Hal in the Armstrong building's lobby Sunday night.

Her mouth was dry by the time she finished, and not only from the talking. The look on Rob's face told her that Hal had not yet talked to his lawyer about all this.

She took a sip from her water glass.

"What the heck have you gotten me into?" Rob said.

"I'm so sorry. If I'd known this… Well, I still think he's innocent but… I probably would have let him find his own lawyer."

Rob blew out air and deflated against the back of his bench. He rubbed his hand over his chest. "It won't be the first criminal case I've lost."

The tension in her shoulders relaxed some. He wasn't going to dump the case. "I hope you don't say that to the client," she said in a teasing tone, trying to lighten the mood.

One corner of his mouth quirked up. "No, I will give a brilliant performance of optimism around him. Can we get Skip to do some investigating? The ideal outcome here would be to find who really shot Manny."

She shook her head. "More bad news. Skip's agency was the one investigating the industrial spying. He thinks our client is guilty. But then, he hasn't met him."

Rob groaned. "If we're dependent on winning the jury over with his personality, we're doomed."

"I'll look for another P.I. Skip said he'd give me some names."

"Things have got to be awkward at your house."

"A little," Kate said. "I can't remember when we've been on opposite sides of the same case. But we'll deal with it."

Their food arrived. Smiling her thanks at the waitress, Kate slathered tartar sauce on the bun of her crab cake sandwich. "The, uh, client didn't indicate to you that he'd been there Sunday night?"

"No, I'll call him when I get back to the office. He called yesterday, late afternoon, but I've been in court and haven't had a chance to call him back."

Kate slowly breathed out a soft sigh. Hal *had* intended to tell his lawyer what he'd done but hadn't had a chance to do so yet.

She ignored Rob's thick fingers snitching her pickle slices from her plate. He piled them with his own on his crab cake.

Kate took a bite of her sandwich and rolled her eyes in pleasure. The decor of Mac's Place might've changed, but the chef still made the best crab cake in Towson, maybe in the whole state of Maryland. Which was saying something.

~~~~~~~~~

At the hearing the next afternoon, Kate sat with Rob at a table, Hal in between them, in his orange jumpsuit. She didn't know if Rob would mention who she was or let the judge assume she was another lawyer.

As she'd suspected, the prosecuting attorney put his witness on the stand.

He was a sturdy man, fortyish, soft-spoken, and with kindness in his eyes. His skin was swarthy. Greek, Kate suspected, based on his name.

He was identified as the janitor for the Armstrong building. "I come in at night and clean whole building," he said, "but not third floor. That company, they got their own cleaning people."

Kate didn't remember seeing the guy Sunday night, but then the police would have intentionally kept them apart.

The prosecutor established that the police had asked the janitor to identify the man he had seen in the lobby of the Armstrong Building from a line-up of six men. He had readily picked Harold Murdock.

Kate hated witnessing Rob's cross-examination. He was normally an easy-going guy, but in court he could turn into a barracuda. Now he paced in front of the witness stand, his six-two, barrel-chested frame imposing, despite the middle-aged spread pulling against the button of his suit jacket. He was hammering on the fact that the lobby was dark.

"Sir," the janitor said, his accented voice patient, "as I say, I come down to the lobby to let the police in. I see a tall, thin man run across the lobby. He stop for a… He stop and turn at the door. The light from the big lamps around the parking lot, they show me his face."

"He stopped for how long?" Rob's tone was hard.

"Not long. A few…" He shrugged and made a helpless gesture toward his watch. "I don't know the word."

Rob was silent. Kate suspected he wanted to supply the word, but the judge had already chastised him once for asking a leading question.

Finally the judge said, "Seconds or minutes?"

"Seconds, they are parts of minutes, yes?"

"Yes," the judge said.

The janitor nodded. "Yes, then, a few seconds. Thank you." He smiled at the judge. "I learn new word today."

"You're welcome." The judge's tone was neutral, but his mouth twitched a little at the corners.

Don't try to crucify this guy, Rob. The judge likes him.

"Just a few seconds," Rob's voice was gentler.

Good, he caught the twitch.

"And you're sure you can identify him, based on that?"

"Pretty darn sure." The man grinned, pleased with himself that he knew the slang phrase.

"Pretty darn, but not absolutely sure?"

"What absolooty mean?"

"You're totally positive? No doubt at all?"

The janitor paused and looked at Hal. "Pretty darn sure," he repeated, with less enthusiasm this time.

"Thank you, sir," Rob said. "No further questions."

The judge excused the witness, and the assistant state's

attorney stood to give his final *spiel*, recapping the evidence. He waved the affidavit he had presented earlier, with Skip's signature on it.

It sounded rather thin to Kate's ears. Hal worked in the department where the leaks of confidential information were occurring, Skip's investigation pointed toward him as the industrial spy but with no hardcore proof, and the janitor said Hal was there, but he could have been mistaken in the dark lobby.

She wondered if the prosecutor had another ace or two up his sleeve. What he'd presented today would probably get Hal bound over for trial, but it wasn't really enough to convict him.

Rob rose. "Your Honor, except for the janitor's testimony, the prosecution's evidence is all circumstantial. I'm asking for a dismissal, and in lieu of that, a reduction in bail. Mr. Murdock does have ties to the community. He lives with his elderly mother, who is willing to put up her house as bond for his bail." He waved in Kate's direction, at the end of the table. "Mrs. Huntington is his counselor and is prepared to attest to his character."

Please don't call me, she silently prayed to the judge. She might not have social anxiety but testifying in court always made her "pretty darn" nervous.

The judge glanced her way, but the prosecutor jumped out of his chair. "Your Honor, we are working on other evidence that will prove Mr. Murdock was there that night, in the lab itself where the shooting occurred, but the police have not completed that aspect of their investigation yet."

"Objection," Rob said. "Mr. Bennett can't just say that he has other evidence without actually presenting it."

The judge raised a hand in the air. "Gentlemen, enough." He turned his gaze to Hal. "Mr. Murdock, ASA Bennett has shown probable cause to try you on the charge of attempted murder, but I will reduce bail to $100,000." He lowered his chin and stared at Hal over his reading glasses. "You do realize your mother will be homeless if you don't show up for your court date?"

Hal's Adam's apple bobbed in his narrow neck. He opened

his mouth, but nothing came out. Kate put a hand on his arm.

He licked his lips and tried again. "Yes, sir," he said, his voice barely above a whisper.

The judge scowled, and for a second Kate worried he would change his mind, but he tapped his gavel. "Next case."

Kate squeezed Hal's forearm, then let go as a bailiff came over to lead him away. "Tell your mom to call me if she runs into any glitches with the bail process."

He nodded. "Thanks, Kate. I really appreciate you coming."

Rob gave him a gentle slap on the shoulder. "Call my office once you're out and set up a time to come in. We need to talk strategy."

Hal nodded again and shuffled away with the bailiff.

Rob motioned for Kate to precede him out of the courtroom. Once out in the hallway, he said in a low voice, "That janitor is going to be hard to shake in court, which may mean we have to put Hal on the stand to give his story of why he was there. We really need a P.I. to try to find out what happened."

"I'll work on that," Kate said.

Rob walked her to her car on the street behind the Towson courthouse. She shivered despite her warm wool coat. The January day was damp and raw.

Rob put an arm around her shoulders, which helped a little.

"You do believe him, don't you?" Kate asked.

Rob was silent for a beat. "Yes, I do. Your assessment of him works in his favor, of course. My gut says he's harmless. Sell his company's secrets, maybe. I don't know him well enough to speak to his ethics. And I can imagine him knocking Manny over the head to get away, but then shooting him in the back. No way."

It wasn't a resounding endorsement of Hal's innocence, but Kate was grateful for it. Decades of being a lawyer had made Rob skeptical about human beings.

At her car, Rob gave her a bear hug. As he let go, he said, "Pray Manny is okay."

"I already am."

"Pray extra hard." Rob's expression was grim. "Not just for Manny's sake, but for Hal's. If he dies, I wouldn't put it past Bennett to go for first-degree murder."

CHAPTER FOUR

Skip had texted mid-morning that Manny was awake and relatively coherent. He was being moved out of the ICU.

Kate couldn't wait to get to the hospital and see for herself that he was okay. Fortunately, her first afternoon client wasn't until two, giving her a long lunch break.

At the hospital, she knocked gently on the half-open door of Manny's room. A female voice cheerfully called, "Come in."

She pushed the door all the way open and stepped into the room.

A young woman in blue scrubs was taking Manny's blood pressure. "I'm so glad you're doing better, Mr. Ortiz." She batted her eyelashes at her patient, who gave her a wan smile.

The nurse's fussing gave Kate time to recover from the shock of seeing Manny for the first time since Sunday night.

He didn't look all that good, but then again, conscious was a distinct improvement over unconscious. He was a relatively short man, but muscular—Skip had once described him as built like a fireplug. But today he seemed too weak to lift his own head.

A big bandage covered most of the left side of his head, its whiteness in stark contrast to his tan skin with grayish undertones. His dark hair had been shaved off on that side, exposing scalp a shade lighter. A purplish and yellow bruise leaked out from under the bandage's edge and wandered down his temple to his cheekbone.

The nurse tucked a sheet around his thick body. Only his arms, shoulders and head were outside the cocoon. An IV tube extended from one arm. The other arm lay limply on top of the sheet.

The nurse put a small, white plastic box, a wire extending from one side, into that hand. "There now, just push the button if you start to feel any pain."

The young woman moved toward the door, waving her fingers at him over her shoulder. She gave Kate a once-over. "Don't stay long. He still tires easily."

Kate nodded, noting that Manny wasn't even waiting until the nurse was out of the room before dropping the small box and pushing it off the edge of the mattress with the side of his hand.

"What's that?" Kate asked him.

"Morphine drip," Manny said in an irritated tone. "First thing I told them when I woke up was that I'm a recovering addict. They hooked the damn thing up anyway."

"Want me to put the button behind the bed, where you can't reach it."

"Yeah, thanks. But I wish they'd disconnect it completely."

Kate shook her head, as she nudged the plastic box farther out of reach with her foot. "I'm not sure that's a good idea yet, but when the time comes, they can ease you off of it gradually so you're less likely to have cravings."

"I don't need it now." His wince when he tried to shift his position belied this statement. "Get me outta this straightjacket, will ya?"

He twisted again, trying to loosen the sheet. She jumped into action and pulled loose the sides and the hospital corners the nurse had so expertly created.

He started to sit up and winced again.

Kate found the remote for the bed and put that in his hand.

"Thanks." The head of the bed moved slowly upward a few inches.

"Do you remember what happened?" Kate asked as she sat on a vinyl-covered chair next to the bed. She should probably make small talk first, but he might get too tired to answer her questions if she did.

He shook his head slightly. "I'd just found something. Some files. I don't remember what they were, but I remember being surprised."

"By the person who attacked you?"

"Well, that too." He smiled feebly. "But this was surprise over what I'd found, or maybe by where I'd found it."

"These were papers?"

Manny thought for a moment. "No, on the computer. Skip had finally convinced the powers-that-be at Strategic to give me access to the others' computers. It's a violation of their security protocol. The project is compartmentalized."

"What's that?"

"Each person working on it only knows so much about the whole project."

Kate nodded. "What is this project anyway? I mean in general, what's it about?"

Manny shook his head, then winced. "Sorry, can't tell you. I can't even tell Skip. Which has made it rough. I couldn't brainstorm all that much with him and Rose about what's going on."

"I understand." Kate had sat in on such brainstorming sessions on occasion. The ideas flew freely, and fast and furious sometimes. Having to monitor what one said would be both frustrating and limit the effectiveness of the session.

"Anyway," Manny said, "Skip got one of our guys hired on as a security guard and made sure he was on that night. During the day, I was never alone in the lab for very long, so I had to slip in after hours to check out their computers. I was reading something on one of the monitors—the hard drive for that computer was warm. It had been on recently. Then suddenly there was this searing pain in my torso." He gestured vaguely toward his rib cage with his IV-burdened arm. There was a lump there under the blanket—no doubt a dressing.

"And that's all I remember. The bastard must've hit me from behind and then shot me in the back when I was already down."

Kate shook her head. "I doubt it happened in that order."

She leaned closer to examine his bandage and the bruise. "If you felt the pain from the bullet, you were shot first. My guess is you hit your head on something on the way down. Maybe the workbench."

"Doc says I have a pretty bad concussion."

"I'm not surprised, and that's why you can't remember more. It takes a few seconds for memories to consolidate in long-term memory. You were probably knocked out before that could happen."

"So how come I remember the pain?"

"Consolidation involves interpretation and processing." She grimaced. "Pain doesn't take much interpreting."

"Makes sense." Manny's grin was a little lopsided. "You're pretty smart, boss man's wife."

"No point in buttering her up," Rose Hernandez said from the doorway. "She doesn't decide whether or not you get a bonus for getting yourself shot."

Kate turned and smiled. Rose's five-foot, sturdy figure was clothed in her usual uniform of khaki slacks and crisp white, man-tailored shirt. Her black, silky hair was twisted into a bun on the back of her head.

"Hey, boss lady," Manny said.

Rose stepped into the room and put her hands on her hips. "You know darn well I'm not a lady."

"No, but I like watching you get pissed when I call you one."

Rose gave him an exaggerated glare.

Kate's stomach, that had been clenched to some degree all week, relaxed. Manny was going to be okay.

"Have you talked to the police?" she asked him.

"No, they haven't been around yet."

"You might not want to mention I was here," Kate said, "or that I told you the shot probably happened before the head wound. The lead detective and I haven't totally hit it off."

Kate maneuvered around Rose to leave.

"What's with him?" Rose asked under her breath.

"He's a little loopy on morphine," Kate whispered back. To Manny she said, "I'll let you visit with Rose now." She patted his foot under the covers. "Take care."

Turning to the door, she jumped back.

Detective Russell's bulk filled the doorway.

She prayed he hadn't heard her ask Manny not to mention her comments.

The detective's face was neutral. "Don't go away, Mrs. Huntington. I have some questions for you." He stepped past her into Manny's hospital room.

"I'll be back." She turned to walk away. She needed to find Manny's doctor, or at least the shift's head nurse, and get the "as-needed" button removed from his morphine pump.

"Hey," Russell raised his voice, "I said *stay put*."

Kate pivoted. "I will be back in a few minutes." She turned away again and ignored his spluttering behind her as she walked toward the nurses' station.

She found a doctor there, making notes on a patient's chart. "Excuse me, are you Manuel Ortiz's doctor?"

He turned almond-shaped brown eyes on her. A youthful face belied the age suggested by his receding dark hair. "Yes."

"Uh, could I speak to you privately for a moment?"

"And you are?"

"A friend of his."

The doctor stepped away from the nurses' station.

Kate followed. "I know you can't tell me much, but let me introduce myself. I'm a psychotherapist and also the wife of the man Manny works for. Manny has confided in me in the past about his addiction history, and he's concerned about the morphine drip. He doesn't really want it at all–"

"He's got to have painkillers," the doctor interrupted. "Pain will stress his system and raise his blood pressure, which would not be a good thing right now."

"I understand, Doctor, but he seems to be okay with the current level of the drug. He doesn't like having the 'as needed' button. He's afraid he'll abuse it."

"The purpose of that button is to avoid the staff having to run to his room every time he feels pain."

"Trust me, he won't call the nurses unless he really needs to."

The doctor's expression didn't change.

"If you get him through this crisis but he ends up addicted to morphine," her tone was a little terse, but she decided that was okay, "you haven't done him any favors."

He still didn't look happy. "I'll check in on him in a little while and talk to him about it."

"Thank you." Kate pumped some extra gratitude into those two words, to take the sting out of her previous tone.

After the doctor walked away, Kate perched on the edge of a chair near the nurses' station and pulled a pad out of her briefcase. She jotted down what Manny had told her. She had a bad feeling this case was going to get more and more complicated.

When she returned to Manny's room, Detective Russell was standing outside the door, tapping his foot impatiently. "Thank you, Mrs. Huntington, for obeying my orders," he said in a snide voice.

So, we're back to obnoxious.

She kept her voice soft, dripping with sweetness. "Why, Detective, I wasn't aware that you had the right to order a citizen to do anything, if they weren't under arrest."

His body stiffened, then she watched as he seemed to actively will himself to relax.

Oh, yeah, he's only being nice because he thinks I have connections.

Or at least, what passed for nice with this man.

She gestured toward a nearby waiting area. The bland beige-upholstered chairs and loveseat were currently empty. Once they were seated, she said, "What can I do for you, Detective?"

"I'm trying to understand your involvement in all this. I must insist that you explain your relationship with Harold Murdock."

She stared at him with a steady gaze. *Are you really that*

obtuse, Detective?

Out loud, she said, "You know perfectly well what my relationship is to Hal Murdock."

"But you know his lawyer as well."

"Yes, Mr. Franklin is a friend of mine. I referred Hal to him."

"I saw you two outside the courthouse. You seemed like more than friends."

Kate resisted the urge to roll her eyes. "We are very good friends, as is he with my husband and me with Mrs. Franklin. I understand that your work requires you to be suspicious by nature, but…" She intentionally trailed off.

"And you're also *friends* with Manuel Ortiz, so why are you helping his assailant?"

Kate ignored the emphasis on *friends*. "Because I don't believe Hal attacked Manny, and I want his real attacker brought to justice." Mostly she wanted Hal cleared of the charges so he could get on with his life, but she figured the pursuit of justice sounded more noble.

"So what were you and Mr. Ortiz talking about when I arrived?"

"Not much. He was concerned because he couldn't remember the details right before he was attacked. I told him that was normal with head injuries."

"Yes, we wouldn't want him straining to remember who shot him." A hint of the snide tone was back.

"It probably wouldn't do any good if he did strain to remember. He said he was looking at something on a computer when he was shot, so I doubt he saw his assailant. And it *is* normal for events just before a head injury to not be fully recorded in long-term memory."

"Well, I don't appreciate you getting to my witnesses before I can talk to them."

Kate stiffened and gritted her teeth. "I rushed over here as soon as I heard Manny was awake because I care about him. I wasn't trying to pump your witness or influence what he remembers."

He raised his eyebrows at her. "You weren't?"

"No."

Well, yes, a little, but she was really trying to get at the truth. If Manny had said he saw Hal shoot him or come at him to slug him over the head, she would've believed him.

But sadly Manny's memory hadn't offered many clues as to what happened.

Detective Russell was slowly shaking his head back and forth. "There are way too many coincidences here, Mrs. Huntington. You happen to be with the officer who first arrives on the scene, you happen to know the victim and you happen to know the assailant."

She held up a hand. "The alleged assailant."

He narrowed his eyes at her.

"Haven't you ever heard of the six degrees of separation theory?" she asked.

"The what?"

"We're all related in some way or another with only six degrees or less of separation between us."

The furrows in his forehead deepened. He curled his lip. "I wouldn't be surprised to find you're less than six degrees of something with the judge and assistant state's attorney trying this case."

"No, actually I met both of them for the first time yesterday. They seem like nice enough fellows." She probably shouldn't be flip with him, but this guy was getting on her nerves.

The detective pushed himself to a stand and glared down at her. "Just stay away from my witnesses, ma'am." He pivoted on his heel and walked away.

"The hell I will," she muttered under her breath.

~~~~~~~~~

Skip skimmed through Manny's reports on the Strategic Electronics case yet again. He'd been over them so many times the words were running together before his eyes.

His New Year's resolutions to have a peaceful home life and to keep Kate out of trouble were already in serious jeopardy. Of course, he didn't have complete control over either of those things. Still, he had vowed to try.

Had they missed something in their investigation into the industrial espionage? Harold Murdock had seemed to be the most logical suspect. He had the clearances to access a good bit of the information that was leaked. And he was a computer whiz, so how hard would it be for him to hack into his coworkers' files?

Some of those coworkers had reported he was "odd" and "difficult to get to know" while others had called his behavior "furtive." Manny's assessment was that he was mostly shy, but he did act "extremely nervous" at times. And his bank account balances were much higher than they should be for someone making his salary.

But then again, he lived with his mother and their house was paid for. And he didn't seem to date or go out much. So what would he spend money on?

Skip looked over the background reports on Murdock's coworkers, including the engineers involved with the leaked project. Nothing much jumped out at him. Nobody had a criminal record beyond a few traffic violations, and none of them were serious.

John Cochlin, another of the technicians, had worked for Strategic for over a decade. Cochlin was married with two kids and another on the way. His bank balances were low and his mortgage payment was high, plus he had a fair amount of credit card debt. But in the total scheme of things, his debt load wasn't much worse than a lot of Americans.

The lab supervisor, Elaine Patterson, was married with one kid, a boy, age thirteen. In addition to her salary, her husband made good money as a sales rep for a local manufacturer, so the somewhat higher than average balances in their bank accounts made sense.

Everybody else's finances were in line with their incomes, including Fred Latey's, the guy who'd hired Canfield and Hernandez.

Latey had fouled the soup somewhat when he'd called each of his staff into his office six months ago, and told them he thought someone was leaking information and to be on the lookout for anything suspicious.

That had made Manny's job a lot riskier, putting the spy on alert.

When Skip had asked Latey how he knew the information was being leaked, the man had gotten cagey. "I have my ways," was all he would say. Which had led Skip to believe that Latey had his own spy or spies in the competitor's operation.

I should not *have taken this case.*

He quickly reviewed the background checks on the key employees of Strategic's main competitor. Again, nothing new jumped out. A couple of them had received sizeable bonuses lately. That could mean something. Then again, it might only mean they were good workers.

He slammed the folder shut. Grabbing his jacket, he strode out of his office. He was going to get some answers, and the place to start was to re-interview the key players at Strategic.

CHAPTER FIVE

Strategic's Director of Operations was a middle-aged man, medium height, with salt and pepper hair and a spreading waistline. He leaned back in his executive desk chair and smiled at Skip. Latey's face would have been handsome if it weren't for the brown splotch of a birthmark running down his left cheek to his chin. "We certainly appreciate all your hard work, Mr. Canfield, in finding our spy. Please submit a final bill, and we'd also like to offer Mr. Ortiz a bonus for his efforts."

Skip begrudgingly accepted the offer on Manny's behalf. He wasn't about to keep the man from reaping some rewards for being shot.

But he was taken aback by the assumption that the espionage case was closed. "Uh, I need to interview some of your people again, to tie up some loose ends."

Latey sat forward. "Which people?" His tone was a bit sharp.

All of them was the accurate answer, but somehow Skip figured he wouldn't get that. He'd settle for a few of the main players, for now. "Mainly John Cochlin, Elaine Patterson, and Paul Allen." Allen was the head engineer on the leaked project.

"Elaine's out sick, Paul took a long weekend, and I believe John's left for the day. And frankly, I don't see the point, Canfield." Latey stood and stuck out his hand. "Address that final bill to me, and I'll make sure it gets paid promptly."

Skip had no choice but to shake his hand and leave.

From his truck, he called Rose at the agency and told her about the request for a final bill. "I think we need to get it out this afternoon if possible. There's something off here, and I'd like us to get paid sooner instead of later."

"Right," Rose said. "I'll take care of it."

After they disconnected, Skip started the truck's engine but didn't put it in gear. He sat for a moment, replaying his own words in his head. There was something off here.

"What am I doing?" he said out loud. He'd wanted out of the Strategic case practically since he'd taken it on, and now he had his wish. He should take their money and let it go.

But his operative was in the hospital, and his wife believed that the man accused of shooting him couldn't hurt a fly.

He would take their money, but he wasn't ready to let it go.

He reached for the folder on the passenger seat and rooted through it for the information he needed. Putting the truck in gear, he cruised the parking lot, checking vehicles and license plates. No sign of Elaine Peterson's red BMW or Paul Allen's silver Porsche, but Cochlin's modest nine-year-old sedan was parked in the fourth row of the south lot.

Skip backed his Expedition into a space across from it and slid down in his seat until his head blended with the silhouette of the headrest.

He waited.

At five-ten, a thin man, of medium build and dressed all in tan—beige dress shirt, khaki slacks, tan tie, approached. The sedan let out a sickly bleep, then a dull click.

The man scanned the parking lot, before opening the door of the sedan and getting in.

Skip gave him a thirty-second headstart, then followed him to the exit onto York Road. He expected the man to head for his home in a middle-income neighborhood off Dulaney Valley Road.

But first, Cochlin stopped at a small shopping center. He went into the Safeway and exited twenty minutes later with two plastic grocery bags and a large box of toddler's disposable diapers.

Skip ground his teeth. This was why he hated surveillance work.

But then Cochlin did something odd. He veered off into the entrance of a storefront maildrop.

Skip checked his watch. Five-forty-five.

In less than two minutes, Cochlin emerged. His tense, hunched gait had loosened.

Skip dug binoculars out of his glove box. He focused them on Cochlin as the man walked to his car.

A white envelope was tucked into his left shirt pocket.

Skip wasn't sure what to make of Cochlin's actions. His observations were more impressions than anything else. The man had seemed nervous in Strategic's parking lot, his movements anxious and furtive. He hadn't even been able to hit the right button on his car's key fob. But he seemed much more relaxed now.

At home, Skip went into the study. He found the address of the maildrop place on the computer, then dug in a drawer for a plain envelope. He addressed it to John Cochlin at the maildrop and used the agency's offices as the return address, but with no name. He wrote *Address Correction Requested* under the return address.

The doorbell rang as he was sealing the flap of the empty envelope. He tucked it into his own shirt pocket. He'd mail it tomorrow and see what happened.

When he opened the study door, delicious aromas wafted around him. Chinese? Ah, that's what the doorbell was about.

He laughed at himself. *I'm some detective.*

He strolled into the kitchen and gave his wife a peck on the cheek. "Thank God you didn't try to cook," he teased.

Kate stuck out her tongue at him. "Call the kids."

Once settled at the table, Edie and Billy argued over whose turn it was to say grace. They had once vied for the opportunity. Now they tried to pass it off on each other.

"I will say grace." Kate's voice was firm. "Dear God, thank you for all of our blessings. This food you provide for us, our health and most especially these two children who think they are too grown up to say grace. Amen."

She crossed herself, then stared at each of the kids until they mumbled an "Amen."

Skip struggled to keep a straight face.

"By the way," Kate said as she passed him the plate of egg rolls, "a person whom we are both interested in is now out on bail." Her tone was casual, but he noted the tension in her shoulders. She wasn't sure how he would take the news.

Keeping his voice neutral, he said, "Not surprised. Rob's the best lawyer I know."

What did surprise him a little was the fact that Rob had taken the case in the first place. Criminal law wasn't his favorite thing. But then Rob had as much trouble saying no to Kate as he did.

By tacit agreement, he and Kate let the subject drop for now, even though Billy and Edie seemed oblivious. Heads down, they shoveled food into their mouths. Chinese was one of their favorites.

It was good, but Skip still missed Maria's cooking something fierce. Her Guatemalan dishes had been similar to the Tex-Mex he'd grown up on. And he missed the woman herself. She'd been a part of their family for as long as he'd known Kate. But it was a good thing for Maria to be happily ensconced in her own home, mothering Eduardo's three kids and bent on making their widowed father as roly-poly as she was.

They now had a cleaning lady who came in every two weeks. Kate did the laundry, and he did most of the cooking. When he got home in time, that is. When he didn't, Kate usually ordered delivery. A kitchen drawer was stuffed with carryout menus.

He tuned in as Kate attempted to drag information out of Edie about her day at school.

"S'okay," the girl mumbled around a mouthful of Peking duck.

Her parents glanced at each other across the table. Skip gave Kate a slight shake of his head. If anything was bothering Edie, she'd tell him about it at bedtime. And if it was major, he'd tell Kate.

It wasn't the easy way they had all once communicated, and it wasn't ideal, but he suspected it was what they were stuck with until Edie was past the worst of her teen years.

"How about you, son?" Skip asked. "How was your day?"

Billy regaled them for the rest of the meal with a story about his friend, who liked a girl but was too scared to talk to her.

Skip wondered why his wife's face became pinched as she listened.

Edie pushed her empty plate away. "May I be excused?"

Skip caught himself about to shake his head. She managed to make even that simple sentence sound belligerent.

"As soon as you help with clean-up," Kate said in an even voice.

The kids' help consisted of carrying dirty dishes to the counter, where Kate rinsed, and then Skip put them in the dishwasher. Lately Kate had been looking for ways to get the kids more involved in caring for their home. "I figure our future son-in-law and daughter-in-law aren't going to like us much if we produce two lazy slobs," she'd said.

Three hours later, the dishes had been dealt with, homework was done and checked and the kids were bedded down.

Skip settled next to Kate in their favorite spot in the living room. "You know this sofa's starting to sag in the middle, from us sitting here so much. We should probably think about replacing it."

She snuggled against him. "I kinda like the little dip in the middle. When I walk by during the day, I see it and smile."

Skip grinned down at her. "Why did Billy's story bother you earlier?"

"It reminded me of a client."

Not a client, the *client*. The one she was currently obsessing over.

"You do know that this is why you're burning out as a therapist?"

She turned in the circle of his arm and looked up at him. "Hey, who's the shrink here?"

"Lack of credentials does not preclude astute observations by caring husbands."

She chuckled. "Sometimes you're a little too astute for *my* good." Her face sobered again. "Have you come up with a good P.I. I can... suggest to Hal?"

He knew she'd almost said *hire for Hal*. He hated that he couldn't help her. But it really was a conflict of interest, even though Strategic had declared the investigation over.

Damn this case. Despite Cochlin's odd behavior this afternoon, he wasn't convinced that Murdock was innocent. Maybe they were in on the spying together and Cochlin was the shooter, not Murdock?

"Shall I take that as a no?" Kate said. "I can find somebody—"

"Sorry, I was woolgathering. I've been preoccupied with Manny and forgot to ask around. I'll make some calls tomorrow."

Or maybe he would keep investigating on his own, unofficially. If he recommended another P.I., she'd probably pay for it out of her own money. The brokerage fund, set up initially with her late husband's life insurance money, could afford the drain. There would still be plenty left for the kids' college. But still...

She snuggled against him again. "I'm so relieved Manny is awake."

"Me too." He leaned down and kissed her tenderly.

She giggled. He loved that sound.

"What was that for?" she asked.

"I don't know." *For being you, for caring so much, sometimes too much.*

"Do I have to have a reason to kiss you," he said out loud.

She smiled up at him. "No, sir, you most definitely do not."

He kissed her again.

Her arms slid up around his neck and she deepened the kiss.

His body responded accordingly. *Hmm, don't need Viagra yet.* He smiled against her lips.

She broke the kiss. "Now what are you smirking about?"

He grinned at her, then pushed himself off the sofa. Holding out his hand, he said, "You'll see in a minute."

She matched his grin, an impish glint in her eye. Taking his hand, she pulled herself to a stand, then let go. "Last one undressed has to take Edie to the barn tomorrow."

She took off for the bedroom, her laughter floating back over her shoulder.

But he had the last laugh. He won the bet.

~~~~~~~~~~

Kate thought of Saturdays as Chauffeur Day. Today, Skip was taking Billy to basketball practice. And Edie had insisted on going to the farm where her pony Fiddlesticks was boarded, even though the predicted high for the day was forty-six degrees.

Kate had figured driving to the farm was easier than arguing, despite her desire to get on with her own agenda for the day.

She lucked out. One of Edie's friends was riding her pony in circles in the ring beside the barn. Kate arranged with the girl's mother to take Edie home later. Hopefully, Skip and Billy would be back by then.

Back in her car, she instructed her Bluetooth to call Hal Murdock. She let out a pent-up breath when he answered, and then asked him to meet her at a coffee shop near his house.

It was highly irregular to meet with a client outside of one's therapy office, but this would be better than talking over the phone. She wanted to see his body language as he answered her questions.

She'd had a niggling feeling ever since the hearing. She wasn't sure why, but her gut was telling her she might have been wrong to assume Hal's innocence so quickly.

And her gut rarely misled her.

They settled at a small bistro table with mocha lattes. "Let me start," Kate said, "by pointing out this is not a session. This is about your legal case, so what you tell me is not confidential." She wanted to be up front about that.

She asked Hal to tell her again everything he could remember from that night.

Again, he described how he'd gone there to investigate the leaks on his own but had never gotten farther than the lobby. He'd heard someone yelling in the stairwell—which had turned out to be the janitor calling the police—and had fled.

"Kate, I wish I knew more. I wish I could help find out who shot your friend." Hal sat back and ran a hand over his hair, shaking his head slightly. "When I heard you scream, and realized you knew the guy…"

Adrenaline jolted through her body. Strategic's offices were on the third floor, a long way from the lobby.

"I didn't shoot him, honest," he quickly said, apparently misreading her expression.

She paused to choose her words carefully, since her brain was still reeling. "How could you hear my scream, much less my words, if you never left the lobby?"

He slumped back in his chair, shook his head again. "I, uh…" His voice was barely above a whisper.

Kate leaned forward. "You were upstairs, somewhere on that floor."

His eyes went wide. "No. I wasn't. I swear I never went any farther than the lobby that night. But I, um…" He ducked his head. "I planted a bug in the lab, earlier in the day. I got it from that techie website I told you about. But it didn't have the range they claimed. So I went inside the building and hid in the lobby."

Kate wasn't sure she believed him. The ASA had said he had evidence that Hal was in the lab.

"What did you hear?" she asked to get Hal talking again.

"It worked real well, once I was that close." His expression morphed toward excitement. "It was quiet for a while. Then I heard the click of the door lock unlatching, and some scuffing noises. Maybe somebody walking. Then the sound of a computer booting up. Then nothing for a few minutes."

"Wait, what time was this?"

"I went in the lobby about eight-forty. I'd tried listening from my house first, which is only a mile and a half away. It should've been in the range they advertised." His voice sounded aggrieved. "I thought maybe the bug wasn't working. So I drove over and parked on the street—I didn't want anybody to see my car. Then I walked over to the building."

"Was the outer door unlocked like you said?" Kate asked.

"Of course." He looked offended.

Dishonesty includes sins of omission, she thought but didn't say.

"After another little while, I heard footsteps, moving fast, and the door slammed. There were some rustling noises, off and on, for a few minutes. Maybe somebody looking for something? Then the door clicked and the sound of a computer booting up again." He looked her in the eye, his mouth turned down. "Then the shots, two of them. And I heard the janitor, in the stairwell, not through the bug. So I took off."

"Again, how did you hear me?" Kate said.

He tapped his ear. "Through the bug. I was afraid to run across the lighted parking lot, so I slipped around the corner of the building. The reception wasn't as good there, but I heard a lot of it. The cops going into the lab and searching it, finding Luis, I mean your friend, Manuel. One of the cops on his radio, calling in what happened, asking for an ambulance."

He finger-combed hair out of his face. "I was going to leave after the EMTs went inside. I was trying to sneak around the perimeter of the parking lot, beyond the edge of the lights. Then I heard you scream and the officer said your name."

After a moment of silence, Kate prompted, "What did you do then?"

"I dropped to the ground and listened. I heard you say you knew the guy who was shot. Mostly static after that, so I got out of there."

Kate digested his words for a moment. She was inclined to believe him, but she reminded herself that she was always inclined to believe her clients, especially the ones she liked. But just because they might tell her the truth in her office—most of the time at least, when they weren't in denial about what was going on in their psyches—that didn't mean they'd tell the truth about a crime they'd committed.

"I'm finding it hard to visualize you playing James Bond, double-0-seven," she said.

He looked off to the side, toward the coffee shop's display of baked goods, and the chocolate eclairs that were calling Kate's name.

She gave herself a mental slap and brought her focus back to Hal's body language.

"I kinda got into it," he said. "Had fantasies of Fred giving me a promotion, or at least a fat bonus if I caught the spy."

Aha! Several pieces clicked together.

Fred Latey was a father figure to Hal. He never said much about his boss in sessions, but it made sense. It was a common phenomenon, to transfer feelings and issues about one's parents onto one's boss. After all, they were authority figures who controlled your sense of security, your ability to survive really, and therefore you had to please them.

Hal was hoping his "dad" would finally recognize him and praise him, instead of calling him a lazy bum as his real father had.

Another thought made her stomach tighten. "Hal did you wear gloves when you planted the bug?"

"No. I figured it didn't matter. My prints are all over that lab anyway."

She dropped her head into her hands for a second, then looked up at him.

You are so screwed.

Out loud, she said, "It won't look good, though, if they find prints on the bug. That will be further evidence you were the spy."

He gave her a lopsided grin. "They have to find the bug first. I hid it pretty good."

CHAPTER SIX

Skip had dropped Billy off at his school for basketball practice. The team was going for pizza afterwards. He'd given Billy some money and asked another parent to chauffeur him to the pizza place.

So he had two, maybe two and a half hours. He headed for Elaine Patterson's house. He had no specific reason to suspect her, other than that she was the test lab supervisor.

Latey was convinced the espionage was linked to that lab. Some of the leaked specifications were ones that had been changed after the components were tested.

There were two cars in the driveway of the Pattersons' brick, two-story house, but no activity outside. Not surprising in January.

He parked with a large bush between him and the house. It was mostly bare, with only a few withered leaves left hanging, but it obscured the view of his truck from the house. Getting out his binoculars, he watched the property for almost an hour, bored out of his skull. He hated surveillance with a passion, but since this wasn't an official agency investigation anymore, he could hardly pass the task off to one of his operatives.

Finally the front door opened. A dark-haired boy, tall and slender, stepped out onto the porch. The son.

The kid wore a zipper jacket and jeans. The jacket hung open, revealing a blue and white stripped soccer shirt.

A man followed him out the door. He wore a heavier coat than the boy, with a knit cap pulled down on his head. Only a little shorter than Skip's height of six-five, but his build was hard to judge in the padded parka.

The winter wind rattled the few leaves on the bush. The man hunched his shoulders to protect his face from the cold, but the boy seemed oblivious. He was grinning from ear to ear.

He and the man descended the cement porch steps and started along a stone walk to the driveway.

A willowy blonde, Elaine Patterson, stepped out on the porch. She said something.

The man turned slightly and waved to her. He had something in his hand. Tickets maybe? Even with the binoculars, Skip couldn't tell for sure.

"Bye, Mom," the boy called out.

Elaine waved. She wore a blue bathrobe. Skip zeroed the binoculars in on her face. Her nose was red. Apparently she was legitimately sick.

Now what? Sitting around being bored for another hour until he had to go pick up Billy wouldn't accomplish much.

But Elaine knew him. He'd interviewed her before. If she had anything to do with the industrial espionage, she'd be on guard with him now.

But maybe not with someone else, another woman... He pulled out his cell phone and punched a speed-dial number. He couldn't ask an operative to get involved with this, but he could ask his partner.

"Hey, Rose. You busy?"

"Nothin' all that important. What's up?"

He told her what he'd like her to do.

"We closed that case. Sent Latey the final invoice, remember?"

"Yeah, but I've got a bad feeling about that whole conversation. He seemed a little too eager to bring the investigation to a halt, and this after he's been saying for months to give it everything we had."

"I guess he's assuming, like everybody else, that the bozo who shot Manny is also the spy."

"Well, that's kind of a circular argument. The cops suspected

Murdock of Manny's shooting mainly because our investigation was pointing his way for the espionage. But Manny hadn't found anything conclusive yet." Skip brushed hair back out of his eyes. He needed a haircut. "And there's another complication. Harold Murdock is one of Kate's clients."

"Aw, crap."

My sentiments exactly.

A beat of silence. Rose sighed. "Okay, what's the address?"

He gave it to her.

"Be there in fifteen minutes." She disconnected without saying goodbye.

~~~~~~~~

Rose sat across a spacious living room from Elaine Patterson as the blue-eyed blonde sneezed into a tissue.

"Sorry." Patterson rubbed her already raw nose with the tissue. "I hope you don't catch my cold."

Rose wasn't too worried about that. She had a formidable immune system and rarely got sick. Nonetheless, she made a mental note to check her glove box for hand sanitizer when she got back to her car.

She gave the woman a fake smile. "Sorry to bother you when you're not feeling well, Mrs. Patterson. Just a few questions to tie up loose ends in our files."

"Fred, uh Mr. Latey, told me the case was solved."

"Well it is, but we have to submit a final report, and we like to make sure we have all the facts straight."

Or, in this case, assumptions and circumstantial evidence.

Skip had handed the case file over to her when they'd talked briefly in his truck. She'd skimmed Manny's reports and the background check on Patterson, wishing she had time to read everything more carefully.

"When did you first suspect Harold Murdock of being the source of the leaks?"

"About six months ago," Patterson said. "He started acting kind of furtive, and he was staying late more often. He said it was because of that project, the one that the leaks have been about. It was having a lot of problems."

Damn Strategic Electronics for being so tight-lipped about the nature of the project. It made it awkward to refer to in conversation and left them working almost totally in the dark.

Until Manny went undercover, that is. He was cleared to work on the project—something the company was developing for the U.S. Army—but he was also told not to say anything more specific about it to his bosses. Rose understood the need for security, but it made their job harder.

"*Was* the project having problems?"

Patterson seemed to hesitate. "Well, yes. Hal was assigned to solve one of them."

So why was his staying late suspicious?

"Can you say more about how he was furtive?"

"He'd duck his head or look away," Patterson said, "whenever I came near him, like he didn't want to make eye contact."

Rose didn't find that particularly surprising. Manny's reports said Murdock was excruciatingly shy. But then again, he'd worked with Elaine Patterson for several years. Shy people usually got over it once they knew a person well.

"He wasn't that way before?"

"Yes." Patterson rubbed her nose with the tissue again. "When I first started working there, but he unbent eventually and seemed more relaxed with me."

"But then he got uptight again?" Rose asked.

She nodded.

"Anything else make you suspicious of him?"

"He left some components from that project out on his workbench one day, when he went to lunch. John Cochlin noticed and told me about it." She shrugged. "It's against the rules, but we've all done it at one time or another. It's easy to get careless when you know only people with the proper clearances can get into the lab."

"I don't remember seeing that in Murdock's personnel file?" Rose was winging it. She'd never read Murdock's personnel file, but Patterson didn't know that.

"No, I didn't write him up. I just reminded him when he got back from lunch not to do that again."

"So if that transgression is so common," Rose asked, "why did it make you suspicious?"

"Well, it wouldn't have normally, but combined with everything else."

"What else, besides him acting shy again?"

"Look, didn't Mr. Ortiz tell you all this?" Patterson waved a dismissive hand. The early afternoon sun, slanting through the living room windows, glinted off a ring on her finger.

"Well, most of it," Rose said, "but he didn't get a chance to submit a final report, you know, before the shooting."

"Oh." Patterson's fair cheeks flushed a little. "I was going to go visit Luis, I mean, Manuel. But then I caught this cold."

"I think they're limiting visitors right now anyway. He's still in serious condition."

"But stable, right?"

"Yes. So can you tell me anything else about the evidence against Mr. Murdock?"

She waved her hand again. "I don't know what else your man may have found. Fred, Mr. Latey, told me that you all were convinced the leaks were coming from Hal."

No, we all *weren't convinced of that at all.* Latey probably assumed Murdock was the spy, as well as the shooter, because he'd been seen at the building the night of the shooting.

Patterson blew her nose. The ring flashed again in the sunlight.

"That's a lovely ring," Rose said, to keep the conversation going. "Did your husband give it to you?"

Patterson held out her right hand so Rose could get a closer look. She obligingly leaned forward. A fairly large white stone— diamond or cubic zirconia?—was surrounded by smaller blueish-green stones.

"No, I bought it for myself," Patterson said. "The blue ones are aquamarines. My birthstone."

"It's lovely."

Personally Rose had little use for fancy jewelry, except for her engagement ring—a ruby, her own birthstone—and her wedding band.

She glanced at the woman's left hand. Patterson wore only a thick gold band on that ring finger.

"So when did Mr. Latey tell you the case was wrapped up?"

"Oh, uh…" Patterson looked away for a moment. "Friday morning, I think. I don't remember for sure."

"Before you left early because of your cold?"

Her head swiveled back toward Rose, her eyes narrowed slightly. "Yes, that's right."

"So there was no other evidence that you know of that Murdock was the spy?"

Patterson paused for a moment, tilting her head as if in thought. "No, not that I know of, but I'm sure Mr. Ortiz had found other things."

Rose couldn't think of any other way to get more out of the woman. She placed a hand on the sofa cushion to push herself upright. The leather was buttery soft under her palm.

She had no use for fancy jewelry but she sure wouldn't mind owning this couch. Then she visualized Mac spread out on it, dirty shoes and all.

Hmm, maybe not. She loved her husband dearly, but *slob* was an insufficient label for him.

She thanked Elaine Patterson for her time, foregoing her normal offer to shake hands. She might have a strong immune system, but she wasn't going to push her luck.

Patterson made no overtures in that direction either. She walked Rose to the door.

As Rose headed to her car, she tried to figure out what was bothering her gut. Elaine Patterson seemed innocent enough, but…

Ah, the Mr. Ortiz stuff. Okay, the woman probably got his real name from the newspaper. But how did she know he was undercover, investigating the leaks? Strategic had managed to keep all that out of the news. Had Latey told her that, or had she figured it out for herself?

Rose shrugged. Latey probably told her, but that didn't really matter.

One thing she did know. She now agreed with her partner. This case was far from resolved.

~~~~~~~~

Since Paul Allen, the head engineer on the project, was supposedly out of town this weekend, Skip opted to check out the other engineer who'd been involved, off and on. He would have more of the pieces regarding the project than most of the other players, and he would understand better how those pieces fit together.

So again, Skip was staring at a lawn sprinkled with barren trees and bushes and a large house in a middle-class neighborhood. The exception was this one did have activity going on in the driveway. Garrett Watson was washing his bright yellow Corvette convertible.

Granted the temperature was above freezing, a requirement for car washing in the winter if you didn't want frozen locks. But most people used commercial carwashes to knock the salt off their vehicles this time of year.

Then again, Skip thought, if he owned a Corvette, he might not trust it to others to wash either.

What was it with these people and their fancy cars?

He picked up the folder beside him and skimmed through the background check on Watson again. Bank accounts looked about right. Watson's current wife didn't work outside the home though, and he paid child support to an ex for his two teenaged kids—twins, a boy and a girl. Mortgage payment was on the high side too. How could he afford a Corvette?

He found the line for vehicles. A 2013 Chevy sedan was listed along with the convertible, which was ten years old. The car was long since paid for or perhaps had been bought secondhand.

Skip looked up. Watson was now lovingly hand-drying his pride and joy.

Skip glanced down and the date of the report caught his eye.

Crap! These are almost six months old. And the reports weren't as thorough as Dolph's would have been.

Skip indulged in a short mental rant against credit bureaus. Since they themselves conducted financial investigations for customers, they viewed private investigators as competitors, and P.I. agencies like Canfield and Hernandez were denied access to credit reports. But background check companies *were* allowed access, which didn't make a whole lot of sense to him.

Dolph had both the contacts and the computer skills to get the info they needed directly, although his methods sometimes didn't bear close scrutiny. But Sue Randolph, now retired herself, had put her foot down, insisting he cut back his hours. So they were forced to rely on an outside background check company for their routine investigations, and the one they'd hired had been less than impressive so far.

Skip shook his head as he watched Watson gather his bucket and cleaning supplies and head for his garage.

Time to go pick up Billy.

~~~~~~~~~

Kate turned onto her street. Jill's mom waved from her car as she passed on the way out. Kate expelled pent up air. Even if Skip wasn't home yet, Edie hadn't been alone for more than a few minutes.

She chided herself for being so paranoid. The twelve year old was certainly capable of looking out for herself in broad daylight. But so many things had happened in Kate's life—scary things that, for the most part, had been outside of her control—she no longer had much faith in the benevolence of the universe.

As she pulled up in front of her house, she was still trying to figure out how to break the news to Rob that his client had lied to him, again.

It was more a sin of omission really, but still… And Hal also had failed to tell the police the whole truth and nothing but the truth. That was an even greater problem.

She had a bad feeling Hal Murdock was going to spend some time in prison, if not for Manny's shooting, then for industrial espionage. And she doubted he would survive the experience with his mental health anywhere close to intact.

On the sidewalk leading to the porch, she slowed her steps and looked up at the three-story Victorian-style house that she and Eddie Huntington had bought and lovingly renovated. Eddie had almost given her a heart attack when he'd climbed a thirty-foot extension ladder to sand and paint the gingerbread trim along the roof line.

Then he'd been killed before the renovations were completed. Kate swallowed the small lump in her throat. Even after all these years, the grief could sneak up on her.

Inside, she found Edie at the kitchen table, drawing.

"Daddy left a message. Billy's team stopped for pizza after practice." Her tone was normal for once.

"Thanks." Kate wondered briefly why Skip had called the house instead of texting her. "You okay, need anything?"

"I'm fine, *Mother*." The child didn't even look up from her sketch pad.

So much for normal.

Kate risked a glance over her daughter's shoulder. The scene of a barn and field was pretty good. The art lessons she and Skip had given her for Christmas were already paying off.

"Looks like you've been working on that for a while."

"Yeah, I started it last week, but I forgot to take my pad today."

Kate nodded. "Good job." Then she got out of the kitchen quick, before the mundane conversation had time to go south into Pre-Teen Angst Land.

In the study, she sat down at the desk and fished her pad and a pen out of her briefcase. She jotted notes from her conversation with Hal.

When had she stopped trusting her memory?

About the time the hot flashes started.

She pushed that thought aside and picked up the phone's receiver. Taking a deep breath, she dialed before she could lose her nerve.

Liz Franklin answered. They exchanged greetings. Then in a more serious voice, Liz said, "So how are you really, Kate?"

She gripped the phone receiver tighter. "What has he told you?"

"Not much," Liz said. "You know he wouldn't break confidentiality. But he's worried that you've gotten mixed up in a client's legal mess again."

At least three emotions did battle in Kate's chest—warm appreciation that her friends cared, resentment that they thought she couldn't handle herself and resist getting sucked in too far, and guilt because that was probably exactly what was happening.

"Well, I wouldn't say I'm mixed up in it…"

Really? You just spent most of your Saturday playing detective.

"I'm only trying to help," she finished, her voice sounding lame in her own ears.

Liz let out a deep bark of laughter.

Kate visualized her friend in her mind's eye–green eyes sparkling, strawberry-blonde hair now helped along by her hairdresser, figure still slender despite the fact she was pushing sixty. Liz's booming voice and throaty laughter always seemed so incongruous coming from that petite and feminine body.

Since Liz would see right through any further disclaimers, Kate just asked to talk to Rob.

"Sure, I'll get him." A brief pause. "Kate, do be careful."

She stifled a sigh. "I will be, and thanks for your concern."

The sound of footsteps, then Rob was on the line. "What's up, Kate?" His voice sounded more relaxed than it had in a while.

She hated to spoil his Saturday. Taking another deep breath, she said, "Brace yourself." She filled him in.

Rob was silent for a good thirty seconds after she'd finished. Then he didn't directly address what she'd told him. "Afraid I've got some bad news too. I got a call from Bennett this morning."

"Bennett?" Kate said.

"The prosecutor for Hal's case." Rob cleared his throat. "Strategic has an electronic security program that tracks when doors open and close in secured areas. Someone entered the test lab twenty-three minutes before the shots were fired. The door must've been propped open, because it doesn't close until fifteen minutes later. A few minutes after that, the door opens again, using Manny's security badge, and closes right away. Right after the shots were fired, it opens from the inside and closes again."

Kate's brain churned, processing the implications. Excitement bubbled in her chest. "Then Manny's shooter must've come in earlier and hid in the lab. Who was it who came in initially?"

"That's the bad news. The door was opened the first time with Hal's security badge."

The bubbles burst, replaced by a hollow feeling. Kate slumped back in her desk chair. "Then he did go in there."

Half a beat of silence. "Do you believe that?'

"Wait, no." Kate ran a hand through her curls. "I don't know. Hal swore to me he didn't go any farther than the lobby."

"I've got a call into him," Rob said, his voice now sounding tired. "I'm trying to withhold judgement until I can ask him about it."

"Why do you think ASA Bennett is calling you on a Saturday, so generous with information?"

"I think he's going to offer a plea bargain, and there's something else you should know." The sound of air being expelled. "Attorneys usually get along fine outside the courtroom, defense and prosecuting. Bennett and I, however—we have a history. He's John Bennett's cousin, but years ago, I got the job as a new associate lawyer at Stockton and Bennett that he wanted."

"John didn't hire his own cousin?"

"No. John and I got to talking about it awhile back. I had finished much higher in my law school class, and he didn't think his cousin had the patience to practice general law."

"Wow. So ASA Bennett doesn't want to lose a case to you."

"No. The little bit of good news in this is that he probably doesn't think he has a strong enough case to be sure of a win. If he did, he wouldn't be leading up to a plea bargain. Instead, he'd be anticipating trouncing me in court."

Kate was working up the nerve to ask her next question, when Rob cleared his throat again.

"There's a couple other things. Two bullets were fired, one hit Manny and the other the wall. They were nine millimeter caliber. And something else... I'm not sure what to make of it. I asked about surveillance cameras inside Strategic's offices, and Bennett got cagey."

"How so?"

"He admitted there are cameras but wouldn't say what was on them, which tells me Hal wasn't."

A bubble of hope in her chest again. "Then whoever did go in the lab would be."

"Probably not or Bennett would have said so. I think they were jammed."

Her heart dropped to her stomach as she thought of the tracer gizmo Hal had given her. "Uh, I wouldn't be surprised if Hal has a jammer. He likes gadgets."

Rob blew out air and muttered under his breath. "Okay, I'll ask him about it too, and if he owns a gun. But here's my question—why would he jam the cameras and then do something as stupid as use his own badge?"

Kate drew in a breath and held it. "So you are going to stay with his case?"

"Yes, but I might have to advise him to take that plea bargain."

Her lungs relaxed. "He wouldn't fare well in prison."

"I know that, but..." Rob went silent.

"But what?"

"There's another reason a plea bargain may be forthcoming. Bennett may be afraid the feds will grab the case away from him."

"How could they do that?" she asked. Murder wasn't a federal case, unless the victim had been transported across state lines.

"Because treason trumps attempted murder."

"What?" Kate yelped.

"If Strategic decides to press charges for industrial espionage, that would mean Hal had violated the terms of his security clearance."

Edie stuck her head through the study doorway. "You okay, Mom?"

Kate covered the phone receiver. "Yes, sorry. I'm fine." To Rob, she said, "That would be considered treason?"

"Yeah, I'm pretty sure it would be."

"Holy–" Kate caught herself just in time. Edie was still standing in the doorway. "...crap!"

CHAPTER SEVEN

The sound of a ringing phone. Rose smiled at the sight of her husband's name on her dashboard screen. They hadn't seen much of each other in the last forty-eight hours—since Saturday afternoon, when she'd assigned him to watch Elaine Patterson, and she'd begun tailing John Cochlin, the tech Skip had followed to that maildrop on Friday. She'd also put a man on Harold Murdock.

"I think this lady's made me," Mac growled with his usual lack of preamble.

Rose seriously doubted that. He was former Special Forces and had been on covert operations where his life, and those of his men, depended on their ability to be invisible. And he'd now been a private detective for the better part of a decade.

"Why do you think so?" she asked.

"She looked up in her mirror, then suddenly veered right onto a side street. I had to cruise on by."

Rose shrugged one shoulder, even though Mac couldn't see her. This whole thing was probably a waste of time anyway. "Go back to her house. She'll show up eventually."

"I didn't say I lost her." His offended tone said Rose should know better. "Just that she might've realized she had a tail."

Rose stifled a chuckle. "Okay, where's she headed?"

"Looks like she's going around the block. Now she's got her blinker on to head the other way on York Road."

"So she might've remembered something she needed to do."

"Maybe. Where are you?"

"On York Road. Cochlin just turned into the Towson Diner."

Rose sedately followed his dark sedan into the crowded parking lot. At one-thirty, the diner was doing a booming business.

"Well whatdaya know? This lady's about to turn in there too."

Cochlin was still sitting in his car.

Rose watched from her own parked car as Elaine Patterson tucked her red BMW into one of the few remaining spaces and got out. Mac had backed his old pick-up truck—which he kept solely for surveillance—into a spot half a row down from her.

The woman didn't give him a second glance, or even a first one, as she walked toward the diner.

She hadn't made him. So why the trip around the block?

Cochlin now got out of his car and also walked toward the diner.

Mac exited his truck, his disheveled flannel shirt and jeans in harmony with the vehicle's grime and dents.

Rose texted him. *Bring me a coffee.*

He pulled his cell out of his back pocket and tapped it.

Will do popped up on her dashboard screen.

He crossed the lot to the diner. Through its big plate-glass windows, she saw him approach the carryout counter.

Don't see him, flashed on her screen. *She went to back corner booth.*

A few minutes went by. Mac exited the diner and strolled toward her car, his head swiveling as if he'd forgotten where he'd parked. He balanced one of the two styrofoam cups he was carrying on her hood, then scratched his head and scanned the lot again. A nod as he looked in the direction of his truck, and he strode in that direction.

Rose waited a few seconds, then lowered her window and grabbed the cup. It was hot against her fingers. She placed it in the cup holder in her center console, anticipating the jolt the hot liquid would give her. This was the time of day when surveillance was the hardest. One's natural circadian rhythms wanted to lull you to sleep.

She waited while Mac got himself settled back in his own

vehicle. Her phone rang again.

"Yeah," she answered.

"Cochlin came out of the men's room and sat down across from Patterson. I didn't get too close, since she might've made me already."

Rose didn't bother to argue that issue.

"They leaned in real close to each other," Mac said, "and started talkin'. I couldn't hear what they were sayin'."

Are Cochlin and Patterson having an affair? Out loud, she asked, "Did they act like lovers?"

"Could be. The discussion seemed kinda intense."

Rose mulled that over. Patterson might or might not have known Cochlin was going to be there, but had he been waiting for her?

The diner door opened. "Here comes Cochlin," she said.

The man was holding a large plastic cup, a straw sticking out of it. He made a beeline for his car without looking around.

Rose put her own car in gear, ready to follow him. She waited a couple of beats after he'd turned right on York Road before pulling up to the parking lot's exit. Once out on the main thoroughfare, with Cochlin in sight three cars in front of her, she said to Mac, "See ya later."

"Maybe sooner. Here comes Patterson. Looks like she got somethin' to go. She's carryin' a white paper bag."

Following Cochlin, Rose wound her way through the beginnings of rush-hour traffic. It seemed to start earlier and earlier.

"She's headed north," Mac said. "Didn't Cochlin turn south?"

"Yeah, so they're probably not meeting up somewhere else. Why would Cochlin just happen to pop in while she's getting her lunch?"

"And why would she sit down in a booth and then get carryout?"

"She could've changed her mind about staying to eat," Rose speculated, "after hearing whatever Cochlin told her."

"Or maybe it's a coincidence," Mac said, "that he happened

to stop for a cold drink and to use the can, and saw her there."

She glanced at the screen on her dash, and shook her head slightly. "You don't believe in coincidences."

"True. Catch ya later."

A tiny voice in Rose's head said she should've told him she loved him. They didn't say those words often, only when one or both were going into a potentially dangerous situation. It was their version of "be careful." Two words that they would never insult each other by uttering out loud.

She shook her head, this time at herself. There was nothing dangerous about following these two people around. The only risk was they might die of boredom.

Rose tailed Cochlin back to Strategic Electronics. She drove slowly around the lot, as if searching for the perfect parking place, while he headed inside the building.

Then she darted across the road to a strip shopping center. She needed a restroom. Before she finished this cup of coffee, she needed to get rid of the last one.

~~~~~~~

After another twenty-four hours of watching Cochlin do little more than drive to and from work, Rose made a tough decision. All this surveillance was expensive and didn't seem to be producing any results at this point. She called Mac off of Patterson and Bill Young off of Murdock, then went back to the agency herself.

In the operatives' bullpen, she peeked into the pink donut box on an empty desk. There were two left from this morning, one plain and one cream-filled. Her favorite.

Her stomach gurgled. Not the most nutritious lunch, but better than nothing. She grabbed the cream-filled and a couple of napkins and went to Skip's office.

He was bent over a file, reading.

She walked up next to his desk and glanced down. The Strategic file. Make that re-reading.

A frisson of shock ran through her when he looked up. His hazel eyes were clouded with worry, and there were dark circles under them.

"What's wrong?"

"Nothing."

She arched an eyebrow at him. She'd been told she had very expressive eyebrows.

He shrugged. "Nothing new. Just worried about the agency. I went over the books this morning. We're okay for this month. But without the income from the Strategic account, I'm not sure we'll be able to make payroll next month, not without a hefty boost from our reserves."

Her throat tightened. She was worried too but was trying not to think about it. They'd had slow times before, but not for this long.

She placed a napkin on his desk and laid the donut on it, then slid it across the polished wood. "I think you need this worse than I do."

He nudged the donut back. "Thanks, but I'm not hungry."

Rose lowered herself into the chair in front of his desk and struggled to find the right words. Comforting people wasn't her forte. "Worst case scenario, we go under, but none of us will go broke. Mac and I have the restaurant income and you all have got Kate's brokerage account."

She tried for a lighter tone. "You'll become a kept man, and I'll be a lady of leisure, eating donuts all day."

Skip snorted. "What about our people?"

"We don't owe them a living." That sounded colder than she'd intended. "What I mean is, they'll find other jobs. If it looks like everything's going south, we spend our last few thousand on good severance packages, to tide them over."

He nodded.

I can't believe we're having this conversation. Their agency had done a booming business for almost a decade, until six months ago. What had gone wrong?

She picked up the donut, then put it back down again. Suddenly she wasn't so hungry either.

They brainstormed about the case. "Could've been an innocent running-into-each-other thing at the diner yesterday," Rose said, "but Mac felt their conversation was serious. And it looked like Cochlin might have been waiting for her in the parking lot."

Skip sat back in his desk chair, seemed to relax a bit. "So maybe Cochlin's bank accounts are so low because he's trying to keep two women happy."

"Yeah, and if Patterson's living room furniture and the rock on her finger are any indicators, she's not likely to be satisfied with a posy of daisies now and then."

Skip shook his head. "No, that's probably what his poor wife gets."

"Or they simply ran into each other," Rose repeated, "and were sharing office gossip. Hey, was there anything in Manny's reports about Murdock leaving stuff related to the project out on his workbench?"

Skip shook his head again. "No. And there was no mention of it in his personnel records either."

"Patterson said she didn't write him up, just warned him not to do it again, but it was one of the things that made her suspicious of him. But she also said they'd all done it on occasion."

Skip frowned. "I'm wondering why she didn't mention it in my initial interview with her." A wrinkle on his forehead, which hadn't been there until recently, furrowed into a deeper crease. "Damn Latey for telling all of them about the leak. He made them suspicious of each other, and now it's hard to tell if the things they report are really off or just products of their paranoia."

Rose nodded. "Bill Young hasn't reported anything interesting on Murdock." She was laying the groundwork to tell him what she'd decided. It wasn't going to improve his mood any.

Her mind veered to Manny. Anger expanded in her chest. Kate and Rob both believed that Murdock wasn't his shooter. If they were right, then who the hell was? She fervently wished they could afford to keep a full investigation going.

She took a deep breath. "I'm stopping the surveillance. Too expensive for a case that isn't really a case anymore."

His body stiffened for a second, but then he nodded.

"We can keep working on it," she said, "when we're not busy with other things."

"Can we at least keep Landon at Strategic as a security guard for a bit longer?"

She'd forgotten about Phil Landon. "Is Strategic still paying him?"

"Probably, until Latey thinks to terminate him."

Rose paused to consider that. Phil turned his Strategic paycheck over to them. It was only about a third of what they paid him as an operative. But she didn't have any other case she needed him for right now. Might as well get a third of his pay covered.

"I guess we can leave him in place," she said, "until Strategic remembers he's not really one of theirs."

Skip rose from his chair. "I think I'll go have a little chat with Murdock about leaving components for a secret project out on his workbench."

Rose resisted the urge to say he should be out drumming up new clients. That had always been the division of labor between them. She supervised the operatives. He recruited new business. But she knew he would be out shmoozing with people, *if* he had any leads on potential clients.

She stood and they left his office together, the donut still sitting on his desk.

~~~~~~~~

Skip pulled up in front of Hal Murdock's house—a modest bungalow on a street of other modest houses.

A woman answered the door. She was about five-four and average build, except for a slight thickening around the middle. Her brown hair was a little too even to be completely natural, but her face was relatively smooth.

"Mrs. Murdock?"

"Yes."

He hesitated, still unsure if this woman was Murdock's mother. "Is your son home?"

She narrowed her eyes at him. "You a reporter."

"No, ma'am. I'm an investigator."

She moved back, letting him enter, apparently assuming he was from the police, as he'd hoped she would. Although he would have to disabuse her of that notion eventually.

The living room he'd stepped into was overfull with squared-off, sturdy furniture, a bit on the shabby side. But the space was spotlessly clean.

Hoping to butter her up before having to reveal his true identity, he smiled at her. "I gotta say, ma'am, you don't look old enough to be Harold's mother."

"Good genes, clean living," she snapped, seemingly unimpressed by the compliment. "Hal," she called out. "You got company."

After a moment, her lanky son entered the room. He halted abruptly when he saw Skip. "What do you want?"

"I only have a couple questions."

"I don't have to talk to you." Murdock's voice shook a little.

"No, you don't but would you rather talk to the police."

Mrs. Murdock had been glancing back and forth between them. Now her eyes bore into Skip's. "You're not the police?"

"No, ma'am. Private investigator."

Murdock's face had turned red. He glared at Skip. "He's the one who accused me of selling Strategic's secrets."

Skip couldn't say he blamed him for being pissed. "No, Strategic and the cops have accused you. My agency was still gathering information, and we knew what we had on you was all circumstantial."

Murdock ran fingers through his dark hair. Skip noted the hand was shaking as he lowered it again to his side.

Mrs. Murdock placed a gentle hand on her son's arm. "I think you need to leave, sir," she said to Skip, her tone crisp.

"No, Ma." Murdock patted her hand. "I'll talk to him. You'd better get to work."

His mother works? Why didn't that come out in the background check?

Mrs. Murdock eyed Skip, then moved to a gilt-framed mirror by the door. She patted some stray hairs in place. "I'll be home by midnight."

Murdock nodded.

Belatedly, Skip realized the pale blue dress she wore was a uniform. Once the woman was out the door, he asked, "What's your mom do for a living?"

"P-private nurse." Murdock's voice shook a little. He ducked his head. "In-home care for old people."

Ah. That helped to explain their comfortably padded bank accounts.

"She looks so young."

"Sh-she married right outta high school. She's fifty-eight."

Watch what you assume. Skip's mental image of the woman had been a stooped old crone.

Again, Murdock brushed a shaking hand over his hair.

Skip now recalled why he'd thought the man was their industrial spy. The hesitant speech, the nervous gestures—this guy acted like he was guilty of every crime ever committed.

"Can we sit?" Skip asked.

Murdock waved at an oversized armchair. He perched on the edge of the sofa. The young man's eyes never quite met Skip's. He stared slightly off to one side.

Skip resisted the urge to look behind him. He had planned to run Murdock through the whole sorry mess again—the leaks, the night Manny was shot—but he wasn't sure the guy wouldn't have a full blown panic attack before he got to the new questions.

A mild jolt ran through him. *Duh. That's what Kate's treating him for, anxiety.*

Suddenly the discrepancies in his and her perceptions of Hal Murdock made sense. He'd thought the guy was hiding something, acting guilty. She knew he suffered from some kind of anxiety disorder. He was *always* nervous.

Murdock had noticed the shift in his body language. His

eyes had gone wide. His Adam's apple bobbed in his throat as he swallowed hard.

The guy's afraid of me.

Actually more like terrified.

Skip kept his voice low and neutral. "I just have a couple of things I wanted to clear up."

Murdock made the briefest of eye contact, then his gaze shifted to Skip's other ear. He nodded.

"Your supervisor said something about you leaving some components of the project out on your workbench when you went to lunch one day."

Murdock's eyes went wide again. "That wasn't me."

"It wasn't?"

"No. John did that once, and Elaine bawled him out."

"She acted like it wasn't a huge deal," Skip said. "That it happens now and then."

Murdock was now maintaining eye contact. "Of course it's a big deal." His tone was mildly indignant. "We all have top secret clearances, but this project is so sensitive, it's compartmentalized."

Skip knew that but he let the guy keep talking.

"Leaving that stuff out meant either Elaine or I could have examined it and figured out John's part of the design."

Skip nodded, then scratched his chin. "I've wondered about that. How the heck do you all work on part of something, without knowing how the other parts work?"

"We're given specs." Murdock paused, but it didn't seem to be nervous hesitation this time. "Say the company's trying to design that table." He pointed toward the small dining room opening off of the room they were in. "My portion of the project is the legs, and maybe John has the braces and one of the other techs has the top."

Skip noted that the man's anxiety had gone way down as he talked shop.

"I'm told that I need to design a strong wooden pole. I can put curves or such in it to make it more attractive, but nothing that weakens it, and the ends need to be flat."

Skip smiled. "Good analogy."

The corners of Murdock's lips actually curled up a little.

"So who does know what all the parts do?"

"The president of the company knows what the project's supposed to do, and Fred Latey has a general idea. But the head engineer for the project is the only one who has all the specs. He's the one who did the original design."

"So you don't actually design the components."

"No, we build the prototypes from the specs and then test the components to make sure they do what they're supposed to do."

"And you're sure the time John Cochlin left stuff out, that was the only time that happened on this project?"

Murdock nodded. "But he didn't go to lunch. His wife called and said she thought she was going into labor. He just grabbed his coat and ran out of the lab."

"How long ago was this?"

"About mid December."

"But she didn't have the baby."

Murdock shook his head. "False alarm." He looked down at his hands in his lap. "She's carrying twins. The doc said they'd probably come early, maybe real early. John's been worried."

"How did Mrs. Patterson and Cochlin act when she was 'bawling him out?'" Skip made air quotes.

Murdock glanced up, then dropped his gaze again. A few seconds ticked by. "She was saying how critical it was to maintain security and all that, but she didn't seem to be real mad at him. I think she understood he wasn't thinking straight, because of his wife and the babies." Murdock's gaze moved around the room. "John seemed more distracted than nervous, even though he would've been in a lot of trouble if she'd told Fred Latey. He kept looking my way. I kinda wondered if he was mostly embarrassed that she was confronting him in front of me."

"The night my man was shot, you were there. Tell me about it."

Murdock twitched a little on his perch on the edge of the sofa. "Uh, I don't know what I thought I could accomplish. I had some half-baked idea I could look around the lab and maybe figure out who was leaking the stuff. But I chickened out."

"Did you go in the lab that night?"

"No, I never got past the lobby."

Skip pretended to believe him. "So who do you think is the spy?"

The man's head jerked up, but he didn't answer.

"If it isn't you, which of the other techs do you think it is?"

Murdock shook his head. "Not just techs. There are a few engineers involved in the project too. And somebody else in the company could've somehow gotten the specs."

Skip cocked his head to one side. "I was told the original specs wouldn't be enough. Y'all had made modifications after testing the components."

"But somebody else could've gotten into our lab."

"And into your computers?" Skip said, pumping a fair amount of skepticism into his voice. "They're pretty heavily encoded." He'd practically had to give Strategic one of his kids as a hostage in order to get them to give Manny the emergency security codes. And even those were compartmentalized. Latey had some of them, the head of security some more, and the CEO the rest.

Murdock didn't say anything.

"Who do you think could've gotten in there?" Skip asked.

"I don't know." Murdock stood up, wiped his palms on his jean-clad thighs. "Look, I gotta go out soon. I need to get ready."

Skip opted not to push him any further, for now. He rose from his chair.

Murdock bent back over the sofa, as if trying to put more space between them.

At six-five and two-forty, Skip knew he was imposing, but this guy had sat and talked with him for the last twenty minutes. Why suddenly did he seem afraid of him?

"You own a gun, Mr. Murdock?"

The man shook his head vehemently. "I… I don't like them."

Hmmph, doesn't mean you wouldn't use one if you felt threatened.

Skip eased toward the door. "Thanks for your time. I can see myself out."

Once he was out on the porch, the front door slammed behind him. Then the snick of a deadbolt being thrown.

CHAPTER EIGHT

Skip squirmed in his seat, trying not to think about his full bladder. He'd been watching Murdock's house for two hours.

Finally the man was on the move. He pulled his car into the small lot in front of a hole-in-the-wall Chinese carryout, halfway between his house and the Armstrong Building.

Skip blew out a frustrated sigh as he drove on by.

Not much he could read into a man going out for Chinese. But why had Murdock changed into nicer clothes? And his hair was slicked down, as if wet from a shower. All that just to go get carryout?

Since it was after five, Skip headed home instead of back to the office. Kate had a task force meeting tonight. On the way, he contemplated the discrepancies between Elaine Patterson's and Harold Murdock's versions of reality.

Someone had left top secret components out on their workbench. Elaine remembered Murdock doing so. He claimed it was John Cochlin.

So there were three possibilities. Elaine Patterson's memory was faulty, and she'd mis-remembered who had committed the sin of not locking up their work while away from the lab. Or Elaine had lied, or Murdock had lied.

Making a left onto York Road turned out to be impossible at this hour without a traffic light. Skip went right and down a block to make a U-turn.

Murdock had been the *least* nervous during that part of their discussion. He hadn't acted like a man who was lying.

It had happened in December, only a month ago. Surely a forty-year-old woman wouldn't become confused about who did what in such a short time?

And she had no motive to lie. The incident really had happened. Why blame it on Murdock instead of John Cochlin? It was something both Cochlin and Murdock could so easily refute.

But why would Cochlin do so if she was letting him off the hook? And Murdock was already accused of industrial sabotage and attempted murder, so who would believe him?

Which brought him back around to Murdock being the liar.

The man had seemed genuinely incensed by Elaine's implication that it was no big deal. Why would he emphasize that it *was* a big deal if he had been the culprit?

Arrghhh. Skip resisted the urge to bang his head against the steering wheel.

As he turned onto his street, he made a mental note to track down John Cochlin at lunchtime tomorrow and see what he had to say about the incident.

He couldn't do it in the morning because, thank the good Lord, he had a meeting at ten with a potential client.

~~~~~~~

Kate was late.

She hurried down the hall of the state office building in Annapolis and slipped into a conference room. The only empty chair at the large, polished wood table was at the end, directly opposite a small portable podium. Benjamin Horowitz, one of the behind-the-scenes movers and shakers in the state, and the head of the task force, stood behind the podium.

The chairs on either side of the table were occupied by the other members of the governor's police PTSD task force. Several of them were minor politicians from some of the counties. Two were police officials and the rest were a smattering of concerned citizens and health professionals.

The chief of police of Baltimore City glanced over from the chair next to Kate and nodded a greeting.

She nodded back as she pulled her pad out of her briefcase. She quickly flipped the top dozen pages—the ones with her notes from the Strategic case—under the pad.

She hadn't slept well the night before, waking up twice soaked with sweat. Now she prayed she could stay awake through the meeting.

Benjamin Horowitz gave some opening remarks, then gestured toward the door. "Tonight, ladies and gentlemen, we have three members of our various police forces around the state, who are going to talk to us about officers' concerns. They are at different levels within their departments, from a patrol officer to a shift sergeant to a detective."

When Ben introduced the first speaker, Kate gave the young man an encouraging smile. She had been responsible for recruiting him to talk to the task force. He was a rookie State Trooper, only six months on the job, and he spoke about the stresses of a new officer who doesn't quite know the ropes yet.

When he'd finished his remarks, Ben asked him to take a seat off to the side, in case there were any questions later.

The next policeman came through the conference room door and Kate's body tensed. She felt a little queasy as Detective Russell stepped to the podium.

She placed a hand on top of her pad, suddenly quite conscious of the notes hidden under it.

The detective's gaze circled the table, rested briefly on her, then moved on. "Thank you, ladies and gentlemen, for your willingness to help our police officers deal better with the stress of our jobs."

He spoke for a few minutes about the particular stressors that detectives experienced. Kate's tired mind started to wander. Then the word "politics" yanked her attention back.

"It's particularly difficult and stressful to do our jobs when we feel pressured by the powers-that-be to make sure our findings in an investigation point in a certain direction." Russell looked straight down the table at her, his eyes hard. "When we know someone involved in a case has *connections* with local or state authorities, it's very nerve-racking."

Heat spread through Kate's body and up into her cheeks. She gritted her teeth. *You jerk!*

"Will our careers be damaged if we seek the truth?" Russell continued, now scanning the faces of the task force again. "We have a good Samaritan law that protects doctors and others who stop to offer first aid to victims in an accident. Perhaps we should have similar regulations protecting officers of the law from stepping on political toes."

Kate resisted the urge to shake her head. As if there would ever be a way to control politics? But she knew he wasn't actually lobbying for such unrealistic measures. His remarks were aimed at her.

Her stomach twisted as a thought hit her. *Who does he know who got him on the agenda tonight?*

How ironic that she was now the one worried about political fallout. But of course, that was Russell's intention. She had underestimated him, seen him as just an annoying cop.

Next up was the watch sergeant. He talked about his worries for his people, how hard it was to send them out into the streets these days. Again Kate's mind started to wander.

"It's particularly hard when their actions might be second guessed later by not only their superiors but the press and the public."

She sat up straighter. The man now had her full attention. She noted for the first time that all the speakers tonight were male and white. Of course, she had recruited one of those speakers, but still.

"My officers are hesitant now," the sergeant said, "afraid they'll be accused of an unjustified shooting if they protect themselves. This Black Lives Matter stuff, it's stressing them out big time. And me too."

The black police chief beside her was holding a pencil. His hand tightened around it. She heard the soft snap of the wood breaking.

"I'm afraid their hesitation is going to get some of them killed," the speaker continued. "Thanks for listening."

Kate wondered if the sergeant was a member of a twelve-step program.

Benjamin Horowitz asked if anyone had any questions for the officers. When no hands went up, he thanked the three of them for taking their time to speak to the task force. All but Detective Russell took the hint and left the room.

Ben Horowitz scowled at him but Russell avoided eye contact.

Ben turned his attention to the rest of them. "Your thoughts, ladies and gentlemen?"

Todd Anderson, a medical doctor, turned to Russell. "I understand your concerns, Detective. But do you have any concrete suggestions on how we can begin to control political influence?"

The detective shrugged. "That's your job to figure out." His tone was borderline insolent.

Hot anger flared anew in Kate's chest, but she kept her mouth shut.

Ben Horowitz stood. He was at least seventy, a bit shrunken, with gray hair, what was left of it, and a small gray goatee. But he exuded authority. He stared at Russell, his brown eyes piercing. "Thank you for your time, Detective."

Kate felt some satisfaction when she noted that Ben's goatee was quivering. He was as pissed as she was.

Russell took his time as he pushed up from his chair and strolled to the door. Once there, he turned and smiled directly at Kate. "Have a good rest of your evening, folks."

He was no sooner out the door than the black woman next to Ben spoke up. "I'd like to address the issue raised by the watch sergeant."

The city police chief beside Kate held up his hand in a calming gesture. "It is stressful for the good cops to worry about whether they'll end up on the hot seat, or fired or prosecuted, when they're only trying to do their jobs."

The woman, Jasmine—Kate's tired brain couldn't remember

her last name—narrowed her eyes at the chief. "No more stressful than it is to be black in this community, worrying about some cop harassing you and yours or maybe shooting someone you love."

"Is there a way to identify a bad cop," Kate asked, "before they shoot someone?"

"Sure is." This from the sheriff of a rural county in southern Maryland. "Look at their resistin' arrest record." He spoke with a slight drawl in his voice.

"Resisting arrest?" Ben said, confusion on his face.

The city police chief spoke up. "How often their other arrests are accompanied by a resisting arrest charge. If it's often, that can mean they are overly aggressive."

"As in, into power instead of just enforcing the law," Jasmine said.

Darn, what was her last name… Jackson. Jasmine Jackson.

"Aren't we getting a little off topic here?" Dr. Anderson said.

"I don't think so." This from Cheryl Mendez, a white woman and fellow mental health professional, who was married to a Latino police officer. "With all the news media about unjustified shootings, it is a concern for officers now. A big concern."

"Good officers shouldn't be stressed by the actions of bad ones," Kate said. "Not to mention it makes their jobs more dangerous." There had been several unprovoked attacks on random police officers in the last year, the worst of which had been in Dallas last summer.

"So maybe we should give some consideration," Ben Horowitz said, "to including recommendations for how departments can weed out overly aggressive officers."

"Before they're 'weeded out,'" the rural sheriff made air quotes, "additional trainin' might be a good idea."

"As would anger management counseling." Kate smiled at Ms. Jackson. "And if we're making the community safer for African-American citizens, so much the better."

"And how about including recommendations for more funding to pay for all that," the city police chief said, his tone acerbic.

Kate nodded.

A lively debate followed as to whether or not this was within the parameters of their assignment from the governor. Those for including it won out, by a slim margin.

Finally, Ben adjourned the meeting. "Mrs. Huntington, could I speak to you for a few minutes?"

Kate rose with the others, put her pad and pen in her briefcase, but lingered as the group trailed out of the room, chatting amongst themselves.

"Do you know Andrew Russell?" Ben asked.

Kate's stomach tightened. Ben's sharp eyes didn't miss much. But did his use of the detective's full name mean he did know him personally? Was Ben the man's connection within the group?

"You remember I said my husband is a private investigator? He's involved in a case that Detective Russell is assigned to."

Ben gave her his patented hard stare. "Do you wish to recuse yourself from the task force?"

Her hand gripped the handle of her briefcase tighter as she struggled to keep her expression neutral. She would love to get out of the task force, which had turned out to be much more time-consuming than she'd figured on. But not like this. Russell would assume he'd gotten her kicked off.

"No. I can't see how my husband's case would impact on my participation." She was gratified to hear no hesitation in her voice.

Ben nodded, then placed his hand gently on her back in a gentlemanly gesture. They left the room together.

~~~~~~~~

At noon on Wednesday, Kate sat in a booth at Mac's Place and tried to figure out why Skip was being so evasive about recommending another P.I. for Hal Murdock's case. She thought she'd had him cornered on the subject last night, after her meeting. But he'd said that everyone he'd called was too busy to take on more work.

Everyone is so busy, *except* Canfield and Hernandez?

Worry made her queasy. All businesses had their ups and

downs. But Skip had been saying things were slow for a while now. Was there too much competition in the area these days?

Towson had lost its county seat flavor years ago. Today it was more an extension of the sprawling metropolis of Baltimore.

Maybe Skip and Rose should open a second office on the other side of the city, in Essex perhaps. It would be a bold move, when their finances were already tight.

But she could lend them the money for the startup out of the brokerage account. Maybe she'd broach the subject with Rose first.

"Hi, Kate." Rob dropped onto the bench across from her, interrupting her thoughts.

"How you doing?" She noted he looked somewhat less exhausted than he had the last couple of weeks.

The waitress approached and they ordered coffee and their usual crab cakes.

Once she was headed off to place their order, Rob said, "Sorry I've been a grump lately."

"You've had good reason," Kate said. "I'd be grumpy too if a friend referred a case to me that turned out to be impossible."

Rob gave her a small smile. "Believe it or not, that wasn't the main thing stressing me out. Even though I've taught this course three times now, the beginning of the semester is always a zoo."

She'd forgotten all about his class at the law school. "I thought the idea was to cut back on your caseload some and teach instead."

"Best laid plans and all that jazz." Rob nodded a thank you to the waitress as she placed coffee cups in front of them. He took a sip.

Kate glanced around at the crowded tables and the line by the door of people waiting to be seated. "Speaking of a zoo, this place is mobbed today."

"Big trial at the courthouse across the street. Guess it's bring-ing out the looky-lous." Rob placed the heel of his hand against his chest and rubbed.

"What's the matter?"

"I gotta stop drinking coffee. It's been giving me heartburn lately."

Kate shook her head. With her frequent insomnia, caffeine was the only thing that kept her going some days. "I'd hate to have to give up coffee."

"My dad used to complain that getting old meant you had to give up all your vices, one at a time. His favorite line was 'Aging ain't for sissies.'"

Kate laughed, then thoughts of her own hot flashes sobered her mood. "So getting back to our shared case, Skip still hasn't found a P.I. who can take it on."

"No rush. The courts are so backed up, I doubt we'll get on the docket until June."

"That's not good," Kate said. "H... Uh, the client," they avoided using even clients' first names out in public, "he's on unpaid leave until the issue gets resolved."

"I know. I was the one who got the company to change it to that, rather than outright firing him."

Kate's mouth fell open. She stared at Rob. "They were gonna fire him? Before the trial?"

"Yeah. I pointed out that they might be facing a lawsuit if he's acquitted."

"Five months though." She shook her head. "That's a long time to go without a paycheck. His house is paid for, but he's still gotta eat."

"Not going to be a problem," a male voice boomed over the background chatter of the other diners.

Jumping a little, Kate swiveled on the bench. It took her a second to recognize the man in a business suit standing next to their booth.

"Your boy's been arrested again, for murder this time," ASA Bennett said. "The state will be feeding him for the foreseeable future."

Rob's face paled. "Manny?"

Manny can't be dead. Kate felt lightheaded as she fought the sense of *deja vu*. She'd been sitting with Rob in Mac's Place when she'd first learned of Eddie's death.

Rob grabbed her hand and squeezed it.

Belatedly, it registered that Bennett was shaking his head. "Not of Ortiz. This time he killed one of his real coworkers."

CHAPTER NINE

Bile burned the back of Rose's throat. She couldn't seem to stay focused on the meeting.

She'd called off the surveillance. If only they'd still been watching, they might have seen what happened.

Or been able to stop it.

The image of the woman and kids piling into an older model minivan came unbidden into her mind's eye. Mrs. Cochlin had been hampered by her big belly as she'd tried to help her husband strap the children in. Then Cochlin had sedately driven his family to church.

Rose swallowed hard and forced her attention back to the meeting.

She glanced down the conference table at Kate. She looked like she was struggling to hold back tears. She'd been picking at the crab cake sandwich and salad in the styrofoam container in front of her. Now she pushed it away.

"What happened to the whole conflict-of-interest thing?" Kate's tone was angry, even though they'd just admitted to her that they'd been investigating the case. That news should've made her happy.

Skip was standing by the whiteboard, where he'd been listing what they knew. He now gave his wife an apologetic look. "I didn't want to get your hopes up. Not until we'd found out more."

Rose cleared her throat. "I don't think it's a conflict now anyway. Latey said he considered the case closed and sent us a check."

"Which has cleared the bank, by the way," Skip told her.

Rose's insides relaxed a little. At least they'd make payroll for the next couple of weeks, without dipping into their reserves.

She glanced at Mac sitting beside her. With both of them working for the agency, they'd be in deep do-do if it went under. She'd lied to Skip. The income from the restaurant was a nice supplement but it wouldn't be enough to live on, not after all the expenses and wages came out of it. Mac would have to fire the manager and go back to running it himself.

And unless she found other work, they'd have to give up their house and move back into the apartment above the restaurant. She cringed internally at the thought of working for someone else, after a decade of self-employment.

Mac's lips were pursed, but as his gaze met hers, his eyes softened. He gave a slight shake of his head. He was telling her not to worry.

Warmth filled her chest. For someone who usually seemed clueless about emotions, he read hers like a book. And she made a point of being hard to read—except by him.

She felt her facial muscles relax and gave him a small smile.

Skip was telling Kate about following Cochlin to the maildrop place on Friday.

Rose and Mac chimed in with what little they'd found out during their surveillance. They'd no sooner finished when the conference room phone rang.

Skip got to it in two long strides. He picked up the receiver and listened for a moment. A grin slowly spread across his face. "Wait. Let me put you on speaker."

Rob's voice filled the room. "I was telling Skip, I think Bennett's jumped the gun. He doesn't have any solid reason for believing that John Cochlin's death isn't the suicide that it appears to be. He was found in a hotel room, with an empty bottle of pills, his own prescription, by the bed. And his wife told the police he's been preoccupied lately about financial issues."

Rose swallowed hard again. Good news for them and Hal

Murdock. Bad news for Mrs. Cochlin. It would be hard enough for her to raise those kids on her own, without having to deal with the reality that her husband committed suicide.

"He left a note," Rob continued. "Said he was the one who'd sold Strategic's secrets to their competitor. He needed the money to dig them out of debt. But his conscience had gotten to him. I didn't see the note, was told that's the gist of it."

"So why does Bennett think Hal killed him?" Kate asked.

"The note was computer-generated, not handwritten, no signature, so anybody could've written it. And Mrs. Cochlin has no idea where her husband stashed the payoff he got. The police searched their house looking for it. Nada. And it's not in their bank accounts, and the debts haven't been paid."

"That's pretty flimsy," Rose said.

"Which is why I think Bennett's jumped the gun," Rob said. "He doesn't want to give up a case that he now thinks he can win. Sobbing widows tend to sway juries. I'll keep you all posted, but with any luck I'll have Murdock out of jail by the end of the day." He disconnected.

A knock on the conference room door. The agency's receptionist stuck her head in and looked at Skip. "You wanted the mail as soon as it came?"

He waggled his fingers at her in a come-in gesture. She handed him a bundle of letters. He leafed through them, took one out and handed the rest back to her. "Thanks, Ginny."

He held up the envelope as the young woman left. "I mailed this Saturday to the maildrop address, with Cochlin's name on it. It's come back as undeliverable."

"Which means he closed his mailbox there, once he got that envelope he was carrying?" Kate asked.

"Maybe," Rose said, "but usually they forward anything that comes in for at least a week or two."

"If you give a forwardin' address," Mac said.

Good point, Rose thought.

Skip, still standing, propped one foot on a chair and leaned an elbow on his raised knee. "The other possibility is that the box was rented with a fake name."

Mac scratched his stubbled chin. "Which ain't as easy to do these days as it once was."

Rose shrugged. "Just because they're supposed to ask for I.D. doesn't mean they do."

"And I.D. can be forged," Skip said.

As we well know. They had developed several false identities to be used in undercover work. One of which—Luis Gomez—was now blown, thanks to the Strategic case.

"Do you know anything about the gun Manny was shot with?" Kate was asking. "Rob said it was a nine millimeter."

"Dolph got his hands on a copy of the police report," Skip said. "No gun was found, but yes, the bullets were nine millimeter. Fortunately, only one hit Manny. Went in through the back." He turned slightly and pointed to his own back. "Collapsed his left lung, took out a chunk of rib on its way out the front."

Kate winced.

Rose figured Manny was lucky to be alive. A nine millimeter slug at close range could've done a lot more damage. As it turned out, the doctors had been more worried about his head injury.

"That janitor's quick thinking," Skip said, "and Officer Peters—the guy you were riding with, Kate—getting there so fast, that probably saved his life."

Rose nodded. "People think gunshot wounds kill because of tissue damage. They can, but more often it's loss of blood that gets people."

Kate glanced her way, then turned her gaze back to Skip. "So where's this leave us?"

Rose suspected the words had been chosen carefully. Kate wasn't only asking where they should go next in the investigation. She was asking if the agency was going to continue to investigate.

"I think one thing's legit about Cochlin's suicide note," Skip said. "He was the spy."

Kate leaned forward and tapped the pad in front of her. "Hal reported to me that he overheard a phone conversation, in the lab the day Manny was shot. It was a man, but the guy's voice was too low to recognize it. It might've been Cochlin. From what Hal could make out, the guy was talking about coming into the lab that night. That's what inspired Hal to go there."

Skip shot his wife a sharp look.

"What?" Kate said, her voice rising some. "You kept telling me you couldn't investigate, and your client had closed the case. How would I know you were still poking around and could use that information?"

Rose held her breath, but before Skip and Kate could get into it further, Mac jumped in. "How come he couldn't tell who it was?"

"He said he got up to see who was on the phone, but they'd hung up already. There were four men in the lab at the time."

"Can you get their names?" Rose said.

Kate nodded.

"So it's lookin' like Cochlin's our spy," Mac said, "but did he shoot Manny?"

Rose shook her head. "I don't see it. I don't think he'd have the gumption. Hit him on the head maybe, but shoot him in the back? Nuh-uh."

"Fred Latey was awful quick to call the case closed," Skip said. "I want to take a closer look at him. He could've been the person Murdock heard, or Allen, the head engineer."

Kate frowned. "I didn't write down his exact words, but I got the impression the people in the lab were peers, not someone above him in the hierarchy."

"We need those names," Mac said.

"I was gonna call him later," Kate said, "to check on him. I'll get them then."

Skip waved the undeliverable envelope in his hand. "We should dig deeper into Cochlin."

"Won't the police be doing that now?" Kate asked.

Rose grimaced. "Yes, but we're not necessarily looking for the same things."

"Dolph's coming in tomorrow," Skip said. "Put him on Cochlin. And ask him to check out Paul Allen too."

Rose nodded. Despite being the oldest member of the staff, Dolph was the most computer savvy.

Mac snorted . "If there's anythin' there, Dolph'll find it."

~~~~~~~~~~

After the meeting at Skip's agency, Kate headed home. With her reduced client schedule, she now had most Wednesday afternoons off. Once she started teaching, they would be filled with paper grading and class preparation. Today, however, her only obligation was to make a couple of calls regarding the PTSD task force.

Inside the front door, she kicked off her shoes and looked longingly at the sofa.

She forced herself to make the calls, then tried to reach Hal. It went straight to voicemail. Perhaps he wasn't out of jail yet. She pushed aside the worrying thought that Rob might not be able to get him released. Best not to cross bridges prematurely.

She flopped down on the sofa.

Toby took her semi-prone position as an invitation to saunter over and request a few pets. She obliged with a scratch behind each silky ear. Then her hand dropped to her side.

Discontent with such a mediocre show of affection, the dog maneuvered his nose under her palm and nudged her hand upward.

Normally this would elicit a chuckle and more petting. But not today. "Go lie down, boy."

He slowly walked to his bed across the room, glancing back over his shoulder twice to see if she'd changed her mind. She smiled a little at the exaggerated poor-me look on his face.

She swung her feet up onto the sofa. Her body felt like lead.

Why was she so tired? She'd slept okay last night, for a change. All too often lately she woke up in the wee hours soaking wet from night sweats.

Okay, I'm not just tired, I'm depressed.

How much of that was about Hal Murdock and how much

was menopause?

"Dear God," she muttered out loud. She'd just admitted she was menopausal. Well, technically the term was perimenopause, the period leading up to true menopause, the cessation of ovulation.

The end of a woman's reproductive years.

Butterflies fluttered in her chest. Realistically she and Skip had no desire for more children. But still...

Tears sprang to her eyes. Suddenly she was plunged back to the time when she and Eddie were trying to get pregnant. They'd gone through so much—craving a child, discussing *ad nauseam* the options of *in vitro* fertilization, fertility hormones, adoption. And then she'd found out she was pregnant, weeks after Eddie's murder.

She swallowed hard. This was ridiculous. She had a good life, a great life. What did she have to be upset about?

Why am I arguing with my hormones?

She pushed up off the sofa and headed for the kitchen, seeking a distraction.

Forty minutes later, Kate had tossed the last of the iffy leftovers into the kitchen trashcan. The refrigerator was now spotless.

The phone rang. "You okay?" Liz said. "Just heard from my husband that your mutual case has gotten a whole lot messier."

"Yeah. Did Rob say if he got the client released?"

"He did."

Kate blew out air. "Good." But she didn't particularly want to talk about the case right now. "Hey Liz, how long does menopause last?"

A beat of silence. "You've been having symptoms—what five months now?"

"It's that obvious?"

"Probably only to women who've been there, done that."

"So I'm about halfway through?"

Another pause. "The first year."

"What?" Kate yelped. "How long did yours last?"

"Three years."

Her heart sank. She had two and a half more years of this!

"The good news is," Liz said, "you feel a whole lot better after it's over. I think the average is two years."

"Only slightly better. Especially since Edie's showing significant signs of puberty these days."

A low chuckle. "Poor Skip. Surrounded by out-of-control female hormones."

"Don't feel sorry for him. He's still perfect Daddy, while I've become the mother from hell."

"It's a rough age," Liz agreed. "Remember what we went through with Samantha?"

Kate groaned. "Don't remind me." The Franklins' youngest had rebelled in every way imaginable, with the exception of drugs, thank heavens.

"But she's delightful now," Liz said. "You all will survive, honest you will."

The front door opened, then slammed shut again. Billy's footsteps pounded up the stairs. Edie's somewhat lighter ones trudged toward the kitchen.

"I'd better go," Kate whispered into the phone. "The hormonally-challenged offspring has arrived."

Another low chuckle. "Hang in there. This too shall pass."

"Not nearly soon enough."

~~~~~~~~~

Kate sank down on the sofa. Finally, the kids were in bed. Why was that such a struggle these days?

Because everything with Edie is a struggle these days.

Skip came down the stairs and settled onto the cushion beside her. "You okay?"

"I'm fine." It was a semi-lie. She was sort of okay, but really not fine.

He dropped an arm around her shoulders. "It's been a crazy week."

"And it's only Wednesday."

He let out a soft snort. "At least we're now on the same side of the Strategic case."

She swallowed, took a deep breath. "Hal told me some things." Things she hadn't felt ready to share with the whole crew earlier that afternoon.

He leaned slightly away and turned his head to look at her. "Oh?"

"I still think he's innocent." Did she really believe that?

Skip's face went blank, but his jaw tensed.

"Tell me."

She told him about the bug Hal had planted and what he'd heard the night Manny was shot.

Skip was now scowling.

She hurried to get the rest out. "Rob found out that Hal's badge was used to get into the lab that night. Hal told him the badges can be cloned. He doesn't know how to do it exactly, but theoretically, it can be done."

Skip sat rigid, his face still turned in her direction, but he stared past her. "Can we trust anything Murdock says?"

Kate wasn't sure how to respond to that.

She took another deep breath. "Here's what I know. Hal Murdock is a gentle soul. I don't believe he would intentionally hurt someone physically. But he's not a coward. So I *can* believe that he would attempt to investigate on his own, to find out who was selling secrets that would damage his employer."

Skip still wasn't looking at her, which was starting to annoy her. She squashed the feeling, for now.

Suddenly, he said, "Does Murdock have an anxiety disorder?"

That jolted her. Not at all what she'd expected him to say. She didn't know how to answer him, since confidentiality demanded she not discuss Hal's diagnosis. She went with a lighthearted tone. "I can neither confirm nor deny that statement."

He met her gaze. "I need to understand him."

She took a deep breath, let it out slowly. "I can only talk in generalities."

He nodded.

Kate sank back into the circle of his arm and looked across the room.

Toby lay on his bed, snoring away. She envied him.

"Anxiety and fear are first cousins," she said, "but they're not exactly the same emotion. Fear is more concrete, related to specific concerns. Anxiety is often more free-floating."

She paused to think through how to explain it. "For most of us, anxiety, while more vague, is still related to reality, such as being anxious before a big presentation. But in some people it's a more chronic thing. Sometimes it's brain chemistry, a biological predisposition to anxiety. Sometimes that generalized anxiety is programmed into us by early experiences."

She turned her head and made eye contact with her husband. "And then there's social anxiety."

"That's what Hal has?" Skip asked.

Again, she had to answer with generalities, but she knew Skip would understand what she wasn't saying. "Social anxiety is often one part genetics and one part, or sometimes several parts, environment. Take a person who's genetically predisposed to be shy and/ or anxious. Add an abusive environment to the equation, and you can end up with someone who is terrified of rejection and ridicule."

Skip tilted his head in a half nod. "I met his mother today. She didn't strike me as the shy type, and if his father was abusive, well, that doesn't sound like a shy man to me."

She shifted around to face him. "Genetics can be more complicated than that. Sometimes it's a matter of a combination of genes from both sides, or a throwback to an earlier generation."

Skip's eyes drifted off to the side for a moment, then his gaze returned to her face. "His nervousness was part of why we suspected him."

She wasn't surprised. Shy people were misread all the time, as aloof, stuck up, and sometimes, as in this case, nervous liars.

"That's why Rob's worried," she said. "If he has to put Hal on the stand, he'll come across as a bundle of nerves and the jury might conclude that he's lying."

Skip nodded and once again gazed across the room.

She followed his line of vision. Dust bunnies had taken up residence along the far baseboard. She'd have to talk to the cleaning lady about that.

"You're doing it again, you realize?" He didn't elaborate, but she knew what he meant.

"I've been trying not to get too involved," she said.

He sighed and tightened his arm around her shoulders. "You care. It's what makes you good, as a therapist and as a mother."

She snorted softly. "I haven't exactly been feelin' the love there lately."

"It's a rough age. We'll survive," Skip echoed Liz's words from earlier. Suddenly, he stood and held out his hand.

She let him pull her to a stand.

He wrapped his arms around her and dropped a tender kiss on her lips. "The fact that you care," he whispered, "it's a big part of why I love you."

She circled his waist with her arms and smiled up at him. "I love you too."

He claimed her lips again, this time more passionately.

Heat surged through her. *Hot flash or turn on?*

The heat settled into her core and burned a path southward.

Turn on. It was her last coherent thought for several moments.

They came up for air, panting. Somewhere along the way, her fatigue had melted away.

Skip ran his hands down her sides, then up again to cup her breasts.

Self-conscious worries intruded. Her sides were fleshier than they'd once been, her breasts sagging a little lower.

He skimmed his thumbs across her nipples.

Even through layers of fabric, the gesture sent a jolt of electricity through her.

Again he lowered his mouth to hers. She opened her lips, inviting him in.

CHAPTER TEN

At a traffic light, Skip caught himself drumming his fingers impatiently on the steering wheel. Normally he was a pretty laid-back person, but lately...

Despite the sweet lovemaking of last night—he smiled at the memory—he was wound tighter than a drum.

At least, he and Kate were on the same side again.

He fisted and relaxed first one hand, then the other, a trick she had taught him for stress management. He tried the same tactic with the tight muscles in his neck and jaw, tightening and releasing them, with minimal results.

Too much stress. Maybe they should take a vacation somewhere.

Scratch that. Even on vacation, Kate usually managed to end up in somebody else's mess.

This time, she'd landed in the same mess he was in.

Before leaving the office, he'd added Fred Latey's name to Dolph's list of dig-deeper background checks. Although they'd ordered a routine check from the outside company on him, they'd never considered him as a serious candidate for the leaks since he was the one who'd hired them.

A horn blasted. Skip jerked his head up. The light had turned green. He hit the accelerator.

If Latey was in on the espionage, why hire a P.I. to look into it? Had the powers above him in Strategic's organization demanded an investigation? If so, why hire Canfield and Hernandez? They had a good reputation for being thorough.

Not that we did such a hot job this time around.

He almost overshot the entrance to the Armstrong building. Slamming on the brake, he spun the truck into the turn. Tires squealed in protest.

The receptionist placed the phone receiver back in its cradle. "Mr. Latey can see you now."

Skip blew out a quiet sigh of relief. He hadn't called for an appointment, hadn't wanted to give the man a chance to ask questions or to prepare his own answers.

Skip smiled at the young woman behind the oversized desk. "Thanks. I know the way." He held out a hand for the temporary badge she proffered.

Elaine Patterson passed him in the hall, outside the test lab. She gave him a big smile. There was a glint in her eye.

Was she coming on to him? Lord knew he should be used to it by now, but the scrawny teenager he'd once been was still alive enough inside of him to be surprised occasionally by female reactions to his adult physique.

Latey's office door was open. He stood behind a desk even bigger than the receptionist's. His ruddy cheeks were a little redder than usual and the birthmark was a murky purple. It reminded Skip of an eggplant.

Latey's white dress shirt was partially untucked on one side. Jamming it back into his waistband with one hand, he gestured with the other toward a chair in front of his desk. "What can I do for you, Canfield?" The calculating look in his eye belied the friendly tone.

"Just a little follow-up on the case." Skip settled his tall frame into the chair. "I figured I should touch base in light of John Cochlin's death."

Shaking his head, Latey sat down. "A sad development. Very sad."

"Do you believe that he was your leak?"

"Harumph. Why shouldn't I?" Latey waved a big hand in

the air. Light from the florescent tubes overhead glinted on a gold wedding band. "A confession in a suicide note after all. I'm surprised you all didn't find anything on him."

"We found that he was in a lot of debt, but other than that he checked out clean. Still does."

And his debts haven't been paid off, so where's the money? Skip didn't ask that question out loud.

"I don't see the point of all this," Latey huffed out. "You've already been paid, even though your investigation didn't turn up the real culprit."

"We would have soon enough," Skip said, "if our man hadn't been shot."

Latey narrowed his eyes at him. "You're not thinking of instituting some kind of lawsuit, are you? I'd think those would be the risks you take, when you're a P.I."

"The thought had never crossed my mind. But I'm feeling like we didn't get a chance to finish the job. Everybody jumped to the conclusion that Harold Murdock was at fault..." Skip let his voice trail off.

Latey waved his hand in the air again. "We'll make it up to him. He's coming back tomorrow, and I'm going to get him back pay for the time he was off."

Previously Skip hadn't had any particular opinion of this man, but now he decided he didn't like him. "That's good of you." He managed, barely, to keep the sarcasm out of his tone.

Latey stood, a not so subtle dismissal.

Skip remained seated. "I'm not convinced we've found all the spies."

Latey put his hands on his hips. The pose would have looked more impressive if his spare tire wasn't hanging over his belt.

"It you're trying to drum up more work, forget it. I don't throw good money after bad."

Skip's body tensed. But he kept his face and voice neutral. "I'm not sure I get what you mean."

Again, the dismissive flash of his hand. "It was a bad decision.

We all make them sometimes."

"Which decision?"

Latey's ruddy cheeks turned brick red. A muscle in his lower jaw twitched, giving the eggplant birthmark a heartbeat. "To hire you, or at least to keep you on after I heard…"

Skip's chest tightened. He stood up, towering over the man. "Heard what?"

Latey broke eye contact. He stared at the right front corner of his desk. "A rumor, that's all, that you weren't as good as you'd once been."

Skip's stomach churned. "Exactly where did you hear this rumor?"

"Look, I'm not gonna say. I was told this in confidence."

Convenient.

"Thank you for your time, Mr. Latey." Skip didn't bother to offer his hand.

Once out of the building and in his SUV, he shifted his body to settle it more comfortably in the seat, but his insides were nowhere close to settled.

He'd gotten no answers, except to one question that he hadn't asked—why business had been so slow lately.

He felt like he'd been punched in the gut.

~~~~~~~~

Hal Murdock was Kate's last morning client. She never had been able to reach him last night, but maybe it was for the best. Better to be able to read his reactions when she asked him about the people in the lab when he overheard that conversation.

He was ecstatic about being reinstated in his job. Although most people wouldn't know he was ecstatic. He was a master at hiding all emotions except anxiety, and embarrassment. That one showed up on his cheeks as a pink tinge on a regular basis.

Good at hiding feelings. Have I given him too much benefit of the doubt? Could he be capable of shooting people and staging suicides?

The pink tide was moving up his face. She yanked her attention back to his words.

"I went out for Chinese last night." He gave her a slight smile and then ducked his head. "To celebrate."

Kate could guess where this was leading. "Was she there?"

He raised his head, nodded, then actually grinned. "And she smiled at me, and spoke."

Kate hid her own smile. "What'd she say?"

"Something about not usually seeing me there on Wednesdays. I blurted out that I was celebrating." He paused, ducking his head again.

"What did she say to that?"

"Oh, well, she asked what I was celebrating. I didn't want to go into the whole mess, so I just said a new job. Is that lying to her? You said it's important to always tell the truth to someone you're interested in."

It was getting harder to suppress her own grin. This guy had a degree in computer technology and probably made more money than she did, but he was such an innocent when it came to relationships. "Small white lies are allowed. What'd she say then?"

"Congratulations, but she smiled again, and then said something like see ya later."

Now Kate let her grin surface. "And I'll say it too. Congratulations, the ice is now officially broken. Next time you see her there, you smile and say hi. Can you do that?"

"Yeah, I think so." He looked her right in the eye, his gaze soft. "She has a real pretty smile."

Kate almost laughed out loud.

As the hour was winding down, she found her opening when Hal mentioned the leaks. "The day you overheard that phone call, you said there were four people in the lab. Who were they?"

He gave her a funny look. "Why?"

"Mr. Franklin has a private investigator looking into the case." She wasn't totally clear why she didn't want to get into her connection to that private investigator. It was all so complicated, and she wasn't sure how Hal would react to the revelation that the "security guy" his firm had hired was actually her husband.

And a quick glance at the clock on her wall told her they were almost out of time.

"But John confessed?" Hal's tone conveyed a question mark.

"Do you believe him?"

"I don't know. He might have been the spy. He was worried enough about money. But I find it hard to believe he committed suicide."

"He was one of the people in the lab that day, wasn't he?"

"Yeah, and two of the other techs." Hal gave her their names.

Kate jotted them down. "You said four people."

"Garrett Watson. He's one of the engineers. He was way down by Elaine's desk though."

"Elaine Patterson? Was she there?"

"No, she was out to lunch. Watson was leaning over her desk, like maybe he was leaving her a note."

Or using her phone, Kate thought as she added Watson's name to her note.

She changed the subject. "So next week, we can go back to your usual appointment time?"

Hal took the hint and stood. "Yeah, that works."

"Congrats again." Kate grinned.

He returned the grin, then blushed and headed out the door.

Kate stood in the middle of her office and listened. The cacophony of noises from the street below sounded normal— mostly traffic going by and the occasional distant horn. Still she couldn't resist the urge to go to her window and watch as Hal walked to his car, unlocked it and got in.

No policemen came by to arrest him today.

Twenty minutes later, she was parked outside the Cochlins' house, unsure if she should go in. Would the police see this as interfering in an official investigation?

Worse yet, would Skip see it as interfering in his?

"I'm only here to express my condolences to the woman," she

said out loud. Her steering wheel offered no reply.

I can't sit here forever. She had a client at three.

Squaring her shoulders, she pushed her car door open.

After dispensing with the awkwardness at the door and politely turning down refreshments, Kate sat across from Mrs. Cochlin in a modestly furnished living room.

"Johnny's sleeping, so we need to keep our voices down." The woman brushed a stray clump of brown hair out of her face. "Who did you say you were again?"

"My husband's been involved in the investigation at Strategic Electronics."

The woman's forehead creased in a confused frown.

Kate leaned forward. "Don't worry, I'm not some sick, nosy person looking to intrude on your grief. I... well, I lost my first husband... years ago, suddenly and tragically. And I was pregnant at the time."

Mrs. Cochlin dropped her head. She patted her round stomach with one hand while swiping a tear off her cheek with the other. "I, uh..."

"You don't have to make polite conversation. I just wanted you to know you're not alone." Kate pulled a brochure out of her purse, the one she'd extracted from her file cabinet before leaving the office.

Mrs. Cochlin took it with a shaky hand. A tear fell on the front, leaving a gray spot that slowly spread.

"It's about a support group, for those dealing with grief." Kate paused. "Would you like to talk about things now? Or not?" No matter how much she wanted more information, she wasn't going to push the woman.

Mrs. Cochlin shook her head, then nodded. She put her hands on the edge of the sofa and pushed herself farther back into the flower-covered cushions. She had reached the awkward stage of pregnancy where there's no such thing as a comfortable position.

"John's a good man, a good father." Like many newly bereaved loved ones, she didn't seem to notice that she was using the present tense. "But now all anyone will think about is…" She dropped her gaze to the brochure still in her hand. "Is that he was a thief."

Kate didn't say anything. She knew there was nothing *to say*, nothing that would really help.

"He worried so about money." Mrs. Cochlin still wasn't looking her way. "I told him I'd go back to work, once the babies were born, that we'd be okay."

Babies? The poor woman's carrying twins?

"But he said the daycare would cost too much to be worth it. And he knew how I really wanted to stay home with the kids." The last sentence was punctuated by a stifled sob. "Now I'll have to go to work."

Why would this man commit suicide, knowing it would leave his family worse off?

Throat constricted, Kate kept quiet. She knew she was wearing what Rob called her "therapist face." It wasn't hard to feel sympathy for this woman. If Eddie hadn't had the foresight to take out a sizeable insurance policy on himself, she would have been in the same boat. Instead, she'd been able to hire Maria and to stay home until she truly wanted to go back to work.

"I'm sure John must have been preoccupied lately," Kate said, to get her going again on her husband.

She nodded. "But then he came home Friday and he was all smiles. He said our troubles were over and we could relax. He'd found a way to get rid of all the debt. But he had to wait for the bank to open on Tuesday, on account of Monday being Martin Luther King day."

"Was he still in a good mood over the weekend?"

"Yes, even on Monday morning when he left for work." She hung her head. "But I guess he started feeling guilty when he was going to deposit the money in the bank on Tuesday. I wish I knew where he put the money. I'd give it back to the company."

"I wouldn't worry about that," Kate said. "You've got enough to deal with." Besides, the harm done to Strategic Electronics by the competitor who had bought their secrets would hardly be compensated for by a few hundred, or even thousands of dollars.

Kate wracked her brain to come up with anything else she could ask this woman. She remembered something Skip had complained about.

"Did John talk about his work? What kind of project was he working on?"

"He didn't talk about it. He couldn't. But I think it had something to do with drones. He'd get real interested whenever a report came on the news about the military using them. And one time, when a drone had accidentally hit a civilian target, he said something like, 'that won't happen when they have our....' And then he caught himself."

Kate chatted with the widow for a few more minutes. On an impulse, she gave the woman her cell phone number. "Call me if there's anything I can do." She doubted the woman would call, but it made them both feel a little better.

Rustling and a low whimper came from the baby monitor sitting on a side table. Little Johnny was awake.

Kate stood. "Go on and get him. I'll let myself out."

.

The unmarked police car behind her didn't even try to avoid being made. It tailed her, tailgated her actually, all the way back to her office.

She exited her car at the same time as Detective Russell did his.

"What the hell were you doing?" he yelled while still several feet away.

Kate ground her teeth. "I was consoling a bereaved widow. You know, it's what I do. Strive to make people feel better."

Russell closed the gap between them, standing too close. "And who said it was okay for you to interview a material witness?"

Hands on hips, Kate raised her chin. "I didn't know that I needed your permission to talk to a private citizen in her home."

Detective Russell paused for a second. She doubted he was

intimidated by her retort, but perhaps she'd scored a point. He had no right to tell her who she could or couldn't visit.

She watched as he plastered a fake smile on his face and adjusted his body into a somewhat less belligerent stance. "You find out anything interesting?"

"No."

"You do realize that withholding evidence from the police is against the law."

She did not honor that with a reply.

"I checked you out, Mrs. *Huntington*-Canfield. You're a bit of black widow, aren't you? You were a suspect in your first husband's murder."

She resisted the urge to roll her eyes. He might have caught her off guard, if he hadn't led with the "I checked you out" remark.

"Yes," she said, "and you should take note of what happened to the lazy and incompetent detective who assumed I'd killed my husband."

"Your connections won't protect you this time."

She huffed out air. She wanted to tell him he was an idiot, but decided that was probably not the best approach. In a more neutral voice, she said, "I didn't have the, quote 'connections,' then that you think I have now. I was thirty-eight years old. I'd been a therapist for a little over ten years in a not-for-profit agency. My boss, the *director* of my agency would have been flattered if you'd suggested that *she* had connections."

He scowled at her.

"Look, Detective, I have no desire to interfere in your investigation. I'm only trying to..." She trailed off. What was she trying to do?

She stood up straighter, not about to show this man her indecision. "I was *just* consoling a grieving widow."

He took a step back from her car, barely giving her room to maneuver past him.

She stayed where she was. Two beats of silence stretched between them.

He took another step back.

She brushed past him and strode quickly to her office building's entrance.

~~~~~~~~~

Elaine Patterson exited the Armstrong building at one-ten and approached her red BMW. Its locks clicked open as she neared it.

Skip stepped out from between his Expedition and the van next to it.

She jumped, a hand flying to her throat. "Oh, you scared me."

"Sorry. Didn't mean to startle you." Indeed, that was exactly what he'd intended, to throw her a little off balance.

A nervous hand smoothed blonde strands of hair back in place. She gave him a tentative smile. "Mr. Canfield, right?"

"Yes. I need to talk to you about John Cochlin."

She averted her gaze. When she looked back at him, she was blinking rapidly. "Such a tragedy." Her voice was a little choked up.

"We've had you under surveillance. You met with him on Monday, at the Towson diner. What were you two talking about?"

Her fair skin paled to stark white. "I uh… I don't know what you mean?"

"Don't play innocent, Elaine. Two of my operatives saw you having what they described as an 'intense' conversation with Cochlin."

Suddenly she let out a sob. "Please," she managed to choke out, "not out here in the parking lot." She glanced around nervously while she fumbled blindly in her purse, finally pulling out a tissue. She dabbed at her eyes.

He waited to see if she'd reveal more.

"There's a coffee shop," she said, "in the strip mall across the street. Meet me there."

He considered the possibility that she might rabbit. But he knew where to find her. He nodded and watched as she climbed into her car.

The coffee shop had a straggling line of people looking for a caffeine hit to get them through the evening. Elaine Patterson was already in that line when Skip arrived.

He took a seat at a table and waited for her to join him.

Once she'd sat down, he didn't give her any time to collect herself. "You and Cochlin were lovers, weren't you?"

Her eyes went wide. She dropped her gaze to the cup grasped in both her hands. "Please don't tell anybody."

She raised her eyes, now red-rimmed. "It started a couple of months ago..." She trailed off, looked away again. "There's no reason to cause his wife more pain."

Skip wondered how much of her concern for privacy was about preserving her own marriage.

"He was so sweet, and so worried about his kids."

"Is that why you lied about who left components out on the workbench?"

Her head snapped back around. "Wha'?"

"You said it was Murdock who did that, but it was really Cochlin, wasn't it?"

She nodded, biting her lower lip, reminding him for a moment of Kate.

"Luis, I mean Mr. Ortiz, saw the components lying out on the bench. But he didn't know who'd left them there. He'd been at lunch when John got a call from his wife and ran out, but he saw me putting the components away. I was afraid he might've put something about the breach of protocol in one of his reports to you all." She dropped a hand on top of his on the table.

Skip resisted the urge to pull away.

"You know how it is," she said in a low voice, almost a whisper, "when you love somebody. I didn't want John to get into trouble."

Now he did pull his hand loose. "So you blamed it on Murdock instead."

She stared down at her coffee cup, took a small sip. "I know that wasn't very nice of me, but he'd already been identified as the spy. I figured it wouldn't do any harm."

"But he wasn't the spy." His voice came out harsher than intended. He decided that was okay. "John Cochlin has now confessed to that, in his suicide note."

You do realize, lady, that you probably contributed to that suicide.

He didn't say that out loud. His goal here wasn't to make her feel any worse than she already did, it was to get answers. If she had any answers to give him.

Both hands wrapped around her mug again, she took another sip of coffee. "I'm surprised you're still investigating. I thought… I mean Mr. Latey told me that he'd closed the case."

"He did, and we're not investigating officially. But I don't like loose ends." Skip wasn't about to tell her, or anyone else at Strategic, how he himself was connected to the case, through his wife and Hal Murdock.

"Do you believe that Cochlin committed suicide?" he asked her.

Her mouth formed an O of surprise. "Well, I guess so. I mean he left a note and all."

He didn't want to give her any details she didn't already have nor let on that Murdock had originally been accused of killing Cochlin. "But do you think he was the type to kill himself?"

Skip had his own doubts. Would the man abandon his pregnant wife and kids? But the information that he was having an affair put a new light on things.

"No, I wouldn't think that he was," Elaine said. "But sometimes people just get overwhelmed."

Skip could certainly see how John Cochlin might've become overwhelmed by the mess he'd made of his life.

He stood. "Thanks for your time, Elaine, and sorry for your loss."

CHAPTER ELEVEN

"You did *what*?"

Kate stiffened. Anger flared in her chest. She tamped it down. "I talked to Cochlin's widow."

She and Skip stood in the kitchen, just feet apart. The frozen lasagna sat on the counter, the oven preheating.

Skip stared at her. "This case is complicated enough. I don't need you interfering."

She counted to five in her head, then used as calm a tone as she could muster. "I found out a couple of things."

He leaned forward slightly.

Sweet. His ears were practically vibrating.

But he wasn't getting rewarded yet, not until he shifted his mood a bit. He needed a 'tude adjustment, as Billy would say.

Skip scrubbed his face with a long, slender hand and blew out air. "Look, this hasn't been my best day. Can you just tell me what she said?"

Relenting, she relayed her conversation with the grieving widow.

He leaned back against the edge of the counter. "So it's true, there's no trace of the money he was paid?"

She shook her head. "Nada."

"You don't think she's found it, and is lying to everybody?"

She paused to give that some thought. "I doubt it. She seemed too upset to do an effective job of lying."

"And she thinks he was working on drone technology?"

"Seems that way, from what he let slip."

Skip tapped an index finger against his lips.

"Does any of that help?" Kate asked.

He gave her an apologetic smile. "Probably. Every little bit of info helps. But I'm not sure how this fits yet. And I found out another major piece today. Elaine Patterson and Cochlin were indeed having an affair."

Her mouth fell open. "Wow. And I was thinking the meeting at the diner was indeed a coincidence."

"Me too, until I met with Elaine today. She seemed pretty broken up over Cochlin's death."

"So maybe guilt over the affair played a role in his committing suicide."

"Maybe."

Another thought hit her, making her growling stomach tense. "Unless Cochlin's plan for getting the family out of debt was a life insurance payout."

"I'll ask Dolph if he uncovered a policy, but they usually have a suicide exclusion clause."

"Only for the first year or two... On second thought," she waved a dismissive hand in the air, "that's unlikely. I got the distinct impression that Cochlin had actual money to deposit. He told his wife he had to wait for the bank to open. Anyway, Hal gave me the names of the guys in the lab, the day he overheard that call. Cochlin and an engineer named Watson, and two other techs. I've got their names written down. I'll get them for you after dinner."

A sharp ding sounded. Skip grabbed the pan of lasagna and shoved it into the oven. As he set the timer on the stove, he asked, "Why are you so sure Murdock didn't play any part in the espionage or Cochlin's death?"

"I'm not sure. How can we ever be one hundred percent positive about others?" She started to bite her lip, then caught herself. She was trying to break that habit.

"You do realize that people tell you what they want you to hear?" Skip said. "They probably put on their best face, motivation-wise, in your office."

The gurgling in her stomach turned acidic. "Actually they don't always, not once they've gotten comfortable with the process. They trust me not to judge them, and the ones who are serious about getting better realize they have to be honest with me."

Even though it would be awhile before the lasagna was done, Kate grabbed plates from the cabinet and started setting the table. She needed to move. "Bottom line, I don't believe Hal is capable of violence. And he's a very loyal person."

She started to say more and realized she was skirting close to the edge of confidentiality boundaries.

As she went to move past him to get the silverware, Skip grabbed her around the waist and pulled her close. "I just don't want you feeling bad if it turns out he's the spy and/or a killer."

She wrapped her hands behind his neck. "I'll be disappointed, but it won't rock my world."

He lowered his head and gave her a long, tender kiss.

"Eeeeww" came from the kitchen doorway.

Skip broke the kiss. The corners of his mouth twitched. Kate rolled her eyes at him.

"Is your homework done, son?" Skip held out his hand.

"Yup." Billy handed over his homework log.

Kate gently pulled loose from Skip's embrace and stepped over to the cutlery drawer. "Dinner will be ready in forty-five minutes."

"Did you cook it, Mom?"

She rounded and shook a fork at him in mock anger. "No, Mrs. Stouffers did."

Billy grinned and took off up the stairs.

~~~~~~~

After dinner, Skip checked backpacks for random permission slips that needed signing and to make sure all books and homework assignments were accounted for.

Kate was supervising "bath time," which consisted these days of making sure that Billy got in the bathroom first. Otherwise his sister would use up all the hot water taking a twenty-minute shower.

He was trying to decide what, if anything, to tell Kate about Fred Latey's comments. He didn't want to worry her, and he really didn't know much yet. Latey may have made up the stuff about hearing a rumor. Skip didn't trust the man as far as he could throw his hefty bulk.

His gut twisted. If Latey wasn't lying, then who in the hell was spreading rumors about Canfield and Hernandez? Would he be able to find enough proof to go after them legally, to make them stop?

Maybe he'd call Rob in the morning.

If the agency went under, he and Kate would be okay. Push came to shove, they could live off the interest on the brokerage account from Ed Huntington's life insurance.

His throat closed. *Suck it up, Canfield.*

The blow to his ego was nothing. His family had to eat.

They'd be okay, but their employees... His chest tightened.

He had to find out who was spreading the false rumors. But rumors were damn hard to chase down. Where would they even start?

His hand froze in the act of putting Billy's homework log back in his backpack. What if the rumors weren't false?

They hadn't done so well with the Strategic's contract, but that was outside their normal areas of expertise. Were there other clients who'd made nice-nice to their faces but were actually discontent?

He dropped into a chair at the kitchen table. His chest felt hollow. He and Rose had worked so hard to build up the agency.

Rose. He might be able to keep what was going on from Kate, but his partner had a right to know. He checked his watch. Eight-thirty. Pulling out his cell phone, he punched the speed dial number.

He sucked in a deep breath. "Hey, Rose..."

~~~~~~~~~~

Her partner might not know where to start, but Rose did. Howard Kaplan, the most sleaze ball member of a profession that tended to attract sleaze balls. Her own profession, sadly.

Kaplan would rat out his elderly mother for a fifty dollar bill.

His small reception area was empty except for cheap metal furniture, a desk and a couple of folding chairs. She shoved his office door open. It slammed back against the wall.

Kaplan jolted a foot in the air. His feet, which had been propped on the corner of his desk, landed on the floor with a thud.

The desired effect. Rose stifled a grin. A little intimidation wouldn't hurt, so the fifty would seem sweeter, since he was getting it instead of a punch in the nose.

Kaplan was now standing behind his desk, his mouth hanging open. "Uh, g… good morning, R…Rose."

"Actually, I'm having a crappy morning, Howie. I hear you've been spreading rumors about us."

"Dear God, not me."

"But you've heard them." A statement not a question.

"Well, uh, yeah."

"From who?"

He shuffled his feet, gestured toward the ratty armchair sitting in front of his desk. It looked like the prize from an evening of dumpster-diving.

She ignored the nonverbal invitation. He shuffled his feet some more, gave a nervous laugh.

She hardened her voice. "From who, Howie?"

He sat back down in his desk chair, laughed again. It sounded no more relaxed than the first chuckle. "Shouldn't that be *from whom*, Rose?"

She crossed the room in three strides and slammed a palm down on his desk, missing a full ashtray by less than an inch. "Skip the grammar lesson, Kaplan. Who'd you hear it from?"

"Now, nobody works for free, do they?" He gave her a sickly smile, leaning away from her.

She stood up straight and held up a ten dollar bill.

Kaplan snorted.

"That's ten per name, but they'd better check out."

He still sat there, fiddling with a pencil.

She leaned forward across the desk, a sneer on her face.

He pulled farther back.

She chuckled inside. She might only be five foot even, but few men who knew her were willing to tangle with her.

"Here are your choices, Howie," she said softly in his face, "You give me names and make a little in the process, or I break you in two."

Gawd, I sound like something out of a grade B movie.

But it worked. Howie coughed up a name. "I swear, Rose that's the only person I heard it from directly, but I got the sense the rumor was makin' the rounds."

She believed him. If he were lying, he would have made up more names to get more money out of her.

Rose pulled out another ten and dropped the two bills on his desk. "I'm feeling generous. Stay outta trouble, Howie."

She waited until she was out in the dingy hallway of the office building before allowing a grin to spread across her face. A woman coming the other way stepped farther to her right, giving her a wide berth.

Rose decided it was a good morning after all.

~~~~~~~~

"Hey, Kate," Hal said on the other end of the line. "I wanted to let someone know what's going on." His voice sounded odd, rushed.

His call had caught her between clients. She glanced at the clock on her office wall. Three minutes of ten.

"You see, I hacked into my company's employee files to check on something–"

"You did *what?*" The irony of Skip's words echoing in her own voice was not lost on her.

"Don't worry," Hal said. "I'm a pretty decent hacker. Nobody's likely to figure out I've been in the HR files. But I wanted somebody to know that I emailed the names of the two guys I suspect to my personal account, you know, just in case."

Holy crap, he's getting off on the cloak and dagger stuff.

Kate flashed back to her conversation with Skip. No, this guy did not lack guts. Common sense, maybe, but not guts.

She didn't quite understand what was going on, but she knew she needed to discourage his snooping. "Hal, at this point, the police don't think you did anything." She didn't know that for a fact. Indeed, she doubted it, but she was desperate for something to say that would get him to leave things alone. "But if you give them any excuse to pin something on you, they're gonna grab it. If you get caught or let slip that you know stuff from those files…"

"I won't. I'll be careful. But I overheard something, on the bug in the lab, as I was pulling into the parking lot at work this morning."

"Where are you now?"

"I'm out in my car. I heard somebody rustling around in the lab, and then they were talking, real low, like they were on the phone but afraid of being overheard. I only caught a few words, but it had something to do with my project."

"What project?"

"The one there's been leaks about. Anyway, I couldn't tell for sure who it was, but I think it was one of these two guys, two of the engineers who've worked on the project." His words were tumbling out, excited. "I got on my laptop—I keep it in my trunk so I can use it during my lunch break—and I got into the fi–"

"You need to give those names to the police, or to Mr. Franklin. He'll tell the police."

"No." Hal's tone was the most emphatic she'd ever heard it. "I know what it's like to be accused when you're innocent. I need to check this out first. After I go through the files I copied from human resources, I'm gonna strike up a conversation with each of these guys and see if I can recognize the voice."

Oh, and that won't seem the least bit suspicious. Shy Hal suddenly making small talk. She kept that thought to herself.

"Hal–"

"Gotta go." He disconnected.

She dialed his cell phone number. It went straight to voice-mail. She recalled him saying once that they weren't allowed to bring their phones inside the building.

He'd already turned it off and it was probably sitting in his car's glove box.

Damn. If nothing else, he's going to get himself fired.

Another thought sent adrenaline jolting through her system. Hal was about to chat up someone who might have tried to kill Manny and maybe murdered John Cochlin.

She glanced at the wall clock again. Her next client would be waiting in the outer room by now. She quickly dug out Hal's file to get his work number. Heart pounding, she punched it into her desk phone.

"Strategic Electronics. How may I direct your call?"

She blew out air. *What am I doing? Hal's a grown man.*

"Never mind. Wrong number."

CHAPTER TWELVE

Worried re Hal. He heard something on bug. Thinks 1 of 2 engineers involved in spying. Investigating himself.

Skip ground his teeth as he re-read Kate's text. He had enough anxiety gnawing at his stomach lining. He didn't need to be worrying about Kate's overzealous do-gooder tendencies.

He tapped in a reply. *Not ur problem.* His finger hovered over the send icon.

He was already having a stressful day. Did he really want to fight with his wife when he got home?

He cleared the text and replaced it with, *Will check into it.*

He bookmarked the website on military drones he'd been perusing, shut down his computer and grabbed his truck keys.

From the Armstrong Building's parking lot, he called Strategic's switchboard. "Harold Murdock, please."

A few seconds ticked by while elevator music played softly in his ear.

"Test Lab. Elaine Patterson speaking."

That threw Skip for a second. He didn't want to tell Patterson who he was. He deepened his voice. "Hal Murdock there?"

"Sure. Hang on a sec."

Skip took a deep breath. After he talked to Murdock, he needed to go to the gym for a workout. He was wound way too tight.

"Murdock." The man's voice was hesitant.

"This is Skip Canfield," he said in a terse voice. "I need to talk to you. I'm in the parking lot, next row over from *your* car." He wanted the man to know how easily he could be tracked down. "White Expedition."

A beat of silence. "Okay, be there in a minute."

Skip scanned the parking lot. No one in sight mid-morning. He got out of the driver's seat and opened the door to the backseat. His truck's windows were tinted as dark as Maryland law allowed, and that was a lot darker in the back of the vehicle than the front windows and windshield. No one was likely to notice them in the back.

He climbed in and slammed the door.

Murdock was coming out of the building. He headed toward his car. As he got closer, he veered toward the truck, then stopped, staring at the windshield.

Skip leaned over and opened the door opposite his.

Murdock started moving again, his steps dragging. When he got to the open door, he peeked around it.

"Get in."

Murdock shook his head.

Skip's jaw clenched. He forced his voice to a softer tone. "I'm not going to hurt you. Get in."

Still the man just stood there.

"I don't want anyone seeing you with me," Skip said. "It could put *you* in danger."

Murdock climbed into the truck and closed the door. He leaned back against it, half turned toward Skip. "What do you want?" His voice was barely above a whisper.

"I understand you told my wife that you're checking out two people regarding the leaks. Who are they?"

He was pretty sure what the answer would be.

Murdock's eyes had gone wide. "Your wife? Kate! She's your wife? She told you?"

Skip's breath caught in his throat. Hadn't this guy made the connection before that Kate was married to him? His stomach knotted. He'd just put her in a very awkward spot.

Murdock was staring at him, his mouth partway open. "B-but

I thought anything I told her was confidential."

"It is, if it has to do with up here." Skip tapped his own temple. "But this is about *my* investigation."

Murdock's face pinched up into an angry frown. His hand shook as he ran it through his hair.

"And she was worried about you getting hurt," Skip added in a gentler voice.

Murdock's shoulders relaxed slightly. "You're still investigating? Fred said he fired your agency."

Skip grimaced, his muscles tensing. "Oh, is that what he's telling people?"

Murdock nodded mutely, pushing himself harder against the door.

"He declared the job done when you were arrested," Skip said, "but I don't see it as done. So who are these two people that you suspect?"

Murdock shook his head. "I'm not gonna say until I'm sure."

"Look–" Skip caught himself. He'd been about to say *kid*. Since when did thirty-somethings start looking like kids to him?

He made the effort to soften his voice again. "Hal, you troubleshoot electronics for a living. I investigate things. I think I'm better qualified to check these guys out than you are."

He let the silence stretch between them.

Finally Murdock said, "Two engineers, Paul Allen and Garrett Watson. I heard someone in the lab earlier. I think it was one of them." He gave Skip a furtive glance, then hurried on. "They've both worked on that project, so they know a lot of the stuff that's been leaked anyway. But there's this one component that kept failing. That's where my group came in. I figured out why it was failing, but I was told not to share the results, not even with the engineers." Murdock paused, took a deep breath. "Because of the leaks, I guess."

"Who told you not to share it?"

"Fred, Mr. Latey. Although I don't know how they can *not* tell engineering eventually. At some point, we'd have to go into production."

"This project has something to do with drones?"

Murdock shook his head vigorously, pushing back against the door again. "No. I can't really talk about it."

"Okay, okay." Skip raised his hand in what he thought was a calming gesture, but Murdock flinched. He lowered the hand. "You need to leave this alone, or you might get hurt. Whoever's behind all this has already shown they're willing to shoot people."

Murdock sat up straighter. "And stage a suicide."

"You don't think Cochlin killed himself?"

"No. He never would have done that to his wife and kids. He was a good guy."

"All the more reason you need to stay out of this," Skip said. "I'll take it from here, and don't talk to Kate about it anymore. You're scaring her."

Murdock's cheeks flushed, "I-I'm sorry. I didn't mean to worry her."

"Oh, and what's this about you having a bug in the lab?"

Murdock's eyes went wide again, but then he nodded. "I planted it that day, you know, before your guy was shot. That's why I was there–"

"Give me the receiver." Skip held out his hand, making a gimme gesture with his fingers.

Murdock froze for a moment. Then he said, "It's in my car."

"Get it."

He fully expected Murdock to bolt, but the man returned with the receiver in his hand, a small metal button attached to a plastic hook designed to go around one's ear. Skip lowered his window and Murdock dropped it in his palm.

Skip's insides relaxed a little. Without access to his bug, this guy might just stop playing James Bond.

Murdock practically ran across the lot toward the building.

Skip stared at the gizmo in his hand.

Damn. He was now in possession of something that gave him access to top secret information. That was probably a federal crime.

He dropped it into a cup holder on his console. Somehow this situation kept getting more and more complicated.

What now? These two guys, Watson and Allen, would be inside the Armstrong building for the rest of the work day. And surely if Skip stepped foot in there, word would get back to Latey.

He sighed. Time to do his second least favorite task of a P.I.'s job. He needed an updated background check on Watson, and he didn't want to wait until Monday when Dolph was in again.

Halfway back to the office, his phone rang. He punched the button to answer it through his Bluetooth.

"Landon here." The operative they'd left inside Strategic as a security guard.

"Hey Phil, what's up?"

"Not sure. The other guy who was on a week ago Sunday, the night Manny was shot. He left on vacation the next day. No biggie. He'd set it up a few days prior. Something about his dad being ill and he needed to go to wherever his parents live to help out."

"Yeah. So?" Skip tried to keep the impatience out of his voice. He was already anticipating the tedium of doing that background check, which didn't have him in the best of moods.

"So he was due back yesterday and nobody's heard from him. Our boss has been trying to track him down but no luck. He called the mother's number from the guy's file and was told her husband died years ago and she hasn't seen her son in months."

"He may be job-hunting," Skip said, but his gut was arguing otherwise.

"Maybe."

"Has Strategic told Detective Russell about him?"

"I don't think so," Landon said. "You think *we* should?"

Skip thought about that for a moment. "Can you get me his name and address? I'll check him out first. He might've gone on a drinking binge or something."

"Guy's name is Carlton Johnson. I'll track down his address and get back to you."

Skip disconnected, then rubbed his chin.

~~~~~~~~~~

Edie Huntington-Canfield trudged up her front walk and tried to remember when her life started to suck.

She'd been so excited at the beginning of the school year. Being a sixth grader meant she was definitely not a child anymore. She was in middle school, after all.

But the new school was so much bigger than she was used to, and she only knew a few of the kids. Turns out her elementary school fed into two different middle schools, depending on where you lived, and most of her friends had ended up at the other school.

The older kids acted like the sixth graders were dirt, and even some of her classmates called her "a baby." She couldn't help it that she was the youngest kid in her class.

At least Connie, one grade ahead, had befriended her. "We're *familia* now," she'd said. Consuela Pérez was Maria's new stepdaughter.

Edie rode Connie's bus home with her sometimes. Then she got to bask again in the warmth of Maria's kitchen, even if it wasn't the same kitchen. Maria always had freshly baked cookies for them. She sat with them and asked about their day, just like when she'd lived at Edie's house.

Edie reached the front door. It was locked. She turned and surveyed the street. Mom's car was nowhere in sight.

Was Billy home yet?

She rang the bell. After a few seconds, she shrugged out of her heavy backpack—teachers gave so much homework in middle school—and rummaged through the smallest of its pockets, looking for her key.

Maria moving out was when life had really started to suck. No more warm-from-the-oven cookies and comforting hugs when she got home, no more delicious dinners served promptly at six o'clock. Now half the time dinner was carryout pizza. She had once loved pizza. Now she was sick of it.

The house was quiet, had that empty feel to it. No Billy.

He'd probably gone to a friend's house and Mom hadn't bothered to tell her.

She left her backpack in the entranceway and flopped down on the living room sofa. Digging out her new smart phone, her birthday present from her parents—at least they were good for something—she texted Connie.

Did u get them?

Not yet. Did u ask ur mom?

Not home.

Let u know when I hear from Zac.

K

Edie hadn't decided yet if she was even going to ask about the concert. She was pretty sure Mom and Dad would say no. They seemed to be afraid of downtown Baltimore, like it was some foreign country. But she'd been to the Inner Harbor a few times with Maria. She knew her way around down there.

Sighing, she got up and retrieved her backpack. Might as well get her homework out of the way.

~~~~~~~~~

Several hours later, Skip was bemoaning the fact that Dolph was off today. All he had for his online efforts was a smattering of information on Garrett Watson, a boring dude who'd never gotten anything worse than a parking ticket. Not a single thread to pull on to find out more either.

And the other two techs on the list Kate had given him hadn't been much more interesting. Maybe Dolph would be able to find out more.

The good news was that his inbox contained the report from Dolph on Paul Allen, the head engineer.

He wasn't in the lab that day, according to Murdock, but he could have been the one on the other end of the line, giving instructions to an accomplice. And he was one of the two guys Murdock might have overheard this morning.

But how much credence should he be giving to what Murdock

said? The guy could be blowing smoke, trying to cover his own trail.

Skip glanced down at Dolph's report in his hand. The background check they'd originally gotten from the outside company a few months ago had indicated a fair credit rating. The Allens were a bit overextended financially but no more so than many middle-class families. The guy had no arrests, not even a parking ticket.

Either the outside company had screwed up or things had gone south for the Allens quickly. Now the credit rating was poor, several credit cards were maxed out and the payments on Allen's car were three months behind. Dolph had also discovered that the Allens' savings account had gone from healthy to pathetic in the same time frame.

Paul Allen was as good a place as any to start, since he knew most of the specs for the whole project.

A twinge of something in his chest. Regret? Sadness? In the past, he wouldn't have had to choose who to follow. He'd have been able to afford to pull in as many operatives as needed to tail everybody, even on a *pro bono* case.

Maybe if he could break this case, he'd not only be in good with Kate again but he might be able to get Canfield and Hernandez in the news. That would go a long way toward getting the agency back on track.

Skip texted Kate. *Gotta do surveillance tonight. Eat without me.*

No response. He checked his watch. It was after three so she should be headed home by now–she didn't like to leave the kids alone for long. He texted again. *U there?*

Driveling. See you later.

Huh. Oh, *driveling* was her Bluetooth's interpretation of *driving.* He chuckled softly, despite the tension in his body, and the fight with her that he was pretty sure he wasn't going to avoid even if he stayed out all night. He was really regretting how he'd handled Murdock earlier.

At the Armstrong building, Skip located Paul Allen's silver Porsche. He found a parking space nearby and settled in to wait.

At four-thirty, Allen exited the building, got in his car and drove toward the parking lot's exit.

Skip jotted the time on his notepad and then followed the man through the clogged traffic in downtown Towson. Friday afternoon rush hour had begun a good two hours ago and was now in full swing.

Allen went home. *Surprise, surprise.*

The other vehicle registered in his and his wife's names, a minivan, was parked in the driveway. Allen pulled past it. The garage door slid noisily open and he drove his fancy sports car inside.

Skip checked Dolph's report. Alicia Allen was a graphic designer. But he'd found no employer. Perhaps she was freelance, worked from home. They had two kids, a teenaged boy and an older girl, away at college. Hmm, that could explain the sudden savings drain.

Leaning his head back against the headrest, Skip fantasized about future years when the kids were older and needed little or no supervision. He and Kate had been in their late thirties when they'd become parents, so they'd be pushing sixty by the time both kids were in college.

He knew they'd miss the kids terribly but part of him was looking forward to the freedom. They could travel whenever they wanted, and make love anywhere in the house.

He yawned. Would he need Viagra by then? He hoped not. That would make things less spontaneous.

His head jerked up. It was full dark. A streetlight shone yellow on the papers scattered on his passenger's seat.

Crap! He'd fallen asleep.

Then he realized what had woken him. The Allens' garage door was rumbling open.

He checked his watch, pushing the little button that backlit the face. It was after eight. He'd slept for almost three hours.

But no harm done. Allen was backing his silver car out of the garage.

The man drove to a section of the Towson business district that was scattered with restaurants and a couple of bars. He parallel parked on the street and entered one of the latter. The sign over the door read *Frankie's Bar and Grill*. Not all that original.

Since Skip hadn't had any dinner, he figured it was time to tail his subject on foot. He went into the bar and stepped back into shadows near the doorway. Allen knew him. He needed to be careful. He looked around. No sign of the man. Had he made him and slipped out the back?

Skip hurried outside again. No Allen on the sidewalk and his car was still in its space.

He waited ten minutes. Still no Allen.

Going back inside, he stood at one end of the bar. On a Friday night, all the stools and tables were taken. He ordered a burger and beer from the bartender and then did a careful sweep of the room with his eyes.

No Allen.

Movement in his peripheral vision. He swiveled his head. A man was going through a door that he closed carefully behind him. The door was plain wood, stained dark, with no sign on it or near it.

The barkeep brought his beer. Skip sipped it with one elbow perched on the bar, casually watching the room.

A few minutes later, another man slipped through the door, and then another a few minutes after him.

Skip had seen the pattern before. Something was going on behind that door, most likely something illegal.

His burger came. He ate it slowly, making a show of savoring it. It *was* quite good.

The bartender stopped to check on him. "Want another beer?"

"Sure."

When it came, he sipped it. He wasn't much of a drinker and

he didn't want to fall asleep again. No one had gone in or out of the plain brown door for the last half hour.

He left the beer half empty, put some bills under the edge of the glass and headed for the men's room, praying Allen didn't come out and leave while he was gone.

While in the hallway behind the kitchen, he checked the back exit. It had a big sign on it stating an alarm would sound if the door was opened. He was tempted to test it, to make sure Allen couldn't slip out that way, but he really didn't want to draw attention to himself.

He sauntered through the bar area, watching the brown door out of the corner of his eye.

Outside, he breathed a sigh of relief. Allen's car was still there. And there was a parking space three down from it on the same side.

Skip moved his truck to that spot, then tilted his seat back so his head wouldn't be silhouetted by the streetlights.

He was stir crazy with boredom by the time Paul Allen exited the bar around midnight. He was walking normally, so either he was a hardcore drinker who could belt down liquor all evening without showing it, or he hadn't had much to drink.

Skip was pretty sure booze wasn't the man's vice. That would be gambling.

Allen glanced in his general direction as he was getting into his expensive sports car. From the pinched expression on his face, Skip guessed he'd not had a good night.

Time to go home. Hopefully, Kate was asleep.

CHAPTER THIRTEEN

Kate jerked awake, pain shooting down her spine from a stiff neck. Despite the tension in her body, she'd fallen asleep, sitting upright on the sofa with her head tilted back.

She checked her chin for drool.

Sounds from the entranceway told her what had woken her. The turning of the front door knob, the jingling of keys being removed from the lock.

She took a deep breath and braced herself for what was to come.

Her anger had fizzled a good bit as she'd waited for her husband to come home. Part of her just wanted to go to bed and forget about it. But she couldn't.

Skip closed the door behind him and took his time hanging his jacket in the small closet in the entranceway. He glanced her way, his expression a mixture of sheepish and grim.

Walking toward her, he said, "I owe you an apology."

"For what?" Her words came out clipped. The anger was coming back.

He stopped a few feet from her, his mouth slightly open.

She resisted the temptation to fill the silence, let it spin out instead.

"I put you in an awkward position," he finally said.

She snorted. "That was only the beginning of the mess you made."

"Then why did you text me about Murdock, if you didn't want me to check it out?"

"I wanted you to check out the lead, not confront Hal Murdock. You scared the crap out of him. *And* undermined his trust in me."

Skip took another step toward the sofa, gestured for her to make room for him. But she wasn't ready to sit next to him. She pointed to the armchair across from her.

Skip sat in it. "Okay, I should've approached it a different way, not told him that you'd said anything to me."

"Yes, you should've."

"Look, I didn't know that he hadn't made the connection between you and me, and I can't help it that our cases have over-lapped here."

Okay, she had to give him both of those points. Perhaps she hadn't been totally clear. That was a problem with cryptic text messages.

She took a deep breath. "It's a sticky situation. But I trusted you to have the good sense to handle it with sensitivity. Instead you came on all Sam Spade."

His body stiffened. "I can't always make nice-nice in my job. And I had no idea he was that fragile."

She took another deep breath, blew it out. No, he would have no way of knowing how scared Hal was of physical violence.

She was tempted to let it go. She hated fighting with Skip. But she gritted her teeth. His biggest transgression had yet to be addressed.

"Why did you tell him not to talk to me about all this?"

He slumped back in the chair. A hand came up and scrubbed his face.

She noted the fatigue in his eyes as they met hers, and felt a twinge of guilt.

"That was a mistake," he said.

"Yes, it was. You were so busy playing protective husband, it never dawned on you that clients have to feel free to tell me everything. It took me twenty minutes on the phone to get him to tell me why he wanted to end treatment. I finally convinced him to come in for an emergency ses–"

Skip's mouth had dropped open. "He fired you?"

"No, he was afraid he was upsetting me." She shook her head. "Do you have any idea how many months it took to get him to relax with me, to stop worrying about my reaction to the things he says? Now he's focused on my feelings instead of his own. That's not okay in the therapeutic relationship."

She felt her face flush, even as her anger was subsiding. A moment of confusion, then her entire body was ablaze. Sweat formed under her armpits, ran down her spine.

A hot flash. Crap!

Skip sat forward, held his hands out, palms up. "I said I'm sorry." His voice sounded slightly aggrieved. "What more can I do?"

She tried to ignore her rebellious body. "You need to realize how serious this is," she snapped, then regretted the words and the tone. Bad enough her hormones were making her depressed, now they were making her bitchy.

"I realized I shouldn't have said it the minute it was out of my mouth." His jaw clenched. "But *you* need to realize how serious this is from my standpoint. Somebody shot Manny, and may have killed Cochlin. Not to mention–" He abruptly looked away.

"Not to mention what?"

He shook his head.

She took a deep breath. There was something else going on here. "Apology accepted, and I should have been clearer in my text." Then she narrowed her eyes at him. "Now, not to mention what?"

He sighed and flopped back in the chair again. "Somebody's spreading rumors about us."

"Us? You and me?"

"No. The agency." He made eye contact. "Our reputation is on the line here."

The remnants of her anger evaporated. Her stomach twisted. "What…"

A muscle in his jaw throbbed. "Things have been slow for

too long. Now we know why. We found out about the rumors yesterday. Rose is tracking them down."

Kate chewed on her lower lip. If Skip's agency was in serious trouble, how could she cut back on her client hours even further in order to teach? Adjunct faculty at Towson University made peanuts by comparison to the income from her practice.

He ran his fingers through the unruly clump of hair that always insisted on flopping down over his forehead. "Apparently these rumors were part of why Fred Latey pulled us off the Strategic case."

"I thought that was because he decided the case was solved."

"Yeah, he did think that, but now he's equally convinced that Cochlin had to be the leak. Either way he thinks we're incompetent. He flat out said so. The man's a little too eager to jump to conclusions, which bothers me."

"It's not that unusual," Kate said. "There's this thing called cognitive dissonance."

"Cognitive what?"

"Dissonance. It's when something is out of kilter with your preconceived assumptions or beliefs. Human beings hate cognitive dissonance. They will often twist things around, reinterpret reality, to come up with neat answers that explain away whatever's making them uncomfortable."

Skip nodded, then rose to his feet. He held out his hand. "Are we done fighting now?" He gave her a weak smile. "Time for makeup sex?"

She returned the smile. "Are you hungry? Did you get dinner?"

"I had a burger earlier, but I wouldn't mind a snack."

She took his hand and let him pull her to a stand. They strolled into the kitchen.

"Edie was acting strange tonight," she said.

"Stranger than usual?"

"Yeah. You might try to talk to her tomorrow, try to find out what's going on."

He grimaced. "About tomorrow, can you deal with the kids

without me? I really should do some surveillance."

Her muscles tensed. He hated surveillance. If he was willing to give up a Saturday to it, things really were grim. And whoever he was watching must be important to the case.

"Tell me," she said.

He walked over to the refrigerator and stuck his head inside. Coming up with a can of beer and a half-full wine bottle, he cocked an eyebrow at her.

Make-up drinks weren't quite as satisfying as make-up sex, but she nodded.

He poured some wine into a glass and brought it, his beer, and a bag of pretzels over to the kitchen table.

He told her about Strategic's head engineer's overly long visit to the back room of a bar.

The fact that Hal's ideas had indeed led to at least one good lead made Kate feel a bit more hopeful. She sipped her wine. "Does this mean you may miss the party tomorrow night?"

Skip's hand, holding a pretzel, stilled halfway to his mouth. "What party?"

"Consuela's birthday party."

Skip's face remained blank.

"Eduardo's daughter, Maria's new stepdaughter."

He grimaced. "I'd forgotten about that. I might not be able to shake free in time. Probably best if you and the kids go over and I'll join you when I can."

If *you can*, she thought but didn't say.

~~~~~~~~

Phil Landon was standing on the sidewalk beside a red brick box the size of a warehouse. A sign next to the door said *Apartments For Rent* in big block letters, followed by a phone number.

The morning sun glinted off of Landon's glasses. He waved as Skip pulled to the curb.

Landon wasn't a big dude like some of their operatives, more the wiry little guy who blended in well. Short brown hair, bland brown eyes. Totally forgettable. He did a fair amount of under-cover work for them.

Once they'd exchanged manly grunts by way of greeting, Skip said, "You look tired."

"I'm on nights this week again." Phil held out his arm in an after-you gesture. "They do this rotating shifts thing that's a killer. One week on days, one on four to midnight, one on nights. Your body never quite adjusts and forget about having a life."

"I wonder why they do it that way."

Phil shrugged as they walked side by side to the outer door of the apartment building. "That's the way they do shifts in the Army most of the time. Security head's former military."

Skip nodded. "I've met him. He kinda gives 'by the book' a whole new meaning."

Phil snorted. "I'm pretty sure he sends his backbone out to get it starched on Fridays."

Skip laughed.

Phil reached out for the door's handle and pulled it open.

"Outer door's not locked?"

"Well," Phil grinned, "it's supposed to be, but I caught it on the way closed last time somebody came out and stuck a little pebble 'tween it and the frame."

At the third apartment down on the left, Phil stopped and knocked on the door. After several seconds, he knocked again, harder this time.

No response from behind the door but the one next to it opened.

"Hey guys, do you have to make so much noise? Some people had to work late last night." The words lost a lot of their force when delivered in a tentative tone, the woman's thin voice rising on the end like a question.

Skip turned and took in a mousy-looking brunette, probably mid-thirties, in a pink bathrobe. "Sorry, ma'am. Didn't mean to disturb you." He gave her his best grin.

She blushed and smoothed her short hair down.

Okay, I've still got it.

"We were looking for your neighbor, Carlton Johnson." he waved a hand vaguely in Phil's direction. "Phil here works with him and he hasn't shown up for the last three days."

She propped one fist on a hip. The other hand held the neck of her robe closed. "Well why should he be at work? He's still on vacation."

"He was supposed to be back on Monday, ma'am," Phil said.

She was shaking her head before he'd even finished the sentence. "No, he's gone for three weeks, to the Bahamas. Won the trip on some radio program."

Phil shot Skip a glance.

"Uh, ma'am," Skip said. "He told his employer he would only be gone a week."

She crinkled up her nose. It was a cute nose.

"Well, they must've misunderstood. He said he'd be back on the fifth of February, and he'd take me out to dinner that night, to thank me for feeding his cat."

Phil started to shake his head. Skip put a hand on his arm.

"You've got his cat here?"

"No, Frisky doesn't like change. So he gave me a key and I go over two, three times a day to check on her."

"Look, ma'am." Skip gave her another big smile. It didn't seem to work as well this time. "I know what he told you an' all," he trotted out the Texas drawl, "but he definitely told his boss one week, an' he never said anythin' 'bout the Bahamas, did he, Phil?"

Phil shook his head.

"We're plumb worried about him," Skip said. "Could we, by any chance, borrow that key?"

Her lips pinched together. "Absolutely not."

Hmm, even the Texan accent wasn't working on this lady.

"Well, have you checked on the cat yet today, ma'am?" Phil asked. "Maybe we could just tag along, check the place to make sure everything's okay."

"I'm sure it's all a mix-up of some kind," Skip said, "but

we'd feel better if we knew there were no signs a foul play or anythin' in there."

She narrowed her eyes at them.

Skip kept quiet, sensing that anymore arguing would come across as too pushy.

"You can wait in the hall while I check on Frisky, and I'll look around a bit." She slammed the door in their faces, then it opened again in a few seconds.

Cinching her bathrobe firmly around her, she shooed them away. As she inserted the key in the lock next door, she said, "You stay back or I'll scream at the top of my lungs."

Skip nodded and took another step backward. He didn't blame her. If anything, she was being too trusting of two male strangers.

She entered the apartment and closed the door behind her. The snick of a deadbolt being thrown.

She was back in less than a minute, her face pale. "All his clothes are gone."

Ten minutes later, Phil hit pay dirt. He came out of the bed-room holding up a plastic card in his latex-gloved fingers. "Looky what I found."

Skip straightened from his inspection of the sofa cushions. "What's that?"

The young woman—she'd told them her name was Sharon—was watching them from her perch on the edge of an armchair, eyes shifting back and forth.

"ID badge for you-know-where."

"So?" Sharon said. "Of course, he wouldn't take his work badge on vacation."

Skip ignored the comment. He had the distinct impression that this Carlton Johnson dude and young Sharon were "an item," as his mother would say. The poor woman was still wrestling with denial that she and Frisky had been abandoned.

"It's not his badge." Phil dropped it into Skip's gloved hand.

Skip looked down. The face of John Cochlin was staring up at him.

"Where'd you find it?"

"Top shelf of the closet," Phil said. "Shoved toward the back. I suspect he missed it."

"Is it a fake?"

Phil shook his head. "Every three months, they change out the badges. We take the new badges to a department and gather up the old ones, bring them back to security where they're deactivated and shredded. The last time we changed out the badges was the Friday before Manny was shot."

"So Carlton helped himself to some of them." Skip turned the badge over, the back held only a magnetic strip and what looked like a small computer chip.

"The departments were in the process of converting over," Phil said, "from the strip readers to the chip version. It can be read from about a foot away. So the person only has to be near the door." He ran a hand over his buzz cut. "Uh, boss, I think we oughta call the police now."

"In a minute." Skip shoved the sofa cushions back in place and sat down to face Sharon. "Has Carlton had more money than usual lately?"

Her eyes flashed at the same time as her cheeks turned pink. "He's *not* a thief."

"I never said he was," Skip backpedaled, trying to appease her anger. He held up the badge. "This was useless. Being replaced. It wouldn't really be stealing."

"I'm not stupid, Mr. Canfield."

He softened his tone. "No, it's just hard to accept."

She dropped her gaze for a second, then pushed back one sleeve of her robe and held out her wrist. "He gave me this." It was a gold bracelet. Expensive, best Skip could tell.

Sharon looked away. "And he said something at the time that has a different meaning now."

A beat of silence. "What was that?" Skip prompted.

"He said it was to remember him by." A tear trickled down her cheek.

Skip swallowed the lump in his throat. "You might want to get dressed, ma'am. The police will be here soon."

CHAPTER FOURTEEN

Kate wasn't surprised when her phone rang at four-thirty.

"Hey darlin'," Skip said. "Looks like you'll need to go to Maria's party without me. My guy's out on the town already."

"Who are you watching anyway?"

"That engineer I told you about."

"You think he's the spy?"

"He's got the best motive. And access to the information. I'm hoping to link him to somebody at the competitor's company."

"So why would he go into the lab that night?"

"Good question, but I've got one answer at least."

Her mouth fell open as he told her about the missing guard and finding John Cochlin's badge in the guy's apartment.

"So this guy must've stolen Hal's badge too," she said.

"That's what makes sense to me," Skip said. "But unfortunately, Detective Russell isn't buying it, or at least he isn't admitting to buying it."

"Sheez, what does that guy want?"

"My guess is he wants someone he can arrest and see prosecuted, instead of a dead man and a guard who's in the wind."

Kate blew out air. "And who probably *is* in the Bahamas by now."

"Yup. Russell wasn't real happy with me. Accused me of interfering with an ongoing investigation."

"Why? Because you found evidence he missed? Most likely nobody would've ever made the connection between this guard and the spying if you didn't still have your man in there."

"Well, that's blown now. Hey, do me a favor." His voice had turned wistful. "Bring me a doggy bag from Maria's."

Aw, poor baby. "Will do," she said into the phone.

~~~~~~~~~

José, Eduardo's eldest, answered the door of the Pérez home. Tall, dark-haired and handsome, Kate suspected he had no trouble getting dates. He stepped back, grinning. "Welcome to the birthday dinner for her majesty, the princess."

"Hi, Joe," Edie mumbled, then she and Connie took off for a far corner of the living room, talking low and giggling. Kate caught a few words—they were apparently discussing some boy in Connie's class. She smiled at the two dark heads bent together, one a mop of curls, the other silky and smooth. Only a year older than Edie, Connie's figure was already filling out.

Kate smiled wider at the warm touches Maria had added to the living room. Brightly colored pillows and a Guatemalan, patterned throw accented the beige sofa and armchairs.

Maria bustled out of the kitchen. "Ah, Kate, Billy. Welcome." She'd worn loose-fitting house dresses around the Canfield home, but tonight she was decked out in a red knit dress, cinched at the waist with a wide belt. The outfit complemented her plump but well-proportioned figure. With her dark hair swept up in a shiny bun, she looked like a different woman.

"*Mi prima* and her *marido* are in the kitchen." Maria made a shooing motion in that direction and bustled off with their coats.

The kitchen smelled wonderful. Kate's stomach growled enthusiastically.

Mac chuckled. His wiry body was decked out in his best clothes—a relatively wrinkle-free plaid shirt and jeans. He'd even shaved at some point in the last twelve hours. He gave Kate's shoulders a one-armed hug. "How ya doin', sweet pea?"

She smiled at the use of his childhood nickname for her. "I'm good."

She turned to Rose, who was in the process of dipping a tortilla chip into a bowl of homemade salsa on the table. "Are your folks coming?" Certainly, Maria's *Tía* Rita and *Tío* Julio had been invited.

Rose shook her head as she chewed. "*Mi madre*'s not feeling good tonight. Just a cold, but *Papi* didn't want to leave her alone."

Eduardo Pérez came into the kitchen. "Kate, so pleased that you and the *niños* could come." He was a slender man, about Kate's height, and he was now sporting a small paunch.

Kate hid a smile. Maria's excellent cooking had its downside.

Ten minutes later, they were taking their seats around the long, mahogany table in the dining room. Carlos, the Pérez middle child, slipped into his chair, a red baseball cap turned backward on his head. Eduardo pointed to the cap and the boy snatched it off.

Connie, as the birthday girl, was nominated to say grace. She did so in rapid Spanish, then finished in accentless English. "In the name of the Father, Son and Holy Spirit. Amen."

A flurry of hands as they made the sign of the cross and murmured "Amen."

Kate was impressed by the Pérez children's fluency in both languages. It wasn't easy to raise bilingual children. They'd tried with Edie and Billy. Maria had taught them quite a few words and phrases, but they were far from fluent.

Noisy conversation accompanied the delicious food, followed by a dark chocolate birthday cake. Kate licked rich icing off of her fork, resisting the urge to have a second piece.

"I miss your cooking, Maria," Edie said from the other end of the table.

Her wistful tone made Kate's heart ache.

~~~~~~~~

It was bad enough that Skip was missing the birthday party, but skipping dinner altogether was unacceptable. Once Allen had been inside the bar long enough to have made his way into the backroom, Skip went in himself.

He kept his head down and moved quickly to an empty barstool at the end of the bar, then discreetly looked around. Allen was indeed no longer in the front of the bar.

The bartender appeared in front of him. "What'll it be?"

Skip ordered a burger, fries and a beer, which he intended to nurse for quite some time. He needed to keep his wits about him.

When the barkeep delivered his food and plopped a ketchup bottle down in front of him, Skip said, "Looks great. You got any mayo?"

Sending the man on an unnecessary errand might not be the best idea, but he needed to keep the guy engaged until he found an opening.

He took a bite of the burger and hastily chewed and swallowed.

The barkeep returned with a little cup of mayo.

"It's as good as it looks," Skip said. "Best burger I've had in ages."

The bartender arched an eyebrow at him. "You had one the other night."

Skip wasn't all that surprised that the barkeep remembered him. It supported his suspicions about this place. This man's job description went beyond mixing drinks.

"Yeah, I did." He grinned. "That's why I came back for one tonight." He grabbed the mayo and started slathering it on the bun. "How does your cook make them so juicy?"

The guy shrugged. "Beats me." He started to turn away.

"Say, you seem like an observant guy. You know where a man can get some action around here?"

The barkeep turned back. "What kind of action ya got in mind?"

"Oh, I don't know." Skip shrugged. "A friendly poker game maybe. I'm fairly new in town. Don't know too many people."

The man grabbed a rag and ran it over the already clean bar. "And who are you exactly?"

Skip was prepared for that question. He pulled out a fake business card that said he was Joseph Marshall, an insurance salesman. He handed it to the barkeep, then picked up a french fry and nonchalantly chomped it down.

The man examined the card before sticking it in his apron

pocket. "I'll see what I can find out for ya. Stop back again in a day or so."

"Hey thanks, man." Skip grinned, then took a big bite of his burger. Now he wanted the conversation to end, before the man could ask any questions.

The barkeep wandered off.

The number on the card was a phone line into the agency that Ginny would answer using the fake insurance company's name. Skip hoped these guys didn't bother to check him out beyond that.

He made a mental note to report this place to the police, once the case was resolved. Hopefully they wouldn't be raided in the meantime, especially while he was here.

~~~~~~~~

Rose had experienced worse weekends, but she couldn't remember when. The birthday party at Maria's had been the only bright spot.

On Monday morning, she knocked on her partner's open door, then stepped into his office. "Been checking out those rumors."

Skip nodded, picking up his coffee mug.

"So far, they track back to a dude named James Kitterling."

The mug stopped halfway to his mouth. "Say what?"

"James Kitterling," she repeated. "He's a retired state trooper, started his own agency about six months ago."

Skip set the mug on his desk. "I know him."

"You have issues with him?"

"No, as a matter of fact, we were sort of buddies." Skip grimaced. "He and I were partners briefly."

When he didn't elaborate, she said, "So is he the type to make stuff up to knock out the competition?"

"I wouldn't think so."

"I've found four other people, so far, in the chain of this particular rumor mill."

"You gonna have Dolph check them out?" Skip asked.

"When he has some time to spare."

He handed her a sheet of paper, a printout from his computer.

"Can you have him dig deeper on these people too?"

She glanced over the list. "These the names Kate got from Murdock?"

"Yes."

"You've got Elaine Patterson and Murdock himself on here too. I thought we'd already dug pretty deep on them?"

"I'd like Dolph to take a second look," Skip said. "That background check service we're using isn't all that good."

"I'll work on finding another one, but Dolph's pretty busy these days with those insurance fraud cases."

Skip nodded, then chugged the rest of his coffee. He rose and lifted the jacket from the back of his chair. "I think I'll pay old Kitt a visit."

~~~~~~~~~

Skip breezed past Kitterling's receptionist.

"Wait, he's on the phone." The petite woman rose from her chair.

But Skip was already rapping his knuckles lightly against the doorjamb of Kitterling's office.

The large, fiftyish man behind the desk had a phone receiver tucked between shoulder and chin. He wiggled his fingers in a come-in gesture without looking up from the pad where he was taking notes. "Yeah, yeah… Okay good, keep on it."

He hung up the phone and lifted his head. His eyes went wide, then lit up. He was out of his chair and around the desk in one stride, extending his hand. "Skip Canfield, you old son-of–a-gun." He slapped Skip's shoulder as they shook hands.

Skip grinned in spite of himself. Warmth spread through his chest. He'd forgotten how much he liked this man. "How're things going, Kitt?"

"Not bad." Kitterling stepped back and gestured toward a visitor's chair next to his desk. "Not bad at all." He settled into his desk chair and leaned back. The chair groaned softly.

Kitt had gained a few pounds around the middle in the last decade and a half, but otherwise he looked about the same. Only a few more lines in his rugged face and a few more gray hairs sprinkled amongst the dark brown ones. He was aging well.

"How's the wife?" Skip searched his memory for her name but came up blank.

"Okay. We split five years ago."

"Oh. Sorry to hear that."

Kitt shrugged. "It happens."

All too often, Skip knew. Being a cop was hard on marriages. But he doubted Kitt actually felt as nonchalant about it as he pretended. He'd adored his wife, had talked about her constantly when they'd been partners.

"Between the fear and the poverty," Kitt said, "she couldn't take it anymore."

Skip nodded. Cops' spouses cringed every time the doorbell rang. Would this be the time they'd find a grim-faced officer on their porch instead of the UPS guy? And poverty might be an exaggeration, but cops certainly didn't make enough to afford many luxuries for their families.

"She's remarried now. Our boy lives with her." Kitt leaned forward and nudged a picture on his desk. "He and I hang out on weekends, as much as I can."

Skip picked up the framed photo. A lanky preteen grinned back at him, red highlights in his dark hair. He held a decent-sized trout up by a string. The boy looked vaguely familiar, but then most kids his age looked similar, their faces still soft like a child's, their bodies either tall and awkward like this kid, or pudgy with baby fat if they hadn't started shooting up yet.

"Handsome kid." He put the photo back on Kitt's desk. "This private stuff allows for more weekends off, but not always when you're working a case."

Like this past weekend. He'd spent most of it in his truck, watching other people have lives and trying not to think about his full bladder.

"So what can I do for you, Skippy?" The man's grin softened the insult of the disliked nickname.

Skip mentally braced himself. "My partner and I have been chasing down some rumors about us."

Kitt's grin faded. He broke eye contact. "Yeah, I heard."

"From who?"

"A couple of people."

"I'd appreciate names. If we've pissed off a client, so be it, but if somebody's spreading false rumors…" He let his voice trail off.

"I heard it first from Howard Kaplan."

Skip barely managed to stop his jaw from dropping.

"I know, Howie's a slime," Kitt said, apparently misinterpreting his reaction. "So I didn't pay much attention. But then I heard the same thing from…other sources."

Still trying to process what he'd just heard, Skip let the silence stretch out. He was pretty sure Kitterling was telling the truth.

The man sat up, swiveled his chair around to an old Mac computer and banged on a few keys. A printer whirred. Kitt grabbed the sheet it spit out and handed it to Skip. "Here's the guy's number and business address. Walk softly, please. He's a client."

Skip glanced at the paper, didn't recognize the name. He folded it and stuck it in his shirt pocket. "Thanks." His stomach tightened as he braced to ask his next question. "Why did you pass the rumor on?" He hoped he'd managed to keep his voice neutral.

"Man, I'm sorry. I didn't mean to. I was talking to another cop, who's thinking of getting his P.I. license when he retires. We were talking about how guys like Howie make it hard, and even when you get a good rep going, it can go down the tubes so easily." Kitt scrubbed his face with a big hand. "That's when I mentioned you and the rumor I'd heard. I wasn't implying it was true, only that it had to be hurting you all."

Skip wasn't willing to admit just how much it was hurting them. "Who's the cop you were talking to?"

Kitt said a name. Skip didn't know him, and he was pretty sure it wasn't one of the four people Rose had mentioned. He pulled out the folded paper and a pencil and jotted the name down. "You got a phone number for him?"

Kitt picked up his phone from the desk and tapped it a couple of times, then rattled off a number. "That's his cell. I don't really know the guy. He contacted me to pick my brain about going private."

"Anything else you can tell me that might help us track down the origin of the rumors?"

His gaze skittered across the room and then back again, locked onto Skip's face a little too intently. "Can't think of anything."

Skip's throat hurt. *He's lying.*

"The other person you heard it from?"

Kitt shook his head a little too vigorously. "Did I say three people? It was just Howie and that client."

Lying again.

Skip let a few seconds of silence tick by. When Kitt didn't fill them, Skip slowly rose and offered his hand.

Kitt stood and shook it. "Good seeing you, man. When you've got this rumor BS straightened out, let's get together for a beer and talk old times."

Skip faked a smile. "Sure. I'd like that."

Up until a minute ago, he would have. His chest heavy, he turned and left Kitt's office.

CHAPTER FIFTEEN

Once in his truck, Skip called Rose. He gave her the names and the contact information Kitterling had provided. "They weren't on your list, were they?"

"Nope, it looks like number three skipped a link in the chain. He said the rumor had come from Kitterling."

"Well, it had, but not directly. He was probably trying to protect his buddy." He didn't mention that Kitt was also apparently covering for somebody.

He sighed. It wasn't going to be easy to track down the source of the rumor, if everybody kept covering each other's butts. "Oh, by the way, Kitt also said that he'd heard it from Howie Kaplan first."

A pause. "What's little Howie up to now?" Rose said.

"Good question. You going to check him out again?"

"Yeah, and I'll get on these other two guys. What are you up to today?"

Skip sighed again. "More surveillance."

Rose chuckled. "You want me to take over later?"

"Actually, I've been sticking with Allen, who seems to have a gambling problem, but it would help if you could take the other engineer, Garrett Watson. He's inside Strategic's offices most of the day, but I'd like to know what he does at lunchtime, and if he goes anywhere interesting after work."

"Okay. I'll meet you in Strategic's parking lot around eleven-thirty."

~~~~~~~

Kate sat at the kitchen table and stared at the empty pizza box. She gave herself a mental pat on the back for having survived another evening.

No wonder Eduardo Pérez had been so anxious to find a mother for his teenaged children. Single parenthood sucked. And the fact that they were more than halfway self-sufficient now physically didn't really help that much. She'd much rather supervise a two year old's bath than deal with a temperamental twelve year old.

Edie had scarfed down three slices despite complaining loud and long that she was sick to death of pizza.

Kate had resisted the temptation to suggest she slow down on the calories some. The child was getting a little pudgy. But she didn't want Edie dieting. That could all too easily slide into an eating disorder at this age.

Her throat thickened with guilt. That pudginess was more than half her fault anyway. She really should learn how to cook some low-cal, nutritious dishes.

She got up and went to the counter where she'd left her purse. She'd find some recipes right now and get the ingredients later in the week to try them out this coming weekend. She dug in her purse for her phone to search the Internet.

Her hand came up with the gizmo Hal had given her instead. She'd forgotten all about it.

Curiosity got the better of her and she turned it on. Her finger hovered over the tiny keyboard on the screen. Sucking in air, she punched in Edie's cell phone number.

A small map appeared with an inverted teardrop-shaped marker in the middle of it. It pointed to her street, Daffodil Lane.

Kate shook her head. Of course it did. Edie was upstairs in bed.

A menu across the bottom included a small telephone receiver. Kate tapped it.

A log of recent calls came up. They either had a P or T next to them.

Probably phone or text.

Two of the numbers were her own cell phone and one was Skip's. They all had Ps next to them. Most of the rest were the same number, mostly Ts next to them. At least a dozen of them.

Kate didn't recognize the number.

The list of numbers jumped on the screen. Kate almost dropped the gizmo.

That same number had appeared again at the top of the list, this time with a P next to it.

Kate noticed another column to the far right. Next to the new phone number, the digits in that column were scrolling quickly—11, 12, 13, 14…

Duh, they're seconds.

Was Edie currently on the phone with this person?

An image rose unbidden in Kate's mind, of a sleazy-looking man with greasy skin and pig-like eyes, on a cell phone, his voice high pitched like a young boy's, making a date with her daughter.

Heart pounding, Kate dug again in her purse and came up with her own phone. She punched in the number from the gizmo's screen.

A tinny voice in Kate's ear, "410-555-1342 is not available. Your call is being forwarded to a voice messaging system."

Then a girl's voice, light and breezy, "Hi, you've reached Connie's voicemail. You know what to do. Talk to ya soon."

Kate disconnected, expelling pent-up air. It was Consuela Pérez's number.

Heat burned her cheeks. She turned off the gizmo and tossed it back in her purse.

~~~~~~~

The bar was almost as crowded as it had been on Saturday night. That was good and bad. Good that it made it easy to duck into a dark corner and avoid Paul Allen's eyes.

Bad in that it was hard for Skip to grab the bartender's attention. Once he had it he wasn't about to let it go. "Bring me one of your great burgers, will ya? And by the way, did you have any luck with that thing you were gonna track down for me."

The barkeep stared at him for a moment, then blinked. "One burger comin' up." He drew a beer without being asked and put it down in front of Skip. Then he disappeared around a corner at the end of the bar.

Skip's stomach growled. *Hopefully he's placing my dinner order.*

Keeping his chin tilted down so his face was in shadows, Skip scanned the room. He didn't find Allen, even though the man's car was parked out at the curb.

Ten minutes later, Skip's beer was down an inch when the barkeep brought a plate with a burger and fries on it. There was even a little paper cup of mayo next to the dill pickle.

This guy was good at his job.

The barkeep placed the plate in front of him, then leaned forward, his elbows on the bar. "Plain door in the back wall. Boss says you got a thousand dollar limit this first night." He eyed the glass of beer. "Not much of a drinker, huh?"

Skip grinned. "I enjoy other vices more."

The barkeep nodded once. "Be discreet." Then he turned away.

When Skip lifted the cup of mayo, a key was under it. So that's what people were doing when they stood for a second in front of the door, before opening it. The door was locked, but the management didn't want that made obvious.

He ate slowly, and sipped beer even more slowly. Finally the event he'd been waiting for occurred. Allen came through the plain wooden door and moved toward the back hall, and the men's room, Skip assumed.

He jammed the last bite of burger into his mouth and picked us his beer. Then he wove his way through the crowd to the wooden door. He blocked the view of the knob with his body and slipped the key in. It turned smoothly. He opened the door and stepped through it.

A short hallway, less than five foot long, ended at another

doorway, covered by a gold lamé curtain. He pushed that aside.

The room was cavernous and not at all what he'd expected. It was a step above the bar in decor. Dozens of people stood around two roulette wheels and several blackjack tables. Two big round tables to his left were the only place where people were seated. Skip suspected they were playing poker.

Before he could see much else, a hulk of a man stepped in front of him, crowding his personal space. "Who are you?"

"Joe," Skip said. He held up the key. "Barkeep said it was okay. The boss gave me a thousand dollar limit."

The hulk grunted softly and stepped aside.

Waitresses in perky, short-skirted uniforms carried trays of drinks amongst the serious-faced patrons, who were mostly male. One of the young ladies was headed his way.

He smiled and lifted his still half-full beer.

She veered off gracefully, giving him a flirtatious look over her shoulder.

Skip quickly positioned himself at one of the roulette tables, his back partially to the door, where he could watch for Allen's return. His eyes veiled by his too long hair, he looked around, searching for familiar faces of people who might know him.

He'd breathed a low sigh of relief when the croupier growled, "Ya gonna bet, sir?"

"Uh, I don't have any chips yet. I thought I'd watch for a little bit first."

The fellow shrugged and spun the wheel, releasing the ivory-colored plastic ball.

Or at least Skip assumed it was plastic, since real ivory was now illegal. Then again, roulette was illegal outside of the state-sanctioned casinos.

But some gamblers liked the extra thrill of going to illicit joints like this one. Others preferred them because they were closer to home or work. He suspected that was Allen's motivation for frequenting this place.

And speak of the devil, the Strategic engineer pushed through the gold curtain, nodding to the goon who guarded the entrance.

Skip turned a bit farther away and watched Paul Allen in his peripheral vision. The man crossed to one of the poker tables and took the only empty chair.

A couple of people joined those already at the roulette table. "Ya gonna play or what, mister?" the croupier asked.

It was far from crowded around the table, and the one woman in the group was also just watching. But Skip got the hint. Checking to be sure Allen wasn't looking his way, he headed for the window on one side of the room where players were buying or cashing in chips.

He smiled at the young woman behind a grill of decorative but sturdy looking white bars. "One hundred, please."

The blue-eyed, blonde returned his smile with a sweet one of her own. "Must be new here, hon. We only do increments of two hundred."

"Two hundred then." He gave her his sexiest grin, the one that always melted Kate's kneecaps. "And yes, I'm a newbie."

He paused to count out the additional money from his wallet. He'd better win some tonight, or at least not lose too fast. He only had one more ten in there.

"How long have you worked here?" he asked the young woman as he handed over the money.

She gave him the same sweet girl-next-door smile but what came out of her mouth was, "On nights like tonight, sugar, the answer is too long."

He nodded and gathered up the stacks of chips she had nudged through the opening at the bottom of the grillwork. He might come back later to mine that field for information. Asking nosy questions now, when she'd made him as a newbie, would raise suspicions.

He turned and walked back toward the clacking sound of the roulette wheels, making sure to keep his face turned away from the poker tables. He was halfway across the room when he stopped in his tracks and barely caught his jaw before it dropped open.

Near the second roulette table was a face he had missed in his first scan of the room. He'd never actually met her in person, but he'd seen her picture in the newspapers in the past. And more recently in the Strategic case file.

With her slender figure poured into a snug black dress and her smooth *café au lait* skin, Beatrice Cooper looked like a fashion model. But she was as much brains as beauty, if not more. Under her sleek black hair was what the *Baltimore Sun* had dubbed the finest mind since Albert Einstein. An exaggeration perhaps, but she was most definitely the local *wunderkind* in electronics.

And she was Fred Latey's counterpart at Enterprise Electronics, Inc., Strategic's main competitor for government contracts.

CHAPTER SIXTEEN

Skip slipped into the house as quietly as he could. Kate had left a small lamp on in the living room and dim light filtered in from the kitchen doorway, but otherwise the house was dark and quiet.

He left his sneakers in the entranceway and padded in his stocking feet into the kitchen to make a sandwich. The burger he'd had at the bar earlier was now a distant memory.

It had been a long and frustrating day. But the evening had paid off, when he'd discovered that Paul Allen, the lead engineer on Strategic's compromised project, liked to hang out at the same illegal gambling joint as the competitor's director of operations.

Way too much of a coincidence.

Beatrice Cooper had spent the evening sipping white wine and watching her male companion play roulette. She had given no indication that she knew Allen. The few times she'd glanced around the room, her eyes had neither avoided nor lingered on the engineer at the poker table.

At midnight, when Allen had thrown down his cards and left the backroom casino, Skip had let him go, more interested in what Ms. Cooper would do next. She and her companion lingered another hour.

Skip followed them to the cashier's window and cashed in his chips. He was pleased to discover he was ten dollars ahead. He hadn't been paying close attention.

Was it beginner's luck, or was the game rigged to allow newbies to win, thus sucking them in further?

Beatrice and her escort had exited through the bar and walked down and around the corner to a public parking lot. There they smooched for a while, with Skip leaning against the corner of a nearby building and freezing his butt off.

She'd donned a dressy black jacket over her skimpy dress, but her legs had to be popsicles. Finally the couple had parted company, getting into separate cars.

Skip wracked his brain as he slapped lunchmeat onto the bread he'd just slathered with mayo. Was Beatrice Cooper married? He made a mental note to check the Strategic file first thing in the morning.

Thoughts of the file reminded him of the more frustrating part of the day—going through the reports from Dolph.

Poking deeper into their finances had revealed nothing all that new or exciting about Patterson or Murdock. Elaine and her husband lived slightly above their means, not all that unusual in middle-class America today. Their credit card debt had been higher two years ago, but then had gradually come down and had been steady for the last year.

Harold Murdock lived considerably below his means and basically had no life.

The report on Latey wasn't very interesting either, except for some hefty credit card charges in December. Nothing he couldn't afford though. Mrs. Latey had apparently had a good Christmas.

The two other technicians on Murdock's list were even more boring. Nothing worse than a speeding ticket or two and their finances were in order—bank balances and credit card debt appropriate for their salaries.

The other engineer, Garrett Watson also seemed to be a good money manager, his finances in sync with his income.

Rose had been tailing him for several days. The only deviation from his commute to and from work had been a stop yesterday, at a small hardware store in a local strip shopping center. She had opted not to go in, concerned he would notice her in such a confined setting where female customers were in the minority.

He hadn't stayed in there long and had come out with a small plastic bag.

After seeing Dolph's report, Skip wished Rose had gone in and observed what Watson bought. Two handguns were registered in his name, a .38 semi-automatic and a .22 revolver. Had he stopped for ammunition?

One handgun was likely for protection. Two or more suggested a gun enthusiast. A man who owned two legal guns might also have some unregistered ones lying around, say, a nine millimeter. Rose was going to see what she could find out about that.

No one else in the group had any handguns in their households, or at least none that were registered.

Rose had assigned Dolph to another insurance fraud case from their newest client. Deep background checks on the links in the rumor chain would have to wait, she'd informed Skip.

He'd been annoyed when she made that pronouncement, but knew she was right. They couldn't afford to lose any of their paying clients, and especially not this insurance company, the last new account he'd managed to land.

His stomach growled, then heaved a little. Anxiety and erratic meals did not mix well.

He sat down at the table and took a bite of his sandwich, his mind veering back to his prime suspect. Did Alicia Allen know about the maxed out credit cards and the overdue payments on Allen's Porsche? Dolph had found that only the mortgage and Alicia's car payments were up to date.

No, Skip decided, Alicia had no idea about the cliff she and her family were about to tumble down.

He glanced across the table and spotted the back of a note, propped against the salt and pepper shakers so that he would see it as he came into the room.

Well, that strategy hadn't worked. He leaned over and grabbed it.

Kate's handwriting.

Talk to Edie if she's still up. Something's going on. Love, K

Of course, technically Edie should *not* still be up, but that didn't mean she wasn't.

Skip dropped the remnants of his sandwich on the plate and stood. He climbed the stairs to the kids' rooms and cracked Billy's door an inch to check on him. The child was sound asleep, but he had once again snuck the dog into his room. Toby raised his golden head in response to the sliver of light angling across the floor.

Skip clicked his tongue softly. The dog stood, shook and came out into the hall.

"You know better," Skip scolded him in a whisper.

Toby just wagged his tail and headed for the steps.

Skip walked to Edie's door. Again, he opened it slowly. A bright flash in the darkness, then a faint pink rim of light on the bed.

Edie's phone, now screen down on her comforter.

He slipped into the room, leaving the door ajar to provide some light. He reached for the phone to move it so he could sit down.

Edie snatched it away and tapped the screen. It filled with icons.

He eased down on the edge of the bed. "You're up late, Pumkin."

"Couldn't sleep."

"Would you like to read a story together?"

She shook her head.

"Mom said she thought maybe something's bothering you."

Edie's head jerked up, her eyes wide. "No, I'm fine."

"What were you doing just now, on your phone?"

She shrugged. "Messing around."

"Texting your friends?"

She shook her head again, a little too vigorously.

"Do you want to talk about your day?" Skip was getting a taste of what Kate experienced every day with this child. And he was rethinking his blasé "we'll survive" attitude. They had six more years of this before they could ship her off to college.

"No." Edie faked a yawn. "I guess I'll try to go to sleep now."

Skip wrapped his hand around the end of her phone. For a second, she resisted giving it to him.

"Your friends need to get some sleep too."

She let go.

He turned the phone off. "It will be down on the table in the morning."

She gave him a sour look.

He ignored her expression and kissed her on the forehead. "Goodnight, Pumkin."

He was halfway out of her room before she relented. "Goodnight, Daddy."

~~~~~~~~

Kate was exhausted, and a bit peeved with Skip. They'd had almost no time together recently. She'd only seen him briefly this morning, just long enough for a whispered conversation about Edie.

He'd acknowledged that their daughter was indeed being secretive but he had no clue what she was up to. "I'm now getting the you're-an-adult-so-I'm-not-telling-you-anything treatment that she's been giving you for a while."

Then he'd pecked her on the lips. "Ill probably be late again tonight." And he was out the door, before the kids had even finished their breakfast.

Kate rubbed her tired eyes and struggled to focus them on the highway ahead. At least there wasn't much traffic this late on a Tuesday evening.

She knew she was being irrational about Skip's long hours. He was working so hard in order to help *her* client—well, that and to restore the agency's reputation.

She yawned and shook her head to clear it. She was more alert for about two minutes.

What happened to the days when she could work ten hours on Tuesdays, to accommodate her clients who needed evening hours? She'd been tired at the end of those days, but not like this.

Of course, the forty-five-minute drive back from Annapolis after the task force meetings made the long day even worse.

She'd dropped the kids off at Maria's earlier. Now she envisioned the Pérez's warm kitchen and anticipated the quick cup of tea she would have with Maria before heading home.

That perked her up some.

At least the meeting had gone well. They'd made headway in several areas, including developing the beginnings of a model for police departments to identify overly aggressive officers and provide them with counseling and additional training in de-escalation tactics, *before* someone got shot.

More than ever, she was having mixed feelings about the task force. Yes, they were making good progress tonight and their report might actually make a difference. But the time commitment—the weekly meetings, the phone calls and consultations in between—all that was adding stress to her own life when there was already too much going on.

She glanced in the rearview mirror. Her tired brain registered that the same pair of headlights had followed her through the last three turns.

Since she was still on a major road, she decided she was being paranoid.

But when she pulled up in front of the Pérez home, bright lights glinted in her rear and side view mirrors. Whoever had been following her had parked behind her and hit his high beams.

She made sure her doors were locked, then blew her horn to attract Eduardo's and Maria's attention.

The car behind her responded with a short blip of a siren. Then the inside light came on as the driver opened his door.

Detective Russell.

Kate gritted her teeth. She climbed out of her car and turned to him.

Maria had come out on her lit porch, Eduardo behind her, which made Kate feel safer about confronting the man.

"What the hell do you think you're doing?"

"Following a suspect."

"What?" she practically shouted.

Lights went on in the front windows of the house next door. Kate lowered her voice. "Suspect in what?"

Eduardo was coming down the porch steps.

Kate held up a hand. "It's okay," she called out.

"I'm wondering if you're in this industrial spy ring, along with Murdock, and maybe your husband as well."

"That's crazy."

"Is it? I've been reading the detective's reports from your first husband's murder case. He thought you and Franklin were lovers, but I've got another theory. You married Canfield pretty darn soon after Huntington died. I think you two were having an affair long before he conveniently got himself killed."

The detective's accusations were ludicrous. Nonetheless they poked daggers into Kate's heart. She might not be able to remember Eddie's face some days, but a part of her still loved him and always would.

She struggled to gather her wits.

Russell smirked.

She took a deep breath. "Detective, what do you hope to accomplish by harassing me? You know damn well that I had nothing to do with any of these crimes. It's a coincidence that I know Mr. Murdock. I helped him obtain counsel. That is all. And I have no *connections*, and if I did, I wouldn't use them to interfere with a police investigation."

"But your husband's still poking around in this."

Not really sure what to say, she passed the buck. "You'll have to talk to him about that."

Sorry, Skip.

Russell widened his stance and crossed his arms. "You know, I'm half tempted to re-open your first husband's murder case."

Kate knew he was just trying to rattle her, and she wasn't going to give him that satisfaction. She narrowed her eyes at him.

"I think you would find that hard to do since his killer confessed and is currently serving a life sentence in the state penitentiary." Turning on her heel, she started around the front of her car.

The scrape of shoe soles on pavement behind her. Russell grabbed her arm.

She fought her natural instinct to pull away from his grasp. She hadn't been to an *aikido* class in a while, but she remembered the simple maneuver that would rid herself of his hand.

"Hey you, let her go," Eduardo yelled, running down the sidewalk.

"Stay out of this, asshole."

A little shocked by his language, Kate held her free hand up to stop Eduardo. She didn't trust Russell not to draw his gun.

Her heart stuttered in her chest when she looked up and saw Edie and Billy standing on the porch with Maria.

Seething, she said in a low voice, "I don't have the connections you think I have, but I do have enough to get you disciplined for assaulting a private citizen and cursing at an innocent bystander who's only trying to stop said assault."

Russell stared at her, still gripping her arm.

"My children are on that porch, Detective." She pushed the words through clenched teeth. "If you do anything that causes them harm, physical or psychological, I will have your badge."

Another couple of seconds ticked by, then he let go of her and stepped back. He gave an exaggerated little bow and returned to his car.

By the time he was pulling away from the curb, Kate was shaking like a leaf.

Eduardo closed the gap between them and put an arm around her shoulders. He led her up the walk.

"Who was that guy, Mom?" Edie asked, concern in her voice.

Kate grabbed the railing to steady herself and climbed the porch steps. "He's a police detective, sweetie. He's..." How could she begin to explain this complicated mess to her children.

She reached out and squeezed Edie's shoulder. "He's not

important. Just somebody connected with the task force."

"But you were arguing with him," Billy said.

"Yeah. He's not a very nice person. Go get your things. We need to get home."

Maria and Eduardo exchanged a concerned look.

Once the kids were out of earshot, Kate said, "Thanks, you two, for coming to the rescue. That scene may have had a different ending if I hadn't had witnesses."

"What mess you in now, Kate?" Maria said.

Kate smiled. This woman knew her too well. "Not one of my own making, but don't worry, Skip's knee deep in it with me."

That news did nothing to shift the pinched expression on Maria's face. She shook her head slightly, then gave the kids goodbye hugs as they returned with their backpacks.

Once home, Kate got the children started on their bedtime routine. Then she sat down at the computer in the study to compose an email.

Dear Ben,

A bit formal for an email, but Ben Horowitz was old-fashioned.

I'd like to address the group next week about something that happened this evening on my way home. It's relevant to one of the issues we've been discussing.

I got a taste of what African-American citizens probably experience all too often, including a threat to my children.

She reread that much, then deleted the part about her children. Ben might perceive that as melodramatic.

After my comments to the group, I will be happy to recuse myself from the task force if you want me to do so.

She reread the entire email, then thought, *Please, please want me to do so.*

She added *Sincerely, Kate* at the end and hit send.

~~~~~~

At eight on Wednesday morning, Rose was watching Howie Kaplan's house, a ramshackle bungalow in a less-than-respectable neighborhood. She doubted Howie was an early riser, but she didn't want to miss him.

He'd been ducking her for two days now, and she was losing patience. Not that she'd ever had much where Kaplan was concerned.

His car, a beat-up older model Chevy, was parked in the driveway, so she knew he was home. It was only a matter of time.

At eight-twenty, her patience ran out. She had better things to do than watch the weeds grow in Howie's front yard. For one, she should be helping Skip with the surveillance on the Strategic case.

She got out of her car and approached the front porch—little more than a cement stoop really—while debating her next move. Knocking would give Howie the option of bolting out the back.

She pulled a small leather pouch out of her pocket.

Five minutes later, she was standing beside Kaplan's bed. The stench of unwashed sheets and stale whiskey made her eyes water.

Again, she contemplated her next move. Howie might have a gun under his pillow.

She retrieved her snub-nosed .32 from her ankle holster, then slid her other hand slowly under the pillow, trying not to think about the vermin that might be living in his sheets.

He snorted in his sleep but otherwise didn't stir.

Nothing under the pillow.

She grabbed a healthy wad of top sheet in her left hand and yanked it off the bed.

No gun under the sheet, but what she saw was almost worse.

Howie slept on, in the raw.

Rose was halfway through her cup of coffee—for a loser, Kaplan had a surprisingly good coffee maker—when Howie finally stumbled out of his bedroom, a grungy bathrobe wrapped crookedly around his scrawny body.

When did he lose so much weight? Was he drinking so heavy he wasn't bothering to eat?

His chest and forearms were red and mottled. She remembered reading an article once about protein deficiency. The pics in that article looked a lot like Howie's skin.

The man was slowly killing himself with booze. She almost felt sorry for him. Almost.

"Rose! What the hell?"

"Good morning, Howie," she said cheerfully. She rose and poured hot coffee into another mug, brought it to him as he flopped into a chair at the folding card table that constituted his kitchen furniture. She returned to her own seat, across from him.

"How'd you get in?" He lifted the mug with both hands. They were shaking so badly, he had trouble getting the coffee into his mouth.

"Your locks are a joke." Her voice was less harsh than it might have otherwise been. She was starting to feel sorry for the guy. She took a sip of her own coffee. "I've been tracing the rumors about us back to the root. Guess what? You're it."

Howie jerked a little, spilling hot liquid onto his fingers. He grimaced.

"Come on, Howie. I don't feel like playing games this early in the morning. Why'd you start the rumor?"

He caved faster than she'd thought he would.

"Four, five months ago. I got an envelope in the mail. No return address. Note inside said I could make an easy five hundred bucks if I started a certain rumor."

He fell silent.

Rose gritted her teeth. Was he going to make her drag the story out of him? "So you started the rumor and then…"

"It was time for the payoff. I got another note, told me to meet some guy at a fast food place on York Road." Howie paused for a coughing fit. It sounded like he was trying to hack up a lung. Finally he found his voice again. "The guy stiffed me. There was only two bills in the envelope."

"What'd this guy look like?"

The description was mundane, could've been a thousand middle-aged guys—until he got to the brown splotch on the dude's chin.

Rose's insides twisted. *Fred Latey.*

"Not like you to do a job without a down payment, Howie."

The man actually blushed. "Well, there were a couple of Grants in the first envelope."

"Anything else you wanna tell me, Howie?" She glared at him. He shook his head.

She rose and extracted two of the ten twenties she'd tucked into her pocket earlier. She dropped them on the table.

Pausing in the kitchen doorway, she said, "You really need to clean up your act, Howie. You're a frickin' caricature."

He stared up at her, his hands shaking around his now empty coffee cup. His eyes were hollow, the dark circles layered under them.

"I'm dyin', Rose. Lung cancer."

Her throat closed. She blinked hard to clear her stinging eyes and wished she could take back her words. "I'm sorry, Howie."

He nodded.

On the way out, Rose dropped the rest of the twenties on a cluttered end table.

CHAPTER SEVENTEEN

Kate braced herself. Hal Murdock was her last client of the morning.

Who knew what fallout there might still be from Skip telling him he shouldn't talk to her about the Strategic mess.

Hal was about as bad as she'd ever seen him, the walking wounded. His voice quavered when he said hello. He trudged to the loveseat where clients usually sat.

She settled into her chair across from him. "How's it going?"

He glanced up, a quick furtive peek, then down again to stare at the carpet. "It's, uh, been a tough few days."

"You want to tell me about it?"

He shook his head. "I'm not supposed to."

Kate leaned forward. "Look, my husband never should've said that, and he knew it. He regretted it the minute he said it."

Hal glanced up again, made eye contact for a second, before ducking his head and looking off to the side.

"Come on, Hal. We need to work on whatever is making you so anxious. We need to keep you in top psychological condition so you can handle the legal case."

Another quick glance. "Mr. Franklin got me out. He said the charges for shooting your friend would probably be dropped."

She hated to add to his anxiety but knowing how relentless Russell was… "I doubt it's over. The police aren't convinced that John Cochlin committed suicide."

Oddly, that seemed to calm him a little. "Neither am I."

She nodded. "You know they're going to keep poking around,"

she kept her voice soft, "and they'll probably question you again."

He stared off to the left, toward her office window. "I want justice for John. I can't imagine what his wife must be thinking, how she's feeling."

"I went to see her," Kate said. "She's hanging on."

He looked her way, held her gaze a moment longer this time before turning his head.

"The names you gave me, the info about the engineers. It helped." She leaned forward slightly. "Hal, let me help you, so you can keep helping *us* with the investigation." It was an unorthodox way to motivate a client, but somehow she felt he needed that sense of purpose. "If John Cochlin didn't commit suicide, his wife needs to know that."

Hal nodded and made eye contact. Fear haunted his eyes. "You said the anxiety is coming from the little kid inside, but that detective, he's pretty scary."

"Yes, he can be." She paused to choose her words. "There's a difference between being afraid as an adult but still able to function, like when you planted that bug." She brought that up intentionally, reminding him that he could be brave. "But sometimes scary stuff in the here and now triggers our old fears too. And that's when we get overwhelmed, feel helpless again, like we did as a child."

She'd been toying with using a particular imagery technique with him that she'd used before. It could be quite powerful, but it required the adult part of the client to be more solid than Hal seemed to be right now.

She'd have to risk it. If he wasn't able to keep his cool with the police he'd likely end up in jail again, where he'd be surrounded by rough men who would most definitely remind him of his father.

"I'd like to try something," she said. "Close your eyes for a minute and just let your mind drift."

His expression turned a bit wary, but he closed his eyes.

She lowered her voice. "Now think about how scared you got when you had to deal with Detective Russell... What memory pops up in your head as you're feeling that fear again?"

"My dad yelling at me. I'm about ten."

"What's your father saying?"

"The usual crap, calling me stupid, accusing me of stuff I didn't do."

Kate nodded, even though Hal couldn't see her. Being accused of a murder he didn't commit would certainly push that button.

"Okay, I'd like you to do something now." Keeping her voice gentle, she walked him through the process of stepping into that scene in his mind's eye, as his current adult self, and standing up for the little boy.

When he seemed to falter, she played a hunch.

"Describe that child's father to me. What do you see?"

Hal scrunched up his face. "He's dirty and smelly, stinkin' of booze. And he's swaying back and forth, like he can hardly keep his balance."

"Sounds more pathetic than scary to me."

Hal gave a slight nod. "Yeah."

"You're bigger and stronger than he is now. Make him stop harassing that child."

Hal was quiet for a full minute, his face turning redder and redder. Kate was pretty sure it wasn't from embarrassment this time.

Finally, his face returned to its normal skin tone.

"What's happening?" she said, barely above a whisper.

"I threw him out of the house. Told him not to come back, that we don't need him."

Kate resisted the urge to do a fist pump in the air. "Good for you. Now tell that little boy that you're not going to let anybody treat him like that again. That anybody who tries, you, the adult, will handle it."

Hal was silent for a few beats, his lips moving slightly. Then he nodded again.

"Now give that child a hug and tuck him away inside of you." The rule in imagery was whatever you took apart, you had to put back together. "And you can open your eyes whenever you're ready."

After another few seconds, Hal did just that, then sat up straighter on the loveseat, a smile growing across his face. "That was awesome."

"Yes, it can be."

His face sobered. "So what does this do, I mean, how will this keep me from being so scared?"

"Scary things are going to happen, but when you start to feel that overwhelming anxiety, the adult part needs to talk to the kid inside. Tell him you've got this, and he doesn't have to worry about it. Visualize yourself standing between him and the threat."

"It's like he's my kid now."

"Exactly," she said. "You're protecting him just like dads do all the time. Your dad was crappy at it but that doesn't mean you can't be good at it."

He gave her a lopsided smile. "I do feel better, calmer. How come imagining all that in my head makes a difference?"

She smiled back, having thought of a way to explain it in terms he'd get. "Okay, your brain is like the hardware of a computer. Your memories are part of the software. They've programmed your brain to think and feel certain ways. Some parts of your brain remember what actually happened, the facts. Other parts are more about processing the feelings. By changing the events in your imagination, having you stand up to your father, we're updating some of the software, basically reprocessing and reprogramming those parts of your brain, changing the feelings, from weak and scared to angry and strong."

Hal's smile broadened.

"Now this may not work one hundred percent yet," she quickly said. "We may need to do that exercise again, with some of your other memories of being scared by your dad. But you keep talking to the kid inside in the meantime. Keep reassuring him that you're gonna take care of him from now on."

Hal looked down at his hands in his lap. "Your husband's

really big."

"Yes, he is. But big men aren't always a threat. He would never hurt anyone unless he was protecting himself or someone else."

Hal's expression was skeptical.

"Trust me, I wouldn't be married to him if he wasn't a sweetheart."

He gave her a thoughtful look. "You wouldn't be, would you? You wouldn't stay."

"No, but I had a lot better childhood than your mother, one that taught me to care about myself, to think I was worthy of being treated right."

He stared into space for a moment.

"Do you think your mom would stay today?" she asked.

He shook his head, then surprised her by chuckling. "No. She'd probably smother him in his sleep."

Kate laughed. "Yeah, I can see her doing that. She's grown and changed through the years, gotten stronger as she's taken care of herself and her boys."

Hal looked at her, his eyes shiny. "But I haven't. I've stayed that little kid."

Kate's chest ached a little. "Freud called it fixation," she said in a gentle voice. "We can get stuck in a certain stage of development because of trauma, but now you're moving forward."

She glanced up at the wall clock above Hal's head and sat back.

"We got time for something else?" he asked.

"A few minutes."

"I'm wondering if I should take that bug out of the lab."

Lordy, that is not a simple question. Her next thought was, *And he thinks he isn't brave.*

"How readily could you do that without getting caught?"

He grimaced. "Elaine's watching me pretty closely these days. She waits until I go to lunch to go herself, and then she's almost always there again when I get back."

Kate doubted Elaine Patterson was doing that on her own. She'd probably been instructed to keep a close eye on him. He might have been reinstated in his job, but that didn't mean the powers-that-be at Strategic trusted him.

"This is a little out of my bailiwick," she said. "But I'm inclined to say leave the bug where it is. Taking it out would technically be tampering with evidence. If you got caught, it could give the police the excuse they need to go after you again."

Hal nodded. They set up his next appointment, then said their goodbyes.

Dear God, I hope I gave him the right advice, she thought as he walked out of her office.

Kate had just finished listening to Rob's apologetic message–his morning court case had unexpectedly extended into the afternoon–when her phone rang in her hand.

She answered it. "Mrs. Huntington."

"Kate." Manny's voice, a bit gravelly. "Uh, are you busy?"

"As a matter of fact, Rob stood me up for lunch."

"I tried to call him first but his assistant said he was in court. Do you know if there are any legal ramifications if I leave the hospital without being discharged?"

"You mean against medical advice?"

"Yeah. The doc says he's transferring me tomorrow to a rehab place. But I gotta get out of here sooner than that."

"Why?" Kate said. Manny was a go-with-the-flow kind of guy. What could annoy him enough that he'd want to leave AMA?

"Lots of things but mainly some ditzy nurse hooked the morphine button back up. She acted like it was an oversight that it was disconnected, and wouldn't listen when I told her I'd asked for it to be turned off. I've buzzed her three times and she keeps insisting she can't disconnect it without a doctor's order."

"What's your doctor's name and do you have his phone number?" She didn't know the answer to his question regarding leaving AMA, but she could try to do something about the morphine button.

"I called his office. They said he's at the hospital." Manny's voice was now distinctly desperate. "The nurse said she didn't know where he was, that he was making rounds and would get to me soon. But that's not the only issue…" His voice trailed off.

"What?"

"I don't want to go to this rehab place. If it's anything like the hospital, it'll drive me nuts."

"Manny, if they're sending you to rehab, it's because you're not in good enough physical shape to take care of yourself at home."

In a low, tense voice, he said, "It's not my physical state I'm worried about."

Duh, she thought, as understanding dawned. He'd been clean and sober for years, but sobriety could never be taken for granted. "Are you sure you'll be better off at home?"

"Yeah. Not great, but better."

"Let me try to track down your doctor and get him in to see you. And since I'm free for lunch, you want me to bring you something decent to eat?"

"Boy, do I." He gave her his doctor's name and the address of his favorite Mexican café. "They're the real deal. Not that crap other places dish out."

She chuckled. "You should know."

She disconnected, then called the hospital's main number. Deciding not to mess with going through channels, she asked for the hospital administrator's office.

It took a few minutes to get past his staff, and then to explain the situation and get across the importance of removing the as-needed morphine button from a recovering addict's reach. When she indicated the hospital might be liable if Mr. Ortiz suffered a relapse, she finally got results.

A sigh on the other end of the line. "I'll page Mr. Ortiz's doctor and have him go to his room asap."

See, that wasn't so hard. She thanked the man, then

disconnected.

Her stomach growled loudly. She smiled. The next part of her mission of mercy would be a real pleasure.

She couldn't wait to get to Manny's room and dig into the goodies in the white paper bag she was carrying. The fragrances it emitted were making her lightheaded.

The low rumble of male conversation told her Manny was not alone. She knocked on the doorframe and entered the room.

Standing at the foot of Manny's bed was the doctor she'd talked to the previous week.

Manny glanced her way and his eyes lit up. "Hey, Kate."

She faked a smile. The bandage was gone and his whole head was now shaved. But in some ways, he looked worse than he had last time she'd seen him.

He was pale and he'd lost weight. Not surprising, but he'd also lost a good bit of muscle tone. His skin was loose on his arms and face.

"This is Dr. Lin," Manny said. "He's the one who patched me up."

The doctor gave her a perfunctory nod, then addressed Manny, "I'll write the order to remove the morphine button, but you really need to go to rehab, Mr. Ortiz. You need nursing assistance for at least another week, maybe longer, and physical therapy."

Manny looked at her, a hint of panic in his eyes, but he addressed the doctor. "Doc, I can't do it. I need to be home. I need a meeting."

"Doctor," Kate said. "Can't we arrange for aides and such to come to his house?"

"I'm going home, Doc, whether you approve or not."

The doctor lifted his eyebrows, but then seemed to thaw some. "Twenty-four hour assistance. No driving. I'll write a prescription for a wheelchair rental. You use it whenever you're going any further than the bathroom until the physical therapist says otherwise. Does your medical insurance cover in-home PT?"

"Yes," Kate answered for him. She didn't know if it did or not, but she'd make it happen. This man had once saved Skip's life and had protected her and other people she loved on multiple occasions.

The doctor nodded. "I'll start the discharge process."

Kate extended her hand. "Thank you so much," she said as the doctor shook it. She hung onto his hand for an extra beat.

He defrosted some more, to the point where he actually patted her arm. "I'll send an aide in to help Mr. Ortiz get dressed."

Kate stepped out of the room to give Manny some privacy as he went through the humiliating process of letting someone pull his pants on for him. She found a quiet corner and called Skip. "What are you doing?"

"I just spent my lunch hour gambling and watching a suspect. What's up?"

Lunch! She'd forgotten all about the bag of Mexican food she'd dropped on a chair in Manny's room. Her stomach grumbled in protest.

But first things first. She filled Skip in.

"Workers' comp should cover all that," he said.

"Will that affect your rates?"

"Oh yeah. And they're already sky high. It's hard for us to get coverage in the first place, considering the danger factor."

"I want to cover it from the brokerage account then. You all don't need higher bills right now."

A long pause, street noises in the background. "Okay, but if the expenses get too high, we can submit some of them to the workers' comp company."

Her throat tightened. His too-easy agreement meant the agency was truly in trouble.

She faked a normal tone. "Sounds good."

"Love you," Skip said.

"Love you too." She disconnected, then called her one afternoon client to reschedule. She had a feeling the whole discharge and getting Manny home process might take a while.

~~~~~~~~~~

Skip disconnected from the call with Kate and blew out a frustrated sigh. He wound his truck through Towson's congested business district. Gambling while spying on Paul Allen was getting expensive. He wasn't always winning anymore. Today he'd moved to one of the blackjack tables and had somewhat better luck there.

The same could not be said for Allen. He stuck to poker and seemed to lose almost every hand. And he didn't look like he was having much fun.

Skip made a mental note to ask Kate about the dynamics of compulsive gambling as he pulled into the public parking lot across the street from his building.

That is, if we ever get more than two minutes of privacy again. These days, Kate was in bed by the time he got home from his evening surveillance. Maybe this weekend they'd get some quality time together.

His mind veered back to the case as he stepped out of his truck. There'd been no sign of Beatrice Cooper since Monday night. He'd checked the file and found that she was indeed single. Had her presence on Monday been a mere coincidence? She'd been too nicely dressed for Frankie's rather dingy place. Had her date brought her there on a whim, for a bit of illicit gambling?

Skip crossed the street. Feeling restless, he took the fire stairs two at a time to the agency's suite of offices.

He was a couple of minutes late for the Wednesday strategy session—Rose refused to call it a staff meeting. He slipped into a chair at the small conference table while she was listing cases on the white board at one end of the room.

Rose turned. "We have eleven paying clients." She pointed to the list to her right.

Skip winced. Normally they had closer to twenty at any given time.

She gestured toward the two lines of writing on the other side of the board. "Plus Strategic and the rumors."

He was surprised she was talking about the rumors, then it registered that only Dolph and Mac were in the room, besides themselves.

Rose made eye contact with him and answered his unasked question. "I didn't invite our other operatives this week. All their cases are going well."

Skip nodded. "I've had a few developments in the Strategic case." He filled Mac and Dolph in on the illicit gambling joint, frequented by Paul Allen and visited at least once by the director of operations of Strategic's competitor. "She hasn't been back since though."

"Beatrice Cooper?" Dolph said. "I saw her on my list of deep background checks."

"I'd appreciate it if you'd make her a priority," Skip said.

Dolph groaned. "I've been working on several things for our new insurance client. I just this morning got to your missing security guard."

Skip stifled his own groan. They needed more research support. He indulged in a momentary fantasy of enticing Liz Franklin away from her career as an insurance actuary. Liz was the only person he knew who rivaled Dolph's computer expertise.

"Carlton Johnson has maxed out all of his credit cards with cash advances," Dolph was saying. "But first he used one of them to reserve a room at a beachfront hotel in Puerto Rico."

"Not the Bahamas?" Skip asked.

"Nope."

"Don't he realize," Mac growled, "that Puerto Rico's a U.S. territory? It ain't outta reach of American law enforcement."

"True," Dolph said, "but he's from there. His mother still lives in San Lorenzo."

"Johnson ain't a Latino name," Mac said.

"Father was white," Dolph said. "Carlton Johnson, Sr., from New York City. They moved there when Junior was three. Mother went back to Puerto Rico after the father died."

"Could he be leaving a false trail?" Rose said.

"Maybe." Dolph scratched his chin. "He could be having one last fling on the beach at San Juan, before he disappears. He drained his bank accounts before he went. He has over twenty grand from them and the credit cards. How much you figure he got from selling secrets?"

"I don't think he sold secrets," Skip said, "just the old badges to whoever *is* selling the secrets. And Latey was real cagey about how much those secrets would be worth."

"So maybe five or ten thousand?" Dolph asked.

"Maybe," Skip said. "But he might have sold more badges in the past, to the same or other customers. An expired badge would only be good for a short time. My guess is their system would flag the old one—or deactivate it—once the employee used the newly issued one."

"Say he's stockpiled another twenty, thirty grand," Dolph said. "He could live comfortably in San Lorenzo for several years. The average income there is only eighteen thousand a year."

"Guess he figured it was time to clear out," Mac said, "before he got caught."

"Maybe whoever bought the badges from him gave him a bonus to leave," Rose said.

Skip nodded. "They're cleaning up after themselves. They got rid of Cochlin–"

"—assuming it wasn't really suicide," Dolph threw in.

Skip nodded again. "And then they pay off Johnson to scram. Could mean the spy is ready to bolt too."

"If there *is* another spy," Mac said, "besides Cochlin."

Rose moved over to a bare spot on the white board. "Possibility number one." She wrote as she talked. "Cochlin was the only spy and committed suicide, out of guilt over it."

"Don't forget" Skip said, "Elaine Patterson admitted to having an affair with him."

Rose nodded, her back to the room. "More reason to feel guilty." She wrote a big *OR* under her number one. "Possibility number two. Cochlin wasn't the spy at all. Somebody else killed him and planted the note confessing to the espionage."

"Not likely," Mac said. "That envelope he picked up at the maildrop had to be a payoff."

She put another big *OR* on the white board. "Number three, he was part of the spying operation but somebody else was also in on it, and that somebody tried to kill Manny and succeeded with Cochlin."

"Paul Allen is my favorite candidate for the accomplice," Skip said.

"What about Patterson?" Rose said. "If she and Cochlin were lovers, they might also have been partners in crime."

Skip turned to Dolph. "We need to go further back in history with some of these people, see what patterns emerge. I doubt Paul Allen's gambling problem is a new thing."

"How 'bout that Garrett Watson fella," Mac said, "the other engineer?"

Skip shook his head. "No motive that we can tell."

Dolph sat up straighter in his chair. "He's a gun owner."

"Okay, add him to the list–"

Dolph let out an exaggerated groan.

Skip grinned for the first time all day. "You shouldn't have reminded me about the guns."

Dolph rolled his eyes.

"Put Watson last on the list. And speaking of guns, do the Pattersons own any?"

"He's a hunter," Dolph said. "Got a couple of rifles, but no handguns registered to either of them."

Mac snorted softly. "Don't mean he ain't got an unregistered one. Lots a hunters carry sidearms."

Rose cleared her throat, her signal that they were moving on. She pointed to the word *rumors* on the white board. "I found out who paid Howie Kaplan for spreading the rumors. Fred Latey."

Skip jolted forward in his seat. "What?"

"Yup," Rose said.

"The slimy bastard," Mac muttered.

Skip ground his teeth as Rose told them about her conversation with Kaplan that morning.

"So if there's a tie-in between the rumors and Strategic," Dolph said. "I guess the folks related to that case are indeed my next priority."

Rose held up a hand. "Not until you finish the background checks for the latest insurance fraud investigation. Paying customers first."

Skip opened his mouth to argue. His chest felt like it was about to explode.

Rose held his gaze from across the table, her lips a grim line. Then her eyes softened and she shook her head slightly.

Damn, she's right. He closed his mouth.

He stood up abruptly, his chair almost flipping over backward. "In the meantime, *I'll* take care of Latey."

CHAPTER EIGHTEEN

It was a good thing Kate had cleared the decks for the afternoon. Lunch–still delicious, even lukewarm–was a fading memory by the time all the forms were signed, a nurse had arrived with the rented wheelchair, and she and Kate had settled Manny into the car.

The forty-something, no-nonsense nurse—obviously not the "ditzy" one Manny had complained about from earlier in the day—handed Kate a fistful of colorful brochures. "The insurance company may have preferences about who you use, but here are some options for home services. Several are all inclusive—nurses, aides, PTs, OTs, the works."

She also handed over a bottle of pills.

Kate peeked at the label—prescription strength ibuprofen. The doctor had gotten the message.

Once they were on the road, Kate said, "Did you hear about John Cochlin's death?" It wasn't a topic one would usually bring up with a convalescent, but she figured thinking about the case might help ground Manny in his work, the part of his life untainted by addiction.

He lifted his head slightly from the headrest and turned to look at her. "Yeah. I was pretty shocked. He didn't seem the type." He dropped his head back and fell quiet for a moment. "And I think I just remembered something, from that night."

"Oh?" Kate glanced over. Despite the fatigue on his face, his color was already better. She quietly blew out air. Getting him out of the hospital was the right move.

"I found some of Cochlin's files on Murdock's computer. That's what I was surprised about."

Her mouth went dry. "I don't understand?" she said, but her gut already knew where this was going.

"The project was compartmentalized, added security because of the leaks. We weren't supposed to share information with each other unless instructed to do so. Murdock shouldn't have had those files."

She struggled to keep her voice even. "So why were you surprised? You all already suspected Murdock."

"I don't know. I just remember feeling that way."

Manny stared out the side window for a few seconds. "I vaguely recall thinking that Murdock wasn't that stupid." He turned slightly in his seat, wincing. "I mean, suspicious files was what I was looking for, but I was expecting the file names to be changed, to disguise them. We all put our initials as part of our file names. These still had JC at the end of them. That seemed a bit too obvious to me."

Kate's insides relaxed some.

Manny shifted uncomfortably in his seat again.

She accelerated as much as she could in the afternoon traffic. "Did you know that Cochlin's suicide note said he was the source of the leaks?"

Manny's eyebrows shot up. "No. And that doesn't jive with what I found. Murdock having John's files pointed toward him, Murdock, as the spy."

A thought struck her. "Maybe Cochlin was trying to frame Hal?"

"That would make sense of the evidence, but it doesn't sound like John. He's... He was a good man. I can see him, maybe, leaking information. He was pretty worried about his family's finances. But set somebody else up for it?" He shook his head.

Kate nodded. "Everyone who knew Cochlin has had the same reaction. They're finding it hard to believe he committed suicide. Even the police. Originally, Hal Murdock was hauled in and accused of murdering him."

Manny turned his head toward her. "But…?"

"But the good detective couldn't make a case against him. All he has is a possible motive, one that I think is pretty farfetched."

"You mean Detective Russell?"

"Yes."

"I should call him, tell him what I remember."

"Tomorrow," Kate said, as she pulled up in front of Manny's apartment complex. "You've had enough excitement for today."

Despite the cold day, Kate had broken a sweat by the time she got him inside, into the elevator, and to his apartment. She took his keys from him and unlocked the door.

He grabbed for the chair's wheels and tried to wheel himself inside. A big wince and a soft "ugh" said that was a bad idea.

She batted at his nearest hand. "Don't you dare pull that wound open, 'cause I'm not dragging you back down to the car to go to the hospital."

He chuckled and let her shove him through the door.

"Couch or bed?"

"Couch is good." He swayed a little as he stood up.

Kate resisted the urge to grab for him, but she hovered nearby.

He turned carefully and sank down on the couch with a sigh. "Home, sweet home."

"You want anything to eat or drink?"

He shook his head. "But I do need to make a call?" His face and whole body were drooping.

"Can't it wait?" she said. "You need to rest."

He shook his head again. It wobbled on his thick neck like a bobble-head doll's. "Sponsor," he mumbled, reaching for the portable phone on an end table. "Tonight's my home group. I need a meeting bad."

Kate had been mulling over what to do about this evening. Manny was too weak to be on his own until an aide could get here. But Skip would most likely be doing surveillance again tonight, and she wasn't willing to leave the kids home alone.

"You mind if *I* call your sponsor? I've got an idea."

He handed her the phone. "Speed dial, under Steve." His head lolled to one side.

She maneuvered a half-asleep Manny into a prone position on the couch. Then she went into the kitchen to make the call.

Steve thought her idea was excellent.

A quick perusal of the brochures the nurse had given her yielded two companies that were full service. She called each of them and made arrangements with the one she liked best, but the earliest they could get an aide to Manny's place was nine p.m.

"Sorry," the lady said. "That's the best we can do on such short notice. Usually these things are set up a couple of days in advance."

Back in the living room, Manny was snoring softly.

Kate wrote a note, propped it against the pill bottle, got a glass of cold water from the dispenser on his fridge and put it next to the bottle. Then she raced home to get the kids.

~~~~~~~~

The crowd of employees coming out of the Armstrong building was beginning to thin at five-fifteen, and still no Fred Latey.

Skip needed to get this confrontation over with so he could get back to his surveillance of Paul Allen, who was now at the top of their suspect list.

But if he was the industrial spy, why had the leaks been a trickle over time? Allen knew all of the details of the project. Had he leaked things slowly so he could set up someone else, like Murdock or Cochlin, as the fall guy? Or did he do so to get more money for each little piece?

Considering how regularly Allen lost at the poker table, Skip suspected the latter. Maybe the man never had intended to leak the whole project. Just enough to fund his gambling until he had the big win that would put him back on top.

Skip climbed out of his truck. After taking off his jacket and tossing it on the seat, he walked to the outside door of the fire stairs. It was locked, as he knew it would be. But he didn't have long to wait until somebody came out. He grabbed the door before it could swing closed.

"Thanks," he said nonchalantly, smiling at the petite woman who'd pushed it open from the inside.

She barely gave him a glance as she barreled past him.

Hmm, losing my touch.

At the fire door for the third floor, he paused. *Okay, Latey, time to see how well you implemented my suggestions.*

Again, he waited for someone to open the locked door from the other side. He stepped forward, nodded politely to the gentleman and walked through the door.

The security guard standing five feet away stiffened. "Sir, you have to check in with the front desk."

Skip waved the temporary badge that he'd neglected to turn in after his last visit. His finger was strategically placed over the date. "I was meeting with somebody and forgot my jacket."

"Still need to check in at the desk."

"Sure thing." Skip sketched him a small salute and veered in that direction.

At quitting time, he had counted on the lobby being in a state of organized chaos. Before employees could exit the double glass doors leading to the elevators, they had to pass two other guards, one male and one female.

One guard had always been on duty, but Skip had suggested the extras, and the pat-downs they randomly administered on the Strategic employees as they left.

All purses and lunch bags were searched. Briefcases and any other containers were prohibited.

Several women waiting their turn chatted near the reception desk. The receptionist was trying to pretend she wasn't eavesdropping.

Skip again flashed the temporary badge, his finger covering the date. "I was meeting with Fred Latey. Just realized I forgot my jacket."

The receptionist nodded.

And he was in. He clipped the badge to his shirt pocket and strolled down the hall, against the tide of departing employees.

Latey's door was ajar. Skip nudged it a little further open. The man was sitting at his desk, his head bent over a newspaper.

Skip slipped into the room and closed the door.

Latey's head jerked up. His eyes went wide in a pale face. "Canfield, what are you doing here?"

"Still trying to track down that rumor you told me about. Turns out a P.I. named Howard Kaplan was paid to start it."

The man's body stiffened. "Oh really?" His attempt at nonchalance fell short.

"Yeah. Seems the creep stiffed him."

"I di–" Latey caught himself. His gaze dropped to the newspaper in front of him.

Skip stepped closer to the desk and perched on the arm of one of the visitor chairs in front of it. "You did or you didn't stiff him?" he asked casually.

"I, uh, don't know what you're talking about. Never heard of the guy." Sweat had broken out on Latey's forehead.

"That's funny." Skip stroked his chin. "He described you to a T."

Latey's face flushed. He rose to his feet.

Skip maintained his relaxed pose. Even standing, Latey wasn't all that intimidating.

The man puffed out his chest.

Nope, still not scared of ya, Fred.

Latey's arm jerked up, finger pointing toward the door. "Get out!"

"Not until you tell me why you paid Howie to sabotage your own investigation. Bet your boss would like to hear the answer to that too."

They stared at each other for several seconds.

Then Latey deflated and dropped into his chair. He slapped a hand on the newspaper. "It doesn't matter now," he muttered under his breath.

"What doesn't matter?" Skip said.

Latey shook his head, still looking at the paper. "I didn't know what the money was for. I was doing a favor for a friend."

"Who?"

He shook his head again. "No way I'm telling you that."

They had another staring contest. Skip kept his voice slow and even. "Who gave you the money, Fred?"

Latey broke eye contact and gave another slight shake of his head.

Skip's jaw clenched. Maybe he would go over Fred's head. He didn't know for sure what the upper management of Strategic would make of the situation, but from where he was sitting, Latey was looking suspiciously like an industrial spy.

Skip rose to his feet. "I'm wondering how Bob Hawthorne will feel about you delivering money to start a rumor that would torpedo the very P.I. agency you'd hired."

"You need to leave, or I'll call security." The words would have been more convincing without the tremor in Latey's voice.

For a moment, Skip's anger got the better of him. He planted his palms in the middle of the desk and leaned into the man's face. In a low, tense voice he said, "I have a very good lawyer, so you'd better stop spreading rumors about my agency."

Latey blanched, his birthmark a livid eggplant silhouette against an almost white background.

That made Skip feel a little better, but only a little. He straightened and lightened his tone. "Thanks for your time, Fred. Don't get up. I'll see myself out."

Skip kept his cool until he was through the door. Then it was all he could do to not punch a hole in the wall.

Striding down the hall, he passed Elaine Patterson. Her smile faded at the sight of his face.

He made sure to rearrange his features into a benign mask when he stopped at the reception desk. Before handing over the temporary badge, he asked if Robert Hawthorne, Latey's immediate supervisor, was gone for the day.

The young woman flashed him a polite smile. "Mr. Hawthorne's out of town this week. Your best bet is to call his admin in the morning and make an appointment for when he gets back."

Skip forced a smile. "Thanks. I'll do that." He handed her the badge, hoping she wouldn't look too closely at the date.

By the time Skip had reached the building's lobby, he'd thought better of contacting Hawthorne. Threatening to go to Latey's superior was one thing. Doing it would most likely come across as petty, and Hawthorne might very well close ranks with his employee.

He stopped in the lobby to buy a newspaper from the coin-operated box there. He was curious to see if its contents had something to do with Latey's mood. Old Fred seemed to have been unhappy, even before his interchange with him.

Once in his truck, he opened the paper. The source of Fred's angst was on page four. *EEI Wins Contract for Top Secret Guidance System for Army Drones.* EEI stood for Enterprise Electronics, Inc., Strategic's competitor—and Beatrice Cooper's employer.

Skip stared out the windshield. Of course, EEI could undercut Strategic's bid for the project now. Bribing someone to leak the project's specs was a lot cheaper than the years of labor Latey's crew had put into developing it.

Skip almost felt sorry for Fred Latey. Almost.

CHAPTER NINETEEN

Edie kept her gaze straight ahead out the windshield, refusing to respond to her mother's attempts at conversation. She was *sooo* tired of her parents acting like she was a baby who couldn't take care of herself for one minute.

No, that wasn't fair to her dad. He didn't act that way. Just… *her*.

Edie shot a glare in her mom's direction.

Mom glanced up in the rearview mirror. "You got much homework tonight, Billy?"

"Nah," Billy yelled from the backseat. "And I got some of it done this afternoon."

Edie stuck her fingers in her ears. "Not so loud, dummy."

Mom shot her a sharp look. "Edie!"

She didn't care. Billy was a dummy. She crossed her arms over her chest and stared out the side window.

"I'll check your homework log when we get to Mr. Manny's," Mom said, "and if you're truly close to done, you can play video games on my phone for a half-hour before starting the rest. But you'll have to keep the phone muted."

Why does Billy always get rewarded for doing his damn homework, but I'm expected to just get mine done?

Edie felt guilty for cussing, even in her head, but she quickly squashed the feeling. She was almost a grown-up. She could use the occasional *damn* or *hell* now. Dad and Mom said worse than that sometimes when they were upset.

The car pulled up in front of a tan building with lots of

windows. Mom shooed them inside. The hallway was lined with doors with numbers on them. An apartment building.

They went up a floor on an elevator. Mom knocked gently on one of the doors and quickly used a key to unlock it. "It's Kate, Manny," she called out as she opened it.

They stepped into Mr. Manny's living room. No, she was too old to be using *Mr.* anymore.

Manny was struggling to sit up on a black sofa.

Mom raced over and helped him to an upright position.

"How long did I sleep?" he asked in a gruff voice.

Mom looked at her watch. "About an hour and a half."

"Wow, guess I was tired."

Mom sat down on the edge of an armchair. "Manny, if this is going to work, you need to promise not to push yourself. You've got to do what the aides and nurses and all tell you, if you want to get your strength back completely."

Mr., *uh*, Manny grinned. "Yes, Mother."

Why's he letting Mom push him around? He's a grown man. Sheez.

Mom smiled back at him. "Your sponsor and I have a surprise for you. You don't need to go to a meeting tonight."

"Wha–"

"Steve's bringing the meeting to you. They'll be here at seven."

"I can't ask them to do that," Manny protested.

"You didn't. We did," Mom said with a small smirk. "Are you hungry? Let me get the kids situated and I'll make you some dinner."

Manny looked past Mom and seemed to notice them for the first time. "Hey, Edie, Billy. How's it goin'?"

"Okay, I guess," Edie mumbled.

Billy practically bounced over to the sofa. "I heard you got shot, Mr. Manny. Did it hurt?"

Manny grinned at him. "Not until I woke up, and by then I was in the hospital."

Billy stood on tiptoes and examined Manny's shaved head. He pointed to a pink, puffy line. "Did they shoot you in the head?"

"No, but I hit it pretty hard on something on the way down."

"Come on, kids," Mom said.

She ushered them into the kitchen and pushed some stuff around on a small table, clearing a space. "You set up here, Edie."

Mom continued out the other door of the kitchen, into a small room with a computer desk and a big old armchair. She gestured toward the armchair. "It might be better," she said to Billy, "if you did a little of your homework, then took your break."

Edie shook her head as she pulled her math book out of her backpack. She still didn't understand what all the fuss was about, even though Daddy'd explained that Billy had a short attention span. He needed things broken down into smaller pieces, and more supervision.

She begrudgingly admitted it must be working. Billy's last report card was mostly Bs instead of Cs and Ds.

She tried to tune out her mother working at the stove to make everybody soup. It was only canned chicken noodle soup, not all that interesting. But Edie was hungry so she ate it.

Halfway through her math problems, the doorbell rang. She turned in her chair to watch a parade of people file in. Some of them were dressed nice but a few were kind of scruffy looking.

One lady was carrying a paper grocery bag and another a big coffee maker. Several of the men had folding chairs under their arms.

Abandoning her homework, Edie got up and peeked around the corner into the living room. The people greeted Manny and told him to get better quick, which was really stupid. He couldn't control how fast he got better.

Then they set up the chairs and put the coffee maker, paper cups and a big plate of cookies on the coffee table.

Edie's stomach gurgled. Could she get away with asking for one of those cookies?

A man stood up. "Since some of us tire easily these days…"

They all looked at Manny and smiled. His cheeks turned pink.

"We'll dispense with the preamble and twelve steps tonight," the man said. "Let's start with the serenity prayer."

They all bowed their heads. "God, grant me the serenity to...."

Giving up on the cookie, Edie went back to her homework. Mom had told them not to eavesdrop, that what people said tonight was confidential, like what her clients told her.

But when she'd finished her homework thirty minutes later, Edie couldn't resist peeking around the doorjamb again.

One of the scruffy looking guys was standing. "Hi, I'm Jack and I'm an alcoholic..."

So that's what this was, one of those twelve-step meetings she'd read about in her Social Studies textbook, in a section called *Current Issues*. It had said something about alcoholism and other addictions being a really big problem in this country.

Mr. Manny's an alcoholic?

The guy was going on and on about how booze ruined his life, but things were getting better now, one day at a time. Then he said, "Thanks for listening."

"Thanks for sharing," everybody said together.

How lame.

Edie's phone pinged in her pocket. She jumped back away from the doorway and pulled the phone out. A text from Connie.

Mom stuck her head around the corner. "Finish your home-work," she hissed quietly.

"I already did," Edie shot back in an angry whisper.

"Then mute your phone." Mom disappeared back into the living room.

Edie pushed the mute button on her phone and looked down at the text.

Still no tickets. Zac says to meet him downtown early. Can u get here by 4 on Friday?

Edie was really glad she'd arranged to sneak out, rather than asking permission to go to the concert. Her parents never would have agreed if they knew she didn't even have a ticket yet.

What if Zac didn't come through? Disappointment made her throat hurt.

But then she shrugged. Worst case was they'd get a look at Shawn Mendes when he went into the Baltimore Arena. Then they could walk to the Inner Harbor, get some ice cream, and catch a bus out to Towson from there. She quivered with excitement at the thought of doing all that on her own… well, she and Connie.

Her phone vibrated in her hand.

U there?

Yes. Can be there at 4. If need be, she'd ride Connie's bus and hide out until time to leave for the concert.

"Kate, can you help me up?" The familiar male voice drew her back to the doorway.

Mom was helping Manny to his feet. "I'll keep this short. You all have heard my drunkalog before anyway. I just want to say how much it means to me…" His voice started sounding funny, kind of hoarse. "It's great to have such wonderful friends." He paused again. "To paraphrase a popular saying, It takes a village to keep a man sober. I couldn't do it without you folks. Thanks for listening."

Everybody called out, "Thanks for sharing." Then they all sprang to their feet and grabbed each others' hands to make a circle. "It works if you work it," they yelled. "Keep coming back."

They started laughing and hugging each other. Even a lady in a really nice dress hugged the scruffy guy.

Edie realized her mouth was hanging open.

Mom came over, smiling, and handed her a cookie. "Thanks for being so quiet, sweetie."

Edie had smiled back before she could catch herself.

~~~~~~~~

Thursday was a normal day.

Kate stopped by Manny's place after work. He seemed better, stronger, and definitely calmer. She decided the shaved head was a good look for him.

The aide on duty assured her that she was on top of things.

"Hon, I won't let him overdo. Don't you worry."

Manny gave Kate a help-me look, which she ignored.

Skip called as she was headed home. "Hey there," his voice came through the Bluetooth.

"Hey yourself, stranger."

He chuckled. "I might actually come home before bedtime tonight. My quarry didn't go gambling for a change. He's headed home. Hey, I've been meaning to ask you about compulsive gambling."

"What about it?"

"I don't know. Is it like other addictions?"

"Yes and no," she said. "Gambling is probably most like alcohol. Lots of people can drink moderately. Likewise, many can gamble without getting hooked."

"But some?"

"Some get addicted to the adrenaline high of winning."

"This guy, Paul Allen, he's not all that high and he hasn't been winning for quite some time."

"Ah," she said. "so he's in the negative reinforcement stage of addiction."

"What's that?"

"The reward for continuing the behavior is the avoidance of the pain of withdrawal."

"Okay. So how does that apply to gambling?"

"He's desperately trying to recoup his losses by the only means he knows, going for the big win."

"Ahhh..." A pregnant pause. "Hmm, our gambler has *not* turned over a new leaf after all. There's a Happy Birthday balloon attached to his mailbox."

"Command appearance," she said.

"He'll probably sneak out later. Expect me when you see me."

Kate shook her head. She'd been thinking earlier that this was a normal day. Since when had checking on a man recovering from a gunshot wound and Skip working eighteen-hour days become normal?

CHAPTER TWENTY

My little girl is growing up. Skip's throat tightened at the thought.

He was sitting in his truck in the Armstrong building's parking lot at noon on Friday—waiting for Paul Allen to make his lunchtime run to Frankie's place—but his mind kept drifting back to Edie.

Last night, she'd been the one to leave a note on the kitchen table. *I really need to talk to you, Daddy*, followed by a little heart.

The lump in his throat grew. *I gotta get this case resolved so I can get back to being a husband and father.*

Edie had been fascinated by the AA meeting Wednesday evening. She'd probably told him more than she should've about what was shared. He'd admonished her for eavesdropping but was glad the experience had opened her eyes some about other people's struggles.

But the rest of what Edie had to say was disturbing. She'd gone on and on about how her mom treated her like a baby. Apparently, Kate was the worst mother ever.

He'd tried one of Kate's tactics, something she'd called "active listening," to draw Edie out. "So you feel like Mom doesn't trust you?"

"Exactly." She crossed her arms, a pout on her face.

Okay, that hadn't worked quite like he thought it was supposed to.

"It's not that *we* don't trust you, Pumkin." He'd emphasized the *we*. "But you're still a little young to stay alone for any length of time."

That last part hadn't gone over well, but somehow the *we* hadn't shifted Edie's attitude—he was still the good guy and Mom was the evil one.

An unhealthy dynamic's developing here.

He laughed at himself. Now he sounded like Kate.

He'd tried another tactic last night. "We've been pretty busy lately. Are you feeling like Mom doesn't spend enough time with you?" He was quite aware that he had the good deal here. He got to spend quality time with the kids at bedtime while Kate spent the afternoons making sure they got their homework done.

Edie's eyes had clouded over for a second, then she'd made a scoffing noise. "Hardly." Her face had twisted into an annoyed expression. "She's hovering over me all the time."

Skip was pulled out of his reverie by the appearance of Paul Allen outside the front doors of the Armstrong building. He seemed furtive today, looking over his shoulder, then scanning the lot as he hurried to his car.

Skip slid down further in the driver's seat.

He hung back as Allen's car headed for the exit, letting a couple of other cars get between them.

Then yet another car nudged its way into the line. *Damn.*

He was too far back now and couldn't see which way Allen had turned. But an educated guess would be left, toward the Towson business district and the bar/gambling joint Allen loved to frequent.

Sure enough, when Skip pulled up in front of Frankie's Bar and Grill, Allen was climbing out of his car.

He gave the man a five-minute headstart, but it turned out not to be enough. Allen was still getting himself settled at one of the poker tables when Skip pushed the gold lamé curtain aside.

He quickly turned, ducking his head and hunching his shoulders to disguise his height some. Sticking close to the wall, he took a circuitous route to the cashier's window.

The same blonde from the first night was behind the white

bars.

"Hey, what's with the poker game?" Skip asked as she counted out his chips.

"Whadaya mean?"

"There's no house dealer."

"It's just a friendly game."

Skip glanced over his shoulder. From the expressions on the players' faces, it didn't look all that friendly. They were as grim as most of the rest of the gamblers in the cavernous room.

"So how's the house make money off of it?"

The young lady gave him a small smirk. "The winner *donates* a percentage of the pot."

"An honor system?" Skip asked, his tone incredulous.

She leaned forward to peer through the grill at an angle. "See the young lady sitting on a stool looking bored?"

Skip glanced in the direction of the poker game again. Allen was now settled in his seat, half turned in the other direction.

Skip spotted the woman the cashier meant. She was dressed in the same uniform as the waitresses bearing trays of drinks. But she had no tray. Instead she looked on casually as the poker players anteed up for another hand.

The cashier said, "That's Lucy. She makes sure the winners put ten percent of the chips from each pot into a small bucket on the table. When the buckets get full, she brings them to me."

"Thanks," Skip said. "Just curious."

He sauntered toward the blackjack table and contemplated the significance of the fact that Paul Allen only played poker.

Did he prefer giving away a percentage of his winnings over the other games, which were probably rigged to make sure he lost more often than not?

He watched Allen in his peripheral vision, while placing a five-dollar chip in the betting box in front of his position. The engineer was already looking desperate and he'd just sat down.

Was he a crappy gambler?

Skip had already figured out that one could stay close to even, losing no more than a little each session, if you were a decent gambler. His own losses had been mostly in the fifty-dollar range, and a couple of sessions he'd come out a few dollars ahead. And his mind was only half on the gambling.

He surreptitiously scanned the room. There were fewer gamblers at lunchtime, but he counted roughly forty-five. The room could easily hold twice that many. So several hundred gamblers came and went during the day and evening. Yes, the house could make a tidy sum, without discouraging the good gamblers from coming back.

He made a mental note to research how such places operated when he got back to the office, to see if his assumptions were correct. Or maybe Dolph would know. He'd worked Vice at one time.

The blackjack dealer cleared his throat.

Skip gave him a small smile. "Sorry, I spaced for a second."

"Ya got two aces in front of you and you're spacin' out?" The man's tone was incredulous.

Skip widened his smile. "Am I allowed to split?" He'd been reading up on the rules of blackjack.

The dealer nodded.

Skip nudged the two aces apart and placed a bet on the second hand. The dealer moved around the table doling out cards.

Skip's mind returned to Allen. "Hey, does the house lend money," he whispered to the guy next to him, "if you get tight?"

The guy had already gone bust, with a ten and a two, and then a king. "Yeah, sometimes," he muttered. "You gotta talk to Frankie."

Hmm, maybe Paul Allen was tapped out, in debt to the house? So he was only allowed to play in the poker game, where the house didn't care if you won or lost.

The dealer came around to Skip. He nodded and the man flipped a card on top of one of the aces. A queen.

The guy next to Skip slapped him on the back. "Blackjack."

Skip grinned, wishing he'd placed bigger bets. He tapped the other ace. The dealer flipped a card. A three. Skip tapped again.

A seven. Twenty-one exactly.

"Man, how'd you do that?" the guy next to him said.

"Luck of the Irish," Skip said.

The guy looked skeptical. "You're awful tall for an Irishman."

"I'm not Irish but my wife is. It rubs off."

The guy held out his arm. "Rub some of that on me."

Skip laughed and rubbed the guy's sleeve.

~~~~~~~

Edie and Connie had left some room between themselves and the other girls at the cafeteria table. Connie pulled her lunch out of a paper sack—an apple, a baggie of homemade chocolate chip cookies and a tortilla wrapped around cold beef, cheese, and Maria's homemade salsa.

Edie's mouth watered. "I'll trade half my sandwich for half of that."

Connie snorted and took a big bite.

"I miss Maria's cooking," Edie said.

Connie nodded as she chewed. "She's pretty good, though not as good as my mother was."

Edie's chest tightened. Heat burned her cheeks. *Maria's the best cook ever!*

She took a deep breath. Insight blossomed. *Connie still misses her mom.* She opted to let the remark slide.

"So'd you ask your parents yet?" Connie said, nudging a cookie across the table.

Edie grabbed it before the other girl could change her mind. "Not goin' to," she mumbled around crumbly, sugary dough and gooey chocolate.

Connie's face sobered, and she chewed more slowly. She nodded knowingly. "I chickened out too. Once they say no, there's no way around it. I'm gonna sneak out. Joey'll drive us down and pick us up later."

"Really? How'd you get him to agree to that?" Connie's older brother rarely gave either of them a second glance.

Connie smirked. "I caught him sneaking *into* the house a

couple weeks ago, at two a.m., *and* he had beer on his breath. I didn't tell on him, so he owes me."

Edie admired her friend's ability to stockpile favors and obligations. "I told my mom I was invited for a sleep-over. Jill's gonna cover for me. I'll ride the bus home with you. Hey, how much are the tickets going to cost?"

Connie had been cagey about that, and Edie was worried she wouldn't have enough money.

Connie smirked again. "Zac's getting them for half price."

Edie narrowed her eyes, suddenly suspicious. "What'd you promise him in order to get these tickets?"

Connie gave her a simpering smile. "Nothing much. I just kissed him a few times behind the gym on Monday."

Edie's jaw dropped. "You kissed him?"

"Yeah, he sorta thinks we're dating."

"You like him that much?"

Connie shrugged. "He's okay."

"So how much is half price?" Edie asked, worry gnawing at her stomach. What if she didn't have enough money?

Connie smiled. "I've got you covered. *Papi* gave me fifty bucks for my birthday."

Edie slumped with relief. "Are you sure Zac's really gonna get the tickets?"

"He says his mom's getting them, that she knows somebody who knows the stage manager."

Edie glanced at her watch. Only five minutes left in their lunch break. She shoved the uneaten half of her sandwich back in her insulated bag and dared to snatch another cookie.

"Hey," Connie protested.

"Hey yourself. You've got Maria full time now. I only get her cookies every once in a while." She leaned forward across the table. "So what are you gonna wear?"

~~~~~~~~~

At one o'clock on Friday, Kate sat in Mac's Place, waiting for Rob and worrying about money.

They'd rescheduled from Wednesday due to Rob's court case. That was easier for her to do these days since she'd stopped taking new clients, anticipating her teaching schedule at Towson University in the fall.

But therein lies the rub.

Part-time teaching didn't pay all that well, and now Skip's agency was in trouble. Should she start taking new clients again? Or maybe try to get a full-time teaching position?

She hated dipping into the money in her brokerage account, originally funded by Eddie Huntington's life insurance. She thought of it as his legacy to her children.

A sudden ache in her chest made her suck in air. Even after all these years, grief for him would strike at the strangest times. What would her life have been like if he hadn't been killed? He was so sweet. He would've been a great dad.

A shadow fell across the table. She jumped.

A large body dropped onto the bench across from her. "Sorry I'm late," Rob said.

Kate gave him a smile, pressing her hands against the cool, shiny black surface of the table, grounding herself in the here and now.

They ordered their usual crab cake sandwiches and side orders.

"So how you doing, Kate?" Rob asked, after the waitress had headed for the kitchen.

"Missing Eddie," slipped out before she could catch it.

Rob's eyes went wide. "Everything okay?"

"Yes, Skip and I are fine. It's not that."

Aw, crap. Her eyes were welling up.

Rob's hand covered hers on the table. "It's okay. This happens."

"What the hell does that mean?" Her tone was far sharper than she'd intended.

Neither his hand nor his expression shifted. "You're menopausal."

She yanked her hand away. "And you're an expert on

menopause?"

He chuckled.

She wanted to smack him.

"Been there, done that. And Liz warned me to expect the unexpected for a while."

Part of her wanted to seethe. Another part suddenly recognized the absurdity of it all. She shook her head.

Now he looked worried. "What?"

She covered his hand and squeezed. "I am so damn lucky."

His cell phone rang. He pulled his hand loose to retrieve it from his pocket.

"It's Murdock," he said at the same instant that her phone rang.

She grabbed it out of her purse and looked at the screen. "Mine's from Detective Russell."

Rob shook his head. "This can't be good."

CHAPTER TWENTY-ONE

Skip was finding it difficult to keep his mind on the blackjack game and his eye on Paul Allen at the same time. He'd lost three times in a row, but he still seemed to be doing better than Allen, who was letting his annoyance show.

Movement in the corner of his eye. Skip turned his head toward the door.

There stood Beatrice Cooper, pausing a moment to make a grand entrance, the gold lamé curtain bunched in one hand, the other hand resting casually on the doorframe. Today she wore a tailored red suit that hugged her curves and three-inch heels that looked deadly.

She caught him staring at her and sauntered his way, a coy smile on her lips. "Didn't I see you in here the other night?"

"You want more cards?" the dealer said impatiently.

"Hit me," Skip said, then held out his hand in a stop gesture without really looking at his cards. Engaging Ms. Cooper in conversation was much more important.

He turned and smiled at her. "Where's your friend?"

She made a small moue with her lips. "He works too hard."

Translation: he doesn't go gambling at lunchtime.

A quick glance over at Allen to see if he'd reacted to Cooper's presence. The man seemed completely intent on, and not very happy with, the cards in his hand.

"So what's your favorite game?" Skip asked, while his mind worked on a strategy to draw her out more.

A toothy smile. "I don't know that I have one yet. I'm just

learning." She waved toward the table. "Looks like you might've won."

He turned to the table. Damned if he didn't have twenty, and the dealer only had eighteen. The man put a five-dollar chip in front of Skip, then scooped up the cards.

"Would you like to try your hand?" Skip stepped back from his spot at the table, and she bellied up to it.

Another glance at Allen. He was still glaring at his cards.

"Hit me." Beatrice looked up at Skip. "That is the correct term, isn't it?" She fluttered her lush eyelashes.

This woman had plenty of brains, but she'd definitely learned how to use her beauty to get what she wanted.

And what does she want? Only male attention, or something else?

"Would you like me to get you some chips of your own?" he asked her. "Unfortunately, it's a two-hundred dollar minimum."

"Could I buy some of yours?" She batted her eyes again.

Skip glanced at the dealer, who was glaring at them. "Is that against the rules?"

The man hesitated the briefest of moments. "Nah, but get on with it." He tapped his deck impatiently.

"Hit me again," Beatrice said. The dealer obliged, and her cards now totaled nineteen. She shook her head, indicating she didn't want any more.

She was either a very quick study or she wasn't the beginner she pretended to be.

While the dealer went around the table, deftly flipping cards to those who indicated they wanted them, she opened the purse on her lap. Handing Skip two crisp fifty-dollar bills, she said, "You think this is enough to get started?"

He nodded and picked up all but twenty of the five-dollar chips. He stuffed his chips in his pants pocket, then glanced over at Allen.

And saw an empty chair. He quickly scanned the room. No Allen anywhere. He looked back at the poker table. Cards had been tossed, face down, at his place. The remaining people at the table played on.

Had Allen gone to the men's room? Or had he left?

"Excuse me a moment," Skip murmured to Beatrice, who barely looked up. Her pile of chips was already growing.

He went through the door into the bar and forced himself to walk, not run across the floor. When he was close enough to glance out the front plate-glass windows, he stopped, patted his pockets as if checking for his keys or phone.

Paul Allen's car was no longer parked in front of the bar.

He cursed under his breath, which would only make his next action more realistic. Snapping his fingers and jerking around, he hoped he looked like someone who'd realized they'd left a crucial item behind.

He moved back to the plain wooden door, unlocked and opened it. He tried to look nonchalant as he pushed aside the gold curtain. The goon on the other side barely glanced his way. Just another gambler who'd had to answer the call of nature.

Beatrice Cooper was no longer at the blackjack table. Nor was she anywhere else in the room.

She couldn't have gotten past him.

He walked as quickly as he could without drawing attention, across the room to the heavy metal door. He reached toward the bar across it.

"Hey," one of the dealers called out. "Don't go out that way. An alarm will go off."

"Oh, sorry."

No alarm had gone off so she had to have gone into the bar. Was she in the ladies' room?

He headed back through the gold lamé curtain, no longer all that concerned whether the staff thought his movements suspicious.

He stopped in the bar, looked quickly around. No Beatrice.

Wait to see if she comes out of the ladies' room, or check out-side for her car? He opted for the latter. If he found her car, she couldn't leave without him seeing her. And she and Allen might be meeting there right now.

Cursing himself now—if the two of them were in league, Beatrice probably noticed him watching Allen—he shoved open the front door of the bar.

Maybe he *was* losing his touch as a detective? He squashed that thought. Now was not the time to be undermining his own confidence.

He turned to his left, intent on checking the parking lot where Beatrice had parked her Audi the other night. As he jogged toward the corner, he scanned the cars parked at the curb, and froze with one foot in the air.

A uniformed police officer was examining the front license plate of his Expedition. The man had a pad in his hand.

Did the meter expire? He'd fed it some quarters before going inside. But the officer wasn't writing on the pad. He was looking at it, then at the license plate again.

Skip decided to walk on past. He needed to find out if Beatrice Cooper and Paul Allen were huddled somewhere nearby, discussing industrial espionage. He'd deal with the parking ticket later.

But the officer looked up and narrowed his eyes. "You the owner of this vehicle, sir?"

Skip's gut clenched. The pad had disappeared and the officer now had his hand on his gun holster. This wasn't about a parking violation. "Is there a problem, Officer?"

"You the owner?" the cop repeated.

He stole a glance at the meter. Still forty minutes on it. "Yes, sir."

"Mr. Canfield, I need you to come with me."

Not good. "Uh, what's going on?"

"Detective Russell wants to speak to you."

"About the Strategic case?"

The officer gave a slight shake of his head. "I wouldn't know, sir. He just put out a be-on-the-lookout bulletin."

A BOLO's out on me? That made Skip more than a little

nervous. He swallowed a sigh of frustration. His chances of shaking loose from this cop in time to catch up with Cooper and Allen were slim to none.

"I'll follow you, Officer."

The man shook his head again. "Orders are to bring you in. Someone will bring you back to your vehicle later."

Skip debated the pros and cons of being resistant. A BOLO meant he was most likely a suspect in a crime or thought to be a material witness. If it was the former, he didn't want to force this cop to arrest him.

"Mind if I reach in my pocket for some quarters to feed the meter?"

"Are you armed, sir?"

"Yes. I have a license to carry concealed. I'm a private detective."

"I know, sir. Where is your gun?"

Skip turned slowly, keeping his hands out away from his sides. "Waistband holster."

He felt cold fingers against his back, then the lightening of the holster as the gun was removed.

"Would you lean against the truck, sir. I need to pat you down."

Skip followed orders, trying to ignore the people on the sidewalk who were stopping to stare.

Hands hesitated over the bulge of gambling chips in his pants pocket, but then they moved on down each leg.

Once the officer straightened, Skip said, "About the quarters for the meter?"

"Go ahead."

The officer watched him carefully as he pulled some change from his pocket and plucked out some quarters.

He had a bad feeling he wouldn't be back before the meter ran out.

~~~~~~~~~

Rob struggled to keep his cool.

He wasn't used to doing criminal work anymore. Mostly now he stuck to civil cases, and his teaching at the University of Baltimore's law school. But Kate had gotten herself embroiled in yet another client's messy life, and he'd let her drag him along with her.

Detective Russell was a bulldog. He kept coming back around, again and again, to Fred Latey's connection to Skip.

Kate sighed. "Detective, I never even met the man."

The detective slid an eight-by-ten photo in front of her. She glanced down, then jerked her head away and shook it.

"You've never seen this guy before?" Russell said.

Kate shook her head again, more vehemently.

Rob pointed to the photo, then to himself.

Russell slid it over to him.

A close-up of a man's head, skin grayish, with salt and pepper hair and a birthmark on his chin. The head lay on a pillow, surrounded by vomit.

Rob felt his own gorge rise. He swallowed hard. "Enough. My client has told you repeatedly that she's never met the deceased."

Russell pushed up out of his chair. "Fine. Mr. Franklin, you and I can now go down the hall and talk to your other client. He has refused to answer my partner's questions until you are present."

"Mr. Murdock is following my orders."

"I wasn't talking about Murdock. Mr. Canfield is down the hall."

Kate's mouth fell open. "Skip?"

Rob wasn't surprised, considering the questions Russell had been asking. He put a calming hand on Kate's arm as he rose from his chair. "Why are you so convinced that Mr. Canfield's connection to Mr. Latey has anything to do with the man's death?"

Russell looked at Kate as he answered. "Because Mr. Canfield was seen leaving Latey's office yesterday afternoon and he was royally pissed."

Rob glanced down at Kate, but she had composed herself.

Unfortunately her face was red and she was sweating.

Rob knew she was having a hot flash, but did Russell get that?

"May I leave now?" Kate asked in an even voice.

"No."

Her body stiffened. "Detective, my children are home alone. If you are done questioning me—which you should be, since I've told you repeatedly that I've never met the man who was killed—I need to go home and make sure they are okay."

Detective Russell narrowed his eyes, but then nodded.

Out in the hall, Rob pulled Kate aside. "Don't say anything to any police officer unless I'm there." He didn't have a grasp on this case and it was making him nervous.

"Don't worry, I won't." She frowned at him. "Your phone call was from Hal. Why did you sit in with me first? He must be a basket case by now."

"I told him not to say anything until I was there."

She continued to scowl at him.

Rob shook his head. "You don't get it, do you?"

Her expression morphed to baffled. "Get what?"

"They did a dragnet. Pulled in everybody remotely related to the case. Murdock's a suspect, but Skip is more so."

"Hunh?" she said. "How do you know that?"

"Educated guess. The lead detective questioned you first because he was hoping you would innocently let something slip that would hang Skip."

Her face shifted from worried and vaguely pissed to terrified. "What motive would Skip have?"

"Don't know, other than Latey fired him."

She lifted a trembling hand to push back an errant curl. "Go."

Rob went, down the hall toward yet another interrogation room.

I'm getting too frickin' old for this.

A twinge in his chest. He slowed his pace and rubbed the heel of his hand against his sternum.

At the door of the interrogation room, he paused. Should he

check on Murdock first? That wouldn't make Russell happy.

Russell's partner, Dave Waters, was headed his way.

Rob waited. "What is Mr. Murdock's status?" he asked when Waters got closer.

"I cut him loose. He's got an alibi for the TOD window."

Rob's eyebrows shot up in spite of himself.

"He had a date. Was eating Chinese with a young lady at the time of death." Waters stopped in front of him. "We'll check the alibi, but my partner and I both like your friend for this." He opened the door. "Shall we?"

Rob resisted the urge to grind his teeth. *What part of "don't say anything" didn't you understand, Murdock?* But the cops had let him go.

Rob felt torn. That didn't bode well for Skip.

He rubbed his chest again as he followed the detective into the room.

Skip was leaning back a little in his chair, trying to buy some extra leg room in the somewhat cramped quarters. The room was stark—cement block walls, metal furniture.

Rob had a dizzying moment of *deja vu.* He'd sat in on a similar interview years ago, when Skip and Kate were newly engaged and had ended up suspects in another murder investigation. He hoped Skip kept his cool as well this time as he had back then.

Russell sat across from Skip, doodling on a pad.

Let the games begin, Rob thought but, of course, didn't say out loud.

Waters went through the process of turning on the recording equipment and identifying those present.

When it became apparent that no Miranda warning would be made, Rob asked Skip, "Were you Mirandized?"

Russell smiled. "No need. This is only a friendly chat. Mr. Canfield came in willingly."

Technically a Miranda warning wasn't required unless someone was under arrest, but Rob was highly suspicious these detectives were up to something. He just couldn't figure out what.

Skip shot Russell a hard look. "I got the distinct impression that I didn't have much choice."

Ignoring the comment, Detective Waters said, "What transpired, Mr. Canfield, in your meeting with Frederick Latey at Strategic Electronics on Wednesday?"

Skip lowered the front legs of his chair to the floor and sat forward. He folded his hands together on the table in front of him. "My partner and I have been tracking down some rumors about our agency. Turns out the person who started the rumors was paid to do so. I was investigating the source of that payment."

After a beat, Russell said, "How so?"

"A Mr. Howard Kaplan started the rumor. He received payment in a plain envelope, delivered by a man he didn't know. But this man had a big birthmark on his chin."

Russell scowled. "So you breached security at Strategic to confront Latey in his office?"

Skip gave the detective a smile that didn't reach his eyes. "Since I suggested most of their security measures, it wasn't that hard to get past them."

"And what did Mr. Latey say?" Waters asked, his tone friendly.

Rob resisted the urge to shake his head. The good cop/bad cop set-up was ridiculously obvious.

"He confirmed that he made the payment but didn't know what it was for."

"Wait," Waters said. "I'm confused. He paid someone to start a rumor about the P.I. agency he himself had hired?"

"Gotta admit," Skip said, "I was pretty confused myself. Still am. Latey wouldn't tell me who gave him the money to deliver. Said he was just doing a favor for a friend."

Detective Russell leaned slightly forward. "What would you say if I told you we have witnesses who heard raised voices coming from Latey's office when you were in there?"

Rob's heart rate kicked up a notch.

He was about to intervene, demand to know who these supposed witnesses were, when Skip said, "I'd say they were lying."

His tone was almost nonchalant.

But Rob knew it was an act. His admiration for Skip Canfield's ability to keep his cool under fire had been one of the things that cemented their friendship early on, despite Rob's misgivings at the time about his intentions regarding Kate.

"You weren't pissed at this man for spreading rumors?" Russell asked.

"I was annoyed at him, but mostly I'm mad at whoever started them."

"And Latey wouldn't tell you who that was." Russell leaned further toward Skip. "Did you threaten him?"

"Only with a lawsuit if he didn't stop defaming my agency." Skip grinned at Rob. "I told him I have a very good lawyer."

Rob stifled a chuckle but couldn't completely suppress a smile. Despite the palpable tension in the room, part of him was enjoying Skip's performance.

"Who else has been helping to spread these rumors about your agency?" Russell said.

"You'd have to ask my partner that. Rose Hernandez. She's been doing most of the investigating there."

"And what have *you* been investigating, Mr. Canfield?" Russell shot back.

For the first time, Skip gave Rob a nervous glance.

He jumped in. "Obviously, Mr. Canfield cannot talk about his clients or other investigations."

"What were you doing at that bar where Officer Michaels picked you up?" Waters said.

"Having lunch," Skip replied.

"Uh huh." Waters' tone was mildly skeptical. "Just having lunch."

Skip smiled at him. "They have great burgers. You should try them out some time."

Rob was trying to figure out what Skip's lunchtime stop had to do with anything.

"What were you doing between six and nine p.m. yesterday?"

Russell said.

Another nervous glance, but then Skip answered, "Doing surveillance."

"Where and for what reason?" Russell said.

Skip shook his head. "Confidential."

"Anybody see you?"

"Nope. I was alone."

"Okay, so let's go over this one more time," Waters said.

Rob softly blew out air. He doubted it would only be one more time. Skip's admission that he had no witnesses to his alibi had bumped him to the top of the suspect list, if he hadn't already been there to begin with.

~~~~~~~~~

By mid-afternoon on Friday, Dolph had finally caught up on the insurance fraud case and had moved on to the deep background check of Beatrice Cooper. Not much had come up, other than a tendency for the young woman to play the field. The society pages of the *Baltimore Sun* were sprinkled with photos of her, with a variety of male escorts.

Ms. Cooper had also made some hefty deposits into her savings account over the last year. They could be honoraria for speaking engagements, but the dates didn't line up exactly.

He turned to the list of rumormongers Rose had given him. She'd added several more names since Wednesday. The question was which of these people were only being human and passing along the dirt, and which had a motive to destroy Canfield and Hernandez, Private Investigations?

He sighed and brought up the site of his favorite data service. He liked doing computer research, but lately that's all he'd been doing. He missed fieldwork. He and Rose needed to have a chat, once this rumor mess was cleared up.

Four names in, his eyes were starting to cross. He was about to call it a day when he glanced at the next name down.

And recognized it. *Interesting.* His fingers returned to the keyboard.

He'd just finished the background check and was printing out the report, when all hell broke loose out in the bullpen.

CHAPTER TWENTY-TWO

Rob's phone vibrated in his pocket. He took it out and glanced at Rose's name on the screen. He let the call go to voicemail and tuned back into the questions the detectives were throwing at Skip.

A purring noise from the phone he still held in his hand. A text message this time.

Call me. Urgent.

Rob held up his hand. "Excuse me, gentlemen. I'm going to have to ask you to suspend this interview for a few minutes. I need to return this call."

~~~~~~~~~~

Connie's brother had dropped them off in front of the Baltimore Arena. Already the crowd was forming. It was like wading in a sea of people.

It had rained earlier in the day, leaving a few puddles on the sidewalks and streets. But now the air was dry and cold.

Edie hugged herself and stomped her feet. Her short-skirted white eyelet dress was completely inappropriate for wintertime, she knew, but it was her favorite. The heavy jacket she wore over it only kept the top half of her reasonably warm. Within seconds, her feet were numb in their Mary Janes.

Connie was only slightly more practically dressed. She too wore a short skirt and blouse under her winter jacket, with bare thighs. But her feet were cozy in knee-high leather boots.

Edie wrinkled her nose. The early evening air reeked of soiled food wrappers thrown in the gutters by passersby and gasoline fumes from the traffic—four lanes across and bumper to bumper.

Horns sounded periodically over the rumble of wheels on the road and the scraping of feet on the sidewalk. Edie looked up at the old soot-covered buildings nearby and could have sworn they were closing in on her. She decided she didn't like the city after all.

But the concert would be so worth it.

Connie was staring at her phone screen. "Zac says to go around the corner onto Light Street. He's down two blocks by a side street. Come on." She turned and started threading her way through the crowd.

Edie wasn't feeling so eager to walk two blocks in the cold. But she didn't want to get separated from Connie, so she followed in her wake.

On Light Street, the crowd thinned from heaving mob to two steady streams of pedestrians moving in opposite directions. People hurrying home from work dodged around vendors starting to set up to sell concert-related wares.

Edie wanted to get a tee shirt and maybe a poster if she had enough money, but first the tickets.

They reached the corner that Zac had designated. The side street was actually an alley.

Connie turned into it, but Edie hung back. Street lights were popping on along Light Street, but the alley was pretty dark in the growing dusk.

"Aren't you coming?" she heard Connie call out.

Edie took a few steps into the alley. Her eyes adjusted to the dim light. About twenty feet away, Connie was talking to a boy. She'd seen him around school occasionally. He, like Connie, was a grade ahead of her.

Okay, so Zac's real.

Edie wasn't quite close enough to hear every word, but it sounded like there was a problem with the tickets.

I knew it!

Disappointment made her stomach feel funny. Her throat hurt and she was afraid she was going to cry.

Zac shook his head. Connie stamped a booted foot.

"I need to talk to Edie," Zac said in a louder voice.

"Why?" Connie asked, but then she turned and motioned impatiently at Edie. "Get over here."

Shivering, Edie moved forward a couple of steps, then hesitated. *Something's not right.*

A large mass loomed out of the shadows.

Connie yelled and ran toward her.

Then Edie was enveloped in darkness, heavy and scratchy, smelling of something that made her eyes water. Heart pounding, she kicked and flailed and screamed, but the noise was muffled by whatever was over her.

She screamed again inside her head, but her mouth had gone dry. No sound came out.

The odor shifted to something else, something stronger. And suddenly she had no strength to fight. Her legs gave out beneath her. She felt someone grab her arms through the scratchy material.

Then the murky darkness around her shifted to solid black.

~~~~~~~~

Kate waited impatiently for word from Skip. She was considering making soup and sandwiches for herself and Billy, since Edie was sleeping over at a friend's house.

Then Liz called. "Rob clued me in. Why don't you come over here for supper. We'll have one of your infamous war councils *when* the guys finally shake free from the clutches of law enforcement?" She came down hard on the *when*, as if there were no doubt that Rob would be able to keep Skip out of jail.

Tears welled in Kate's eyes. She blinked them back. "Sounds like a plan," she managed to get past the lump in her throat.

When did I get so emotional?

Duh, hormones. The last time she'd been this weepy was when she was pregnant with Billy.

She texted Skip that they were going to the Franklins, silently thanking God it was Friday, so no homework to worry about.

It was almost eight-thirty by the time Skip and Rob arrived. Kate had settled Billy in front of the TV in the Franklins' family room, with a sandwich and a glass of milk.

"We stopped to get my truck," Skip said. "Afraid I got a parking ticket, thanks to Baltimore County's finest."

Kate figured that was the least of their problems, but she kept her own counsel. Despite his casual tone, her husband was upset. If the circumstances hadn't informed her of that, the muscle throbbing in his clenched jaw would have.

They compared notes over Liz's gourmet sandwiches. Crustless rye with turkey and chive creamed cheese accompanied concerns over police interpretations of evidence.

Skip's phone rang. He pulled it out and looked at the screen. "It's Dolph. I texted him on the way over and asked him to see what he could find out." He answered the call, then dragged over Kate's pad, on which she'd been listing what they knew.

As he was scribbling notes, the doorbell rang. Liz got up to answer it.

"I hope that's not the police," Rob said. "I'm not sure I'm up for another round tonight."

Kate silently seconded that sentiment.

Skip disconnected as Rose and Mac entered the kitchen. "What'd we miss?" Rose asked.

Rob gave them the gist of the events at the police station. Then he said to Rose, "So how'd it go?"

"How'd what go?" Skip asked.

Rose stared at him for a second. Kate suspected she was assessing her partner's mood. Mr. Easygoing had a high threshold for stress, but once pushed past it, he had a tendency to blow, especially if someone or something near and dear to him was threatened.

That thought made Kate's body tense. Rose had bad news.

"Before I answer that... Rob, your associate was great. She kept them under control." Rose flashed one of her rare smiles in Rob's direction.

"Them who?" Skip's voice rose a little.

"Some cops showed up at our office with a search warrant. They seemed to think it entitled them to rifle through our confidential files."

"Sh…" Skip glanced quickly at Liz. "Crap."

The corners of Kate's mouth twitched upward, despite the gravity of the situation. Skip, ever the gentleman.

"Fortunately," Rose said, "the young woman Rob sent over from his firm was able to disabuse them of that notion."

Skip sighed. "Did they make much of a mess?"

"Not too bad, with Ms. Barrows looking over their shoulders. But they took all of our printers."

"We'll probably get them back eventually," Skip said. "Dolph just called. He got some info from his former colleagues. The two suicide notes both came from the printer in the test lab at Strategic."

"Both notes?" Rob and Kate asked at the same time.

"Yeah," Skip said. "Their initial assumption is that Latey was poisoned. But again it was set up to look like a suicide. He was found in a motel room. Note was to his wife, apologizing for having an affair and saying that he'd been overcome by guilt and couldn't face her."

"So they're not looking at you anymore for it?" Mac said with his usual growl.

Skip grimaced. He glanced from Kate to Rob. "Brace yourselves. They're picking up Murdock again."

Kate's stomach twisted. "But he has an alibi?"

"Guess they're gonna try to break it." Rob pushed his chair back and stood up.

"Does this mean Skip's off the hook?" Kate asked him as he grabbed his suit jacket off the back of his chair.

Rob stopped partway to the doorway. "Not necessarily. They might figure that Skip had access to the lab via Manny."

"That's a stretch," Mac growled.

Skip was shaking his head. "They're at least eight people who had access to that printer. Including Latey."

Rob shrugged, his broad face sagging, and left the room.

Kate felt for him. He looked so tired.

The others were rehashing everything they had already discussed. Kate went back to making lists, one of what they knew and another of what they didn't know. The lists were about the same length, and no new insights presented themselves.

Liz placed a plate of freshly-baked cookies on the table. "If the situation weren't so grim, I'd say it was kind of cool to be at this again, all of us brainstorming together."

Skip frowned at her.

"Like I said, if the situation weren't so grim."

Rose reached out her hand for Kate's pad. She read over the lists, then shook her head. "I don't know what else we can do right now. Let's call it a ni–"

Kate's phone rang. She glanced at her watch. It was after nine. Caller ID read *Maria*.

What the devil?

"Hello."

"*¡Dios mio!* You gotta come quick, Kate. You and Skip. The girls, dey missing."

"The girls. What girls?"

"Consuela and Edie. Dey gone."

CHAPTER TWENTY-THREE

Heart in her throat, Kate pressed the phone against her ear, as Skip wove in and out of Towson's Friday night traffic, Mac and Rose in Mac's Hummer right behind them.

Kate was trying to get the details out of Maria, but the woman's accent had thickened with emotion, making her hard to understand.

"What happened exactly?" Kate said.

"I try tell you. Consuela say she not feel well. José, he say he check on her and she no want dinner, den he go out with his friends. But later I look in Consuela's room and she no there. We search de house, we call all her friends." Her accent grew thicker still, the longer she talked. "Eduardo about to call *policia* and I say no, wait. And den José call and say he cannot find dem."

Kate stuck her finger in her other ear to block out the road noise. "Where couldn't he find them?"

"Downtown. Dey went to some concert. He s'posed to pick dem up. But dey not dere and he look all over and can't find–" Her voice broke.

"Okay, it's gonna be okay. We're on our way. We'll find them. Did they go to the Baltimore Arena?"

"*Sí*. José say dey s'posed to meet him out front but it all crowded and crazy, so he call Consuela's cell phone. But she no answer."

"They went to a concert downtown," Kate said to Skip. "Joe went to pick them up but he can't find them."

Skip hit the accelerator harder.

Kate let out a little yelp as he flew through a yellow light.

"I'll drop you all off," Skip said, "then I'm going down there. Tell her to have Joe meet me in front of the Arena."

Kate conveyed that to Maria, then swiveled around to check on Billy in the backseat. His body was rigid, his gray eyes wide.

Liz had volunteered to go to Kate and Skip's house, in case the girls called or showed up there. Kate had tried to get Billy to go with her, but he'd refused, insisting he had a right to know what was happening to his sister.

"Eduardo say he go downtown too," Maria said in her ear, her voice choked with tears. "He want to call *policia*, but I no like idea. What dey do to little girls?"

"Maria, this isn't Guatemala." Her voice was sharper than she'd intended. She softened her tone. "The police won't hurt them. Yes, he should call. Now. We'll be there in a few minutes."

Kate disconnected.

Even though Maria had said they'd called both girls repeatedly, Kate had to try herself. She tapped the speed dial number for her daughter. Three rings and it went to voicemail.

She tried texting. *Where r u?*

No response.

Oh my God! The gizmo Hal gave me. She dug around in her purse for it, turned it on.

The screen showed the recent calls, her own number listed twice at the top. She fiddled with it, trying to get it to go to the locator map.

"What the hell is that?" Skip said.

Kate shook her head, not sure how to begin to explain it. She punched icons on the tiny menu at the bottom of the screen.

The map popped up. She zoomed in. Everything blurred. She zoomed out instead.

"She's on a side street, off of Light Street two blocks from the Arena."

"What?" Skip said.

Kate held up the small box. "It's a gizmo Hal gave me, called a parental tracker. A GPS that zeroes in on a cell phone."

Skip screeched to a stop in front of Maria's house. He grabbed the box out of her hand. "Okay, go!"

Billy piled out, but Kate froze with indecision. "I'm going with you."

Skip scowled at her. "We might have to search on foot, split up. That area's not safe at night for a woman." His eyes, already red-rimmed, grew shiny. "Please Kate, you'll only slow us down."

Kate ground her teeth. But he was right. Even with her *aikido*, she was vulnerable, and she couldn't run as fast as a man.

Eduardo was waiting on the sidewalk, his expression an odd combination of grim and confused. Kate jumped out and he took her place in the passenger's seat.

Skip leaned forward to look past him. "We'll find them."

She would have been more reassured if he hadn't choked on the words.

The truck roared off, Mac's Hummer on its tail.

Inside the house, Kate tried to send Billy to bed. He crossed his arms and set his mouth in the same grim line she had just seen on his father's face.

Kate's eyes stung. She almost lost it. "Okay," she managed to get out, ruffling his hair.

She took a deep breath to steady herself. "How about you go in the kitchen and keep Maria company? She's pretty upset. I need to make a phone call."

He nodded, then squared his shoulders and marched into the next room.

Kate called Dolph's home number. Sue Randolph answered. Kate quickly filled her in, choking on the words.

"My God, Kate. Let me get Dolph."

When he came on the line, Kate burst into tears. Through her sobs she could hear Sue talking to him in the background, repeating what Kate had just told her.

Then Dolph said in her ear, "Lemme call Judith. Maybe she can help unofficially."

Judith Anderson was Dolph's former partner, now a lieutenant on the Baltimore County police force.

Kate fought her way back to a semi-composed state. "I was hoping you'd be willing to do that."

"I'll get back to you. And Kate…"

"Yes."

"We'll find her," he echoed Skip's words.

"Thank you," she whispered.

Kate disconnected, then dropped heavily onto the sofa in Maria's living room. Her insides in turmoil, she dropped her head into her hands and sobbed.

The cushion beside her sagged slightly. A thin arm circled her shoulders.

She jerked her head up, tears streaming down her cheeks.

Billy's gray eyes stared into hers. "It's gonna be okay, Mom."

Her chest ached. She could hardly breathe. But she managed a small nod and wrapped her arms around him.

~~~~~~~~~

Edie was so excited she was lightheaded. She was here, finally, and Shawn Mendes was singing on the stage right in front of her. He looked straight at her and crooned about how he loved only her. He was walking toward her, and she thought her heart was going to explode.

Then suddenly she was in that alley again, with Connie, talking to Zac. And it was all gray and misty.

She shook her head. Pain gnawed at her temples, made her forehead ache. Where did Shawn go? She wanted to get back to the concert.

"Come on, Connie," she mumbled. "Let's go."

The sound of her own slurred voice brought her more fully awake.

But the gray, misty feeling didn't fade. Where was she? She could hardly see a thing.

She tried to sit up and was yanked back to a lying position.

Oh my God! Her arms were tied to something, just above the elbow.

She tried to kick her feet. Nothing happened. Her feet were numb with cold, but she suspected they were tied too.

Memory flooded back, of the alley, the dark figure looming out of the shadows. The scratchy blanket. A voice screaming, "Zac, get the other one."

Connie had yelled something and then ran. Did she get away?

Tears rolled from the corners of Edie's eyes to her hairline, trickled along her scalp. She wanted to scream but her chest was so tight, she couldn't pull in enough air.

What came out was a groan instead.

An answering moan from the darkness.

Connie?

Heat exploded in Edie's chest. *Damn you, Connie. You got us kidnapped by some creepo. We're gonna be on milk cartons. Have you seen this kid?*

A sob broke loose, then another, then more long wrenching sobs. "Mommy," Edie whimpered out loud.

The thought of her mom comforted her some. She and Daddy would be looking for her. They'd never give up until they found her.

But what did the creepo plan to do to them? Edie didn't want to think about that.

A rustle of movement from her right. Another moan.

Sure sounded like Connie. "Wake up," she hissed.

"Wha?"

It registered that there was some light in the room. It was coming from under a door, across from the end of whatever she was lying on.

The room was chilly, a bit damp. Edie shivered. Cold seeped through the arms of her jacket. Whatever she was tied to was made of metal, cold metal. But it was soft enough under her.

Some kind of cot.

"What the hell?" Connie muttered. "Edie?"

"Yeah. I'm here."

"Where are we?"

"Somebody's basement would be my guess."

"Oh my God!" Thrashing noises, metal scraping on cement, Connie sobbing. "Help! Help!"

"I don't think shouting will do much good," Edie said. "If anybody could hear us they would've gagged us."

"Well, aren't you little Miss Calm?"

Edie clenched her teeth. Getting mad at Connie would be a waste of energy right now. She needed to keep her cool, like she'd seen Mom and Daddy do in tight situations. They didn't fall apart. They thought and they planned and they got themselves and others out of trouble.

"I've been awake longer," she said out loud. "Had more time to get over the shock. We've got to figure out how to get out of here."

The door opened. Edie jerked her head away from the blinding light.

A tall silhouette loomed in the doorway, then shrank to the size of a teenaged boy. The fragrance of chicken wafted into the room.

Edie pulled against the restraints. She wanted to strangle the pimply-faced creep.

"Are you awake, Connie?" His voice was low, tentative.

"You son of a bitch," Connie spit out. "What have you done to us?"

"Sh, sh." Zac walked quickly across the room, set the tray he was carrying down on a small table. "It's gonna be okay. Nobody's gonna hurt you."

"What are you?" Edie said. "The son of a pervert or something? You lead girls into his clutches."

"No, no." Zac shook his head vehemently. "Nothing like that. We just have to keep you here, for a little while. Until we…"

"Until you what?" Connie demanded, straining to sit up. Light from the doorway revealed strips of white cloth holding her arms and hands to the sides of her cot.

Zac shook his head again, more slowly. "I'm not supposed to

tell you too much. But you gotta believe me. You won't be hurt. Everything's gonna be okay." His voice sounded funny, like he was about to cry. And his gaze darted around the room, not making eye contact with either of them.

He's lying. Edie wasn't sure how she knew that, but her mom always said to trust your gut.

She pulled against her restraints and twisted her head around to get a better look at what she was lying on. She flopped back, a bit breathless from her efforts.

"They're the cots we used to use for camping, my dad—" Zac's voice choked up again. He cleared his throat. "My dad and me."

He picked up a bowl from the tray and walked to Connie's cot. "Here, I have to feed you."

The smell of chicken broth made Edie's stomach growl. Too excited, they hadn't worried about dinner, and it had been a very long time since lunch. Her mouth watered.

Then her body jerked as her mind produced a horrifying thought. "Wait! Don't eat it."

Connie already had her mouth wrapped around the spoon. She opened her mouth and yanked her head back, then head-butted Zac's hand that held the bowl. Chicken soup went everywhere.

Zac jumped away. "What'd you do that for? I wouldn't poison you."

"No, you'd just lure us into an alley," Connie's face twisted, "then knock us out and tie us up."

Edie thought an injection of something was more likely than a blow to the head. She'd watched enough TV to suspect that drugs were responsible for her headache. Or maybe a cloth soaked in something. The blanket *had* smelled funny.

"I really was gonna get you the tickets," Zac was saying, "like I said at first. But then…"

"Then what?" Edie said, trying to keep her voice from sounding too harsh. She wanted to know what was going on.

He shook his head. "If you don't want any soup, I gotta go then."

"How about leaving some light on?" Edie said. "It's pretty scary in the dark."

"I guess that'd be okay." He walked to a shadowed corner and fiddled with something.

A light came on, an old floor lamp with no shade, casting a stark glare. They were in some kind of storage room, with boxes piled around the walls, and a few broken pieces of furniture shoved into corners.

Zac looked down at an electric space heater on the floor. "Are you warm enough? I can adjust this."

"No," Edie said quickly, before Connie could answer. It was on the cold side in the room, but the chill air was helping to clear her head.

"I'll be back with breakfast in the morning." Zac started to pull the door closed. "Oh, and I'm supposed to tell you that there's no point in screaming. Nobody can hear you." He pointed to a set of drums in the corner near the lamp. "I practice in here. The walls are soundproofed." The door closed.

Was he lying about that too? She decided not to test it. Yelling for help would only bring Zac back and get them gagged. Or it might bring the person behind their abduction.

She shuddered. She wasn't ready for that.

She was pretty sure the person who was the other part of the *we* Zac kept referring to was indeed going to hurt them.

CHAPTER TWENTY-FOUR

Skip got them to the Baltimore Arena in the inner city in under twenty minutes. The green and blue sign high on its wall reminded him that it was now officially the Royal Farms Arena.

A few people were still milling around outside its doors, but Joe was easy to spot. He waved when he saw Skip's truck.

Skip pulled to the curb, and the young man jumped into the backseat.

Eduardo burst into rapid Spanish.

Skip raised his hand. "Bawl him out later. We need to find the girls."

"I've searched all over," Joe said, a bit breathless. "All around the Arena and down the nearby side streets."

Skip picked up the tracker thing that Kate had given him. The pointer indicated that Edie's phone was still on Light Street, about three blocks away.

He swallowed hard as the implications sunk in. The phone hadn't moved. Either Edie had lost it, or it was on her body, lying unconscious, or worse.

He hit the accelerator, running a yellow light. Mac's Hummer scooted through behind, as the light shifted to red. Ignoring the honking horns, Skip got them to Light Street in record time.

He looked down at the tracker, still clutched in his hand. The map had gotten more detailed now that they were close by. The pointer hovered over an unnamed street about a half block down.

He spotted a parking space big enough for his Expedition and jammed the truck haphazardly into it.

"Down there." He pointed and the three men piled out.

Mac cruised by, searching for a spot for his Hummer.

Skip wasn't waiting. He took off at a run, the tracker held up at eye level. The pointer grew closer.

He stopped at the corner. The tracker said he should turn right. The alley had no street sign, no name, and no streetlights. It was dark as Hades.

He pulled a penlight out of his pocket. It was wholly inadequate but better than nothing. He turned back.

Mac had parked under a streetlight. He and Rose were out of the Hummer, slamming doors. "Flashlights," Skip yelled back to them.

Mac beeped his locks open again and his head disappeared into the truck.

Eduardo and Joe had caught up. "Down there." Skip gestured with the penlight.

Eduardo took off, Joe on his heels. Skip loped behind them, trying to shine the light on the pavement in front of their pounding feet.

"Wait, stop!" He needed the light to check the tracker. Shining it down on the object in his hand, he said, "We passed wherever the phone is."

They backtracked and stopped again. Skip stared at the tracker. Blinding light enveloped him. He held his hand in front of his eyes. The light dropped to illuminate the cement pavement of the alley.

Mac and Rose jogged up. He held a maglite, she a regular flashlight.

Joe took out his phone and tapped it a few times. A barely discernible ringing sound, too muffled to give them much sense of where it was coming from.

The five of them spread out, searching around trash cans, wooden crates and other debris near the back walls of the buildings on either side of the alley. Eduardo must have stepped into a motion detector's field because suddenly a light, attached to the side of what looked like a warehouse, came on.

The circle of light wasn't large, but it helped considerably.

The ringing stopped. Joe tapped his phone's screen and the ringing started again, slightly louder, but still muffled.

They went back over the nearby area.

Blood pounded in Skip's ears as he tried not to think about what might have happened to Edie. He ripped aside a cardboard box. Under it was a gray blanket. Had he just destroyed a homeless person's sleeping spot?

He didn't have time for guilt. Shining the penlight again on the tracker, all he could see was the pointer, filling most of the screen. He zoomed out.

"I'm practically standing on it." It dawned on him that the ringing had stopped. "Call again," he said to Joe.

A ring, much louder but still muffled, near his feet. He yanked away the blanket.

And there was Edie's purse. The small black velvet one that she liked to take to church. He grabbed it up and opened it.

But all that was inside was the ringing phone, a wad of bills and a lip gloss.

Fury at his daughter zinged through his veins. She hadn't even taken any ID with her.

He showed the contents of the purse to the others. He and Eduardo locked eyes.

"She is only twelve." Eduardo's voice was soft, his gaze sympathetic.

Skip almost lost it.

"Should we call the police again?" Joe said. "Tell them we found one of their purses and the phone?"

"Yes," Rose said. There was a tremor in the single word.

Skip's head jerked around to stare at her. Her eyes were shiny in the glow of the flashlights.

His throat closed.

He ground his teeth and straightened his spine. They couldn't afford to fall apart.

"But first we search again," he said, "the whole alley, to make sure they're not here." He barely got the last two words out.

If they were here, they were unconscious, dead to the world if they hadn't heard the five of them searching, banging trash cans and shoving crates aside.

Or they were just plain dead.

His hand shook as he reached for another box to move it.

"*¡Espera un momento!*" Eduardo had picked up the blanket and was sniffing it. "Ether."

"What?" Skip asked, the word not computing.

"I'm a chemist, remember?" Eduardo's tone was irritated.

Skip believed him—Eduardo worked for Grace Chemicals—it had just taken a moment for the significance of the word to sink in.

"How strong?"

Eduardo sniffed again, then yanked his head back. "Pretty strong. I think they were kidnapped."

Skip's knees gave out. He grabbed a trash can as he almost went down.

"Time to call the police?" Joe's voice was little more than a scared squeak.

"Yeah, but we're not stickin' around," Mac growled. "They'll tie us up for hours when we could be lookin' for the girls."

The overhead light went out. Eduardo dropped the blanket and waved his arms in the air. The light blinked back on. "There." He pointed to the ground.

Wet tire tracks on the dry pavement, starting at a puddle and stretching down the alley away from them.

"A truck or van," Skip said.

"Or a car," Mac's voice was gruffer than usual. "They'd fit in a trunk."

He shown his maglite on the cement and they followed the tracks to the next corner. They curved to the right. The vehicle had turned north onto Charles Street.

"Back to the trucks," Skip said.

Once there, he gestured toward his Expedition. "We need to

regroup."

They all climbed into his truck.

He was trying to think what to do next. All they knew was some vehicle had headed north, most likely with the girls inside. "Joe, can you handle calling the police and telling them about that alley?"

The young man's head bobbed up and down in his rearview mirror. Skip made eye contact with Rose and Mac's grim stares.

He turned to Eduardo in the passenger seat. "How hard is it to get ether?"

"Not that hard. Especially if you have a legitimate reason to be using it."

"What is it used for, besides an anesthetic?"

"Actually, it's not used for that anymore. Too volatile. But it is in some other medical compounds, and in solvents, refrigerants, industrial-strength glues." Eduardo scrubbed a hand over his face. "That's all I can think of, off the top of my head."

"Glues? Like those used in airplanes maybe?"

The other man nodded. In the backseat, Joe was talking into his phone, giving a disjointed description of what they'd found in the alley.

Again, Skip made eye contact with Mac and Rose in the mirror.

"Ya thinkin' this is related to Strategic?" Mac said.

"That's a bit of a stretch," Rose said.

Skip's phone rang in his shirt pocket. He hit the button on his dashboard and the ringing sounded through the truck's speakers. He hit another button to answer the call.

"Stop investigating Strategic Elec... or your daughter dies." A low, muffled voice, hard to understand in places. "Do you hear me? Back away from Strategic if... see her alive again. No police. Or both girls die, you hear me." The voice went up in pitch and cracked. "You'll get a call in forty-eight hours, telling you where they are." The caller disconnected.

Skip's body jerked. His heart raced.

He threw an arm over the back of his seat and snatched Joe's phone away from his mouth, hit the end-call icon.

"What the hell?" Joe said.

Eduardo's face had paled. "*¡Dios mio!* This person has our girls."

"Yeah," Skip said, his stomach churning. "And until we've got a better handle on this, we need to back the police off."

His hand shaking, he checked recent calls on his phone. Of course, the number had been blocked.

"Sounded like a kid," Mac said.

"Or a young man with a high voice," Rose said.

"Maybe some of their friends kidnapped them," Joe said, "as a joke?"

Skip shook his head. "No, he mentioned Strategic, twice. Their friends wouldn't know I'm working a case by that name."

Paul Allen. He has a teenaged son.

"But the father of one might." Skip started the truck and put it in gear. He looked in the rearview mirror, expecting Mac and Rose to pile out and run for Mac's Hummer to follow him.

Instead they were exchanging a glance. Rose nodded slightly and Mac got out.

Rose stayed in the Expedition.

My partner, my keeper.

Skip clenched his teeth to keep from saying anything. A more rational part of his brain knew he probably needed one.

~~~~~~~

The doorbell rang.

Kate and Maria took off for the front of the house, Billy on their heels.

Kate got there first. Praying there were two dark-haired, remorseful girls on the other side of it, she yanked the door open.

"Oh." Her heart dropped, and her whole body sagged.

Dolph stood on Maria's front porch, looking more rumpled than usual. "Any word?"

Kate shook her head, struggling not to cry. She stepped back so Dolph could come in.

"Don't know if I can do anything but I wanted to stop by." He pulled a manila envelope, folded in half, from the inside pocket of his sports jacket. "And I wanted to drop this off. Skip probably won't want to bother with it 'til…" He waved his hand in a vague gesture. "But I don't think he'll want to wait until Monday to look into it. There's a connection between the rumors and the Strategic case."

"We already know that," Kate said. "It's Latey, the guy who got himself killed."

"No, another connection. Anyway, don't worry about it tonight. Just give it to him once Edie's home safe."

Dolph's jacket pocket buzzed. He handed the envelope to Kate and pulled his phone out. "It's Skip," he said to her before answering.

Kate's hands flew to her mouth as her throat closed. Heart racing, she prayed that Skip had found their daughter.

"Huh?" Dolph said after a few seconds. He glanced at Kate. "Yeah… Why?"

"Did he find our *niñas*?" Maria demanded.

Tears sprang to Kate's eyes. She had a bad feeling about the expression on Dolph's face. She reached blindly behind her and grabbed for Maria's hand.

"What?" Billy yelled. "What's going on?"

"Shh," Maria said, squeezing Kate's hand.

Dolph had stuck a finger in his other ear. "Yeah… Okay, I'll see what I can do… Where?"

He listened a few more seconds, then disconnected. "He didn't find them, but he knows they're safe for now." He ran a hand through his gray hair, sprinkled with touches of the rust color it had once been, then he gestured them further into the living room.

They all perched on the edges of chairs and the sofa, except for Billy who stood by his mother's chair.

"He got a ransom call," Dolph said. "He'll explain when they get back here."

"Ransom. For money?" Maria said.

"I don't know."

"Why they take our Consuela?" Maria twisted her hands in her lap. "We no have much money."

"Don't worry about that. I do," Kate reminded her. She prayed they didn't want more than was in the brokerage account.

"I'll be right back." Dolph leaned over and whispered in Kate's ear, "I need to try to back the police off."

She nodded.

He went to the front door, opened it and stepped out on the porch, pulling the door closed behind him.

But how did anybody even find out the money exists? They lived on their middle-class incomes, didn't make a big deal about their brokerage account. Only a dozen or so people even knew about it.

She turned to Billy. "Have you ever talked to anybody at school about the money we have for your college?"

He shook his head, his eyes wide.

"You sure?"

"I never even think about it," he said.

Of course, he didn't. College was a lifetime away to a ten year old.

Had Edie bragged about the money to her friends?

Dolph came back inside. "Uh, I should get home." He fidgeted with his phone for a second. "Don't forget to give him that envelope." He pointed to it, lying on the coffee table where Kate had dropped it.

She picked it up and walked Dolph back to the door.

He gave her an awkward hug. "Hang in there. It'll be okay." And he was out the door.

He was acting funny. But then how does one act when dealing with a woman whose daughter has been kidnapped?

Her brain might be tired but it was still a therapist's brain. It struggled for an explanation. Enlightenment dawned. *The old goat wants in on the action.*

Dolph hadn't told her everything. Skip was investigating a lead. She'd bet money on it.

She ground her teeth. Why wasn't Skip telling *her* what was going on?

She turned back to the living room where Maria and Billy were watching her, despair and hope in equal measure on their faces.

She struggled against the sob threatening to escape from her throat. *Sometimes I hate being the strong one.*

Giving Billy a feeble smile, she carried the envelope over to her purse on the sofa and stuffed it down in the top, so she wouldn't forget to take it home with her.

At the moment she couldn't care less about some damn Canfield and Hernandez case, but Dolph seemed to think it was important.

~~~~~~~~

Skip hadn't thought he could feel any worse than he already did. Guilt closed his throat and made his chest hurt. Why hadn't he told Dolph what the "ransom" demand had been? That he leave the Strategic case alone, stop looking for the industrial spy, who had now killed twice.

He hadn't been able to push the words out of his mouth, to admit that *his* case had caused his little girl to be kidnapped.

If anything happened to her, he wouldn't be able to... He couldn't even think about it. He had to get her back.

His eyes stung. He blinked hard and gripped the truck's steering wheel.

The others were quiet, their faces reflecting his own grim thoughts.

He'd gotten Connie kidnapped too. How could he even face Maria?

He ground his teeth and struggled to think.

They had no idea when the girls had been lured into that alley and then taken. Sometime between when Joe had dropped them off at five and gone back to pick them up after the concert.

Where would they look next if this lead didn't pan out?

He shook his head slightly. His gut said it would.

The voice had been that of a teenaged boy. And a teenaged boy could easily lure two young girls into a trap.

He glanced in his rearview mirror.

Joe had taken Rose's hand. Any other time, Skip would have chuckled at her expression. She was obviously struggling not to snatch the hand away.

He turned at the next corner, gliding quietly down the street where Paul Allen lived. As he stopped at the curb, Mac's Hummer behind him, another vehicle also pulled over.

A couple of seconds later, both rear doors of the truck opened at once. Mac piled in from one side, and Dolph from the other.

Skip's chest swelled with gratitude, but his stomach was queasy. He looked up into the rearview mirror, locked eyes with the older man, now wedging himself in beside Joe. "You shouldn't be here, Dolph."

What they were about to do skirted close to the line between legal and illegal, and Skip was prepared to cross that line if necessary. He knew the others were equally willing to go there, but dragging Dolph down with them...

Bushy gray eyebrows pulled together in a frown. Dolph closed his door, then turned to the others. "So what's the plan to get our girls back?"

CHAPTER TWENTY-FIVE

Rob was having trouble staying awake. It was after eleven, and he was not a night person. Plus it had been a long and intense day.

Once again, he had missed the question the detective had asked. He held up his hand before Hal could answer. "Would you repeat the question, please?"

"How long have you been dating this young woman, Mr. Murdock?" Detective Russell said.

Murdock's face flushed. He lifted an unsteady hand to his face, let it drop again. "We're n-not dating, really. I only know her a little."

"But you had dinner with her last night?"

"Sort of."

"How can you sort of have dinner? You either ate with her or you didn't."

"Yes, we ate together, but see, we both go to the Chinese carryout a lot, and it has a couple of tables there. I never sat down to eat there before. I, uh…" Hal ducked his head. "But last night, we both happened to be there, and we decided to sit down and eat together, that's all."

The kid's speech would be more effective if his voice wasn't shaking, Rob thought.

"So you're not dating. You just kinda know each other and you sort of had a date?" Russell's tone was derisive. "I wonder what the young lady will have to say about that?"

The reddish tinge on Hal's cheeks shifted to a darker hue. His fists clenched on the table.

Rob put a steadying hand on his arm. "We need to call it a night," he said for the third or fourth time. He'd lost count. And of course, the detectives were now taking turns so they were much fresher, more alert than Hal or him.

Hal was glaring at Russell. "Leave her out of this."

Rob tightened his grip on the young man's arm.

Hal's face crumpled. "Why are you doing this to me? I finally get a girl to look at me, and you're gonna screw it up. Damn it, leave her alone!"

"They have to talk to her," Rob said. "She's your alibi for a murder."

Hal yanked his arm away, then turned to Rob, his eyes red-rimmed. "She'll think I'm a thug. She'll never talk to me again."

Rob stood, put a hand firmly on the young man's shoulder. "I'm going to insist now. We're done for tonight. I'm instructing my client to refuse to answer any more questions until I am back here tomorrow morning."

Detective Russell rose slowly to his feet. "Okay, Counselor, but we're holding him."

Rob nodded. He wanted to ask if they were going to charge Hal, but decided not to push the issue. They would or they wouldn't at this point. Either way, they could hold him overnight on suspicion of murder.

As Russell took Hal's arm, Rob said, "Mr. Murdock, do not say another thing until you see my face tomorrow. Don't even answer them if they ask you what you want for breakfast."

"Now, Mr. Franklin," Russell smirked over his shoulder as he led Hal out of the room, "what kind of demons do you think we are?"

The kind who would act like you're befriending the guy and try to get him to say something incriminating.

"Not a word, Mr. Murdock," he called after them.

Rubbing his hand against the tight spot in the middle of his chest, he made his way out of the police station.

~~~~~~~~~

"Connie, are you awake?"

"Mhmm…"

"Connie, wake up."

"Wha… Oh my God!" An ear-splitting scream.

Get a grip.

Edie took a deep breath. In as calm a voice as she could muster, she said, "I think I know how we can get out of here. We need to try to scoot our cots together."

"Huh?"

Edie demonstrating by shifting all her weight to her left, then throwing it to her right. The grate of metal on concrete as her cot skooched over an inch or two. "Yes, it works. Come on, Connie."

"Wha' do I do?"

Edie told her, then she demonstrated again. And again her cot moved a little bit. "We need to get close enough to untie each other's hands."

She stopped to catch her breath, heard the scrape of metal on the floor. "You go, girl!"

Then she threw her own weight back and forth, moving her cot slowly a little closer to freedom.

~~~~~~~~~

"Skip, stop," Rose said. "Take a deep breath. We go barging in there and it could get the girls killed."

Skip slowly pulled his truck door closed again and made himself take the suggested deep breath. His partner was right. But he wanted to go rip the front door off of that house and then do the same to Paul Allen's face.

The windows were dark. He glanced at his dash clock. No wonder. It was eleven-ten. Was Allen home or at his favorite gambling spot?

Dolph had asked for a plan, but Skip couldn't think clearly enough to come up with one. He took a deep breath.

One step at a time.

"First we need to check the garage for a silver sports car."

The words were no sooner out of his mouth than the garage door rumbled open and the rear end of said sports car poked its way out.

Skip started the truck and jammed it into gear, hitting the accelerator and the horn together, racing to block the end of the driveway.

Allen's car stopped just short of his front fender. Allen jumped out. "What the hell do you think you're doing?" he yelled.

Skip was out of the truck in a second, Eduardo's words, telling Joe to stay put, barely registering. He rounded the front of the Expedition.

But Rose was even faster. She was already standing in front of Allen. "We need to speak to you, sir."

Mac and Dolph materialized on either side of her.

Allen's eyes went wide and he backed away. "Whadaya want?" Then before any of them could answer, he turned and made a dash for the garage.

Mac was on him in a few strides, tackling him around the knees and bringing them both down on the pavement.

"Owww," Allen howled. He kicked, trying to loosen Mac's grip.

"You might want to keep it down," Rose said. "You really don't want your neighbors witnessing this."

With Mac still clamped onto his legs, Allen managed to twist around to half sit up. "Who are you? What do you want?"

Skip stepped over and grabbed the man by his elbow, hauled him to his feet. "Where's my daughter?"

"Your what? Who?" Allen's head swiveled back and forth between them. "I'll get the money. I just need time. Frankie said I could have some time."

Skip shook him. "You're not listening, man. Where is my daughter?"

Allen's gaze stopped on Rose. "Who the hell *are* you people?"

"They are *familia* of two missing girls who are crazy with worry," Eduardo said from behind Skip, his accent thick with emotion. "I would not mess with them, if I were you, *señor*."

~~~~~~~~~

It was almost midnight by the time Rob got home. Liz had left the lights on in the house.

He smiled to himself, grateful for his Lizzie and the warm home she had created, for him and for the girls when they were growing up.

A twinge of guilt tightened his chest. Hal Murdock wasn't going home tonight to the warm comfort of his own bed.

But there was nothing more he could do about that tonight.

He went into the kitchen, looking for a snack. In the center of the table were two plates, one with three crustless sandwich halves, the other mostly full of cookies.

That was odd. Not like Liz to leave food sitting out like that.

He downed one of the wedges of rye and turkey in two bites, then poured himself a glass of ice water from the dispenser on the door of the fridge. Reluctant to sit at the table—he might not be able to get up again—he juggled the two other triangles of sandwich in one hand, the glass in the other and flipped the kitchen light switch with his elbow. He walked slowly through the living room, munching as he went.

He'd just swallowed and was about to take another bite when a crushing pain erupted in his chest. He staggered against an end table, tried to grab for a teetering vase of flowers and dropped the glass of water in the process. Both crashed to the floor and shattered.

He sank down on the sofa, hands flattened against his chest. Pushing against it, trying to counter the unbearable pressure.

Dear God!

He opened his mouth to call Lizzie's name. Nothing came out. The vise tightened around his chest. He couldn't catch his breath. One hand fumbled in his pocket for his phone.

CHAPTER TWENTY-SIX

Rose stood across the room, observing Paul Allen and his bathrobe-clad wife sitting on the sofa, arguing furiously in whispers. The others, with Allen's reluctant permission, were searching the house.

A few feet away, their son stood, in fleece lounge pants and a gray tee shirt, watching them intently. The kid was about fourteen, pimply-faced, his hands and feet too big for his body. He coughed and his parents looked his way.

"Go to bed, son," Allen said.

Rose took a step toward the boy. "Did your father ask you to make a phone call this evening?"

He shook his head adamantly, maybe too adamantly.

"Your mother?" she asked.

He shook his head again, his barely formed Adam's apple bobbing in his throat.

Poor kid's scared to death.

"Nobody's going to get hurt here, son," Rose said in a gentler voice.

"Go to bed," Alicia Allen said. "We'll talk in the morning." She gave her son a small smile.

Rose followed the kid down the hall, intending to search his room before he went back to bed.

He slowed, allowing her to catch up. "Are you here to collect his debts?" he asked.

"So you know about the gambling."

The little knob in his thin throat bobbed as he swallowed. "I figured it out when things started disappearing from around the house."

"What things?"

"First it was only his stuff, an electric guitar he'd saved from when he was in a band in college, and some other old stuff. Then Mom couldn't find her black pearl earrings that he gave her last year for their anniversary."

They came to an open door. He stopped. "I've been waiting for the Porsche to disappear."

Rose didn't tell him that it was about to be repossessed. "Hey, can I check your room real quick?" she said. "I don't think the guys have gotten to it yet."

"What are you looking for?"

Rose hesitated, not sure she wanted to accuse Allen of kidnapping without proof, especially not to his son. "Let's just say it's bigger than a bread box. I need to look in your closet and under your bed." The men were searching some of the other rooms more thoroughly, looking for evidence of industrial spying as well as for the girls. But she doubted Paul Allen would stash such evidence in his kid's room.

The boy gave a slight shake of his head. "Bigger than a bread box. Where'd that saying come from anyway?"

"In the good ole days," she flashed him a grin, "we actually kept bread in a box on the counter."

He grinned back.

~~~~~~~~~

Billy's eyes had finally drifted shut and stayed that way. Kate stretched him out on Maria's sofa and spread the colorful throw over him.

She and Maria tiptoed into the kitchen, where Carlos sat at the table, an untouched glass of milk at his elbow. He was staring at the tips of his sneakers, stretched out in front of him.

"Go to bed, Carlos," Maria said to the boy.

He gave her a sharp look and opened his mouth. Then manners or something stopped him. "Okay. Call me as soon as you hear anything."

"*Sí, sí.*" Maria made a shooing gesture.

So far, they had heard very little. Skip had called only to say that they hadn't found the girls downtown, but he thought he knew where they were. Before she could ask any questions, he'd disconnected.

Maria had called Rose and had gotten a bit more out of her. "Dey found Edie's phone and purse," she repeated Rose's words to Kate, the phone to her ear. She paused, listening. "Dey think the girls were kidnapped." Her voice caught. She swallowed. "But dey think dey know who…" She expelled air and even smiled a little. "If dey right, nobody has hurt the girls. Dey going there now."

Furious, Kate had grabbed the phone. "What's going on?"

"It's complicated. Can't explain right now," Rose's voice was clipped, sounded distracted. "Gotta go."

"Rose, wait!" Fear for Skip had overridden Kate's anger. "Make him be careful."

Rose had sighed in her ear. "I'll try."

And that had been almost an hour ago. Kate paced the kitchen, trying to decide what to do. Should she take Billy home?

Her phone rang in her pants' pocket. She snatched it out. "Hello?" Blood pounded in her ears, making it hard to hear the frantic voice on the other end. A woman's voice.

"Liz?"

"…I just wanted to let you know I had to leave your house. I'm headed for the hospital."

"The hospital? Why?"

Maria had been giving her anxious looks. Now her hand flew to her mouth.

Kate shook her head slightly, trying to indicate it wasn't about the girls.

"Didn't you hear me?" Irritation, something one almost never heard in Liz's voice. "Rob's had a heart attack."

"What?" Kate yelped, her own heart taking off like a racehorse.

"Rob's had a heart attack," Liz repeated. "Thank God he managed to get his phone out and call 911."

Kate sat down hard in the nearest chair, trying to wrap her brain around the words. Could anything else go wrong tonight?

Don't answer that question, Lord.

"Look, nobody's at your house, if the girls come back there. I wanted to let you know that."

"What hospital?" Kate asked.

"Greater Baltimore Medical Center. They said he's in stable but guarded condition."

Kate hated that *guarded* part. It meant anything could go wrong at any minute.

"I'll–"

Liz interrupted, "You've got enough on your plate."

Kate flashed back thirteen years, to a hospital waiting room where she'd held Rob's hand while they waited to hear if Liz would survive a hit-and-run accident. Eddie had been so solicitous, of her and Rob, and then had joked around to ease the tension once they knew Liz was going to be okay.

Her eyes stung. *Eddie, where are you when I need you?*

In the next second, she felt guilty, disloyal to Skip.

What if I lose Edie? She's all I have left of her father. A sob almost escaped past the lump in her throat.

Maria had been standing at her elbow, hanging on her end of the conversation. "Who in hospital?" she demanded.

"Rob. He had a heart attack, but he's okay." Not completely true but no need for her to worry.

But Maria was shaking her head. "Liz need you." She grabbed a set of keys from a rack on the kitchen wall.

Kate opened her mouth.

"Carlos be here," Maria said. "You take Eduardo's car to hospital. I go to your house."

"Liz," Kate said into the phone, "I'll be there in twenty minutes."

~~~~~~~~~

"Come on, Connie, you can do it."

A sob. "It's too hard. My hand hurts."

"Your hand hurts so much you'd rather die?" She probably shouldn't have said that so harshly but she was losing patience.

Another sob. Then more plucking at her wrist.

The binding felt looser. Edie held her breath. A few more plucks and suddenly her wrist was free.

"Yeah, you did it!" She flexed her fingers, then fumbled for the knot on the cloth strips binding Connie's wrist to her cot.

In a few minutes, Connie's wrist was free.

Edie jerked her body around, maneuvering her cot so that Connie could reach her elbow. Connie untied the strips of cloth there.

One arm completely freed, Edie quickly undid the knots restraining her other arm, then sat up to release her ankles.

She paused a moment to let the circulation return to her feet. When the pins and needles subsided, she swung her legs off the cot and planted her feet on the floor.

Excitement bubbled in her chest as she worked on untying Connie. Her idea had worked. They were free.

Now they needed to figure out how to get out of this room. She ran to the door and grabbed the knob. It was locked, of course. "Find something we can use as a weapon."

"The lamp?" Connie suggested.

"Maybe, but if we use that, we have no light."

They rooted around in the detritus of the room. Edie found a large, dust-coated vase. She sneezed as she picked it up. It had a heavy, round bulb at the bottom, with a thin neck tapering up from there.

She hefted it. "Perfect."

"What now?" Connie asked.

"Stand over there." Edie pointed to one side of the door. She stood against the wall on the hinged side, where she would be behind it when the door opened. "Yell for Zac. Tell him I'm sick and need a doctor."

Edie raised the vase above her head, praying that Zac had been lying about the soundproofing.

Connie yelled, "Help! Zac, please help. Edie's sick."

~~~~~~~~~

Skip and Mac trooped into the Allens' living room, Eduardo and Dolph just behind.

Alicia turned toward them, wide-eyed, clutching her robe closed at the neck.

Rose narrowed her eyes at her partner. He seemed calmer than he'd been earlier, but his expression was determined.

He held up a flash drive. "Looky what we found hidden in a drawer in the study. And it seems to be encrypted."

Paul Allen jumped up, his hand out. "Give me that."

"What's on it?" Skip said.

Allen shook his head.

"Give us the password," Mac growled.

"It won't do you any good. It's designed to only open on two computers, neither of which is here."

"It's from Strategic?" Rose asked. Doubt that Allen was their man had been nibbling at the edges of her brain, but this...

Allen scanned their faces. "I'm not telling you anything more about it. You won't be able to open it."

Skip and Rose both glanced at Dolph, who shook his head slightly.

"Where'd it come from?" Skip said.

Allen sneered. "Seems all your security measures are next to useless. I accidentally brought it home the other day. Forgot it was in my pocket, and I didn't happen to be one of the randomly selected."

"I see you finally figured out who I am," Skip said.

"I didn't recognize you at first, out of context. Especially since you're supposed to be one of the good guys."

"Still am."

"Good guys don't invade people's houses in the middle of the night to find evidence."

"Invade?" Dolph said. "I distinctly heard you give us permission to search."

Rose's doubts were back. They'd been playing it close to their chests, not letting on to the Allens what they were looking for. Allen was acting like he thought they were only after evidence of the espionage, even though Skip had started off demanding where his daughter was. Was Allen just pretending he believed that in front of his wife?

And the Allen kid seemed to have no idea why they were really there. She didn't think he'd made that call about the girls. He'd have been a lot more nervous while talking to her.

Skip turned to her. "We searched the garage and basement thoroughly, and any place big enough to hide them." His voice caught a little on the end.

His gaze veered back to the Allens. "You got any outbuildings?"

Alicia Allen glanced at her husband, then at Skip. "Paul has a workshop out back. I'll get you the key."

They took Paul Allen with them this time, out the kitchen door and along the side of the oversized garage. At the end of the backyard was a small, freestanding building, white clapboard, like the garage.

CHAPTER TWENTY-SEVEN

At three in the morning, Kate hugged Liz goodbye in the hospital parking lot.

"Thanks for coming." Liz sounded as exhausted as Kate felt.

Kate leaned back, holding her friend's shoulders. She looked into Liz's red-rimmed eyes. "He's gonna be fine." Indeed, Rob's condition had been upgraded to stable. The doctors had decided that the heart attack was relatively mild.

Liz nodded, then opened her car door.

"I'll call you tomorrow," Kate said.

"Or sooner," Liz said over her shoulder as she climbed into the driver's seat, "if you hear anything about the girls."

A fresh wave of worry for Edie crashed over her, threatening to drown her. She managed to nod her head.

With traffic practically nonexistent at that hour, the drive home was short—but torturous. Kate's brain kept producing images of what might be happening to her little girl. She'd no sooner push one away than another would pop up, worse than the one before.

As she let herself in her front door, Maria roused from where she'd been lying on the sofa. Her face fell when she saw it was Kate.

I'm not the one who's likely to be bringing her niñas *back to her.*

"How's Rob?" Maria asked, rubbing her eyes.

"Stable. Billy okay?"

"*Sí.* I let him keep the dog in his room."

Kate nodded. "Go back to sleep. There's nothing more you

or I can do tonight."

Maria's face clouded and for a moment, she looked like she was going to cry. Then she nodded again and sank back on the sofa.

Kate trudged into the bedroom and dropped into bed without even bothering to get undressed.

Sometime later, she had no idea when, a rustling noise roused her. The bed shifted as someone slid in beside her.

Half asleep, she rolled over to drape an arm over Skip, but the body she encountered was much smaller.

Kate stared for a moment at her son's tousled brown head on his father's pillow. Then she wrapped her arms around him and drifted back to sleep.

~~~~~~~~~

Edie woke with a painfully stiff neck. No wonder. She was leaning against a wall with her head slumped at an awkward angle.

Her heart raced as it hit her where she was. What time was it?

She peeled cramped fingers from around the vase and pushed her jacket sleeve back to check her watch.

Eight-ten. She assumed that was a.m.

Glancing down at her lap, she noted dully that her favorite dress was grubby. Normally that would have upset her, but right now, as Maria would say, she had bigger fish to fry.

She smiled at the thought of Maria's love for American sayings. Then gulped to swallow back the sob clogging her throat.

She shook her head, setting off another shot of pain from her unhappy neck. Now was not the time to dwell on how much she missed her loved ones.

She turned her head carefully. Connie was slumped over on the floor on the other side of the door.

The door that had never opened, no matter how loud they'd yelled. Maybe it really was soundproofed.

"Connie, wake up."

"Mmm..."

"Wake up!"

Connie's eyes opened. She blinked twice. Then she was on her feet, screaming at the top of her lungs.

Dear God, save me from the drama queen.

Edie rose to her feet. "Zac said he'd bring breakfast. We need to get ready to jump him when he comes."

She thought for a moment, a plan forming. "Untie some of those strips of cloth. We're gonna get behind the door. When he opens it and sees the empty cots, he'll probably rush into the room. I'll hit him with the vase and then we'll both jump on him and tie him up."

Edie figured she'd better get a gag on him quick, if the vase didn't knock him out. Otherwise he'd call out for the pervert he was working with.

Two girls could take down a boy, but she doubted they could subdue a grown man. And he might be armed.

The mental image of a big smelly brute of a man with a gun made her shudder. She recalled the story on the news a couple years ago, of the women who'd been kidnapped as girls and held for years in some guy's house. One of them had even had the guy's baby.

She shuddered again, so hard her teeth rattled together.

Her next thought was that she'd rush the guy anyway, gun or no gun.

~~~~~~~~

Skip struggled to choke down the bowl of cereal Maria had insisted on pouring for him before she'd left. Mostly he was spooning dribbles of milk into his mouth. The thought of swallowing anything solid made his stomach heave. It wasn't even happy about the milk.

His chest felt like it had a huge hole in it, where his heart used to be.

What was happening to his little girl right now?

He had to stop thinking about that. It paralyzed his brain. And he needed to think, plan. Their search of Allen's property hadn't netted them anything but an encrypted flash drive.

Skip touched the outside of his pants pocket, outlining the small rectangle there. Possessing it could probably get him locked up for a long time.

But just because the girls weren't on the property didn't mean Allen hadn't snatched them. Rose was convinced otherwise though. She thought Allen's son was telling the truth when he'd denied making the call.

Dear God, what if Allen hurts the girls because we went there.

He almost jumped up and bolted for the door, but stopped himself. If Allen was the kidnapper, would he have continued to play innocent? Or would he have threatened to hurt Edie and Connie if they didn't back off?

Maybe Allen was innocent and the spy/kidnapper was somebody else altogether.

He considered the suspects. Murdock was still in police custody, out of reach for now, and Skip's gut said the guy wasn't capable of kidnapping young girls.

Maybe the other engineer, Watson? Although Rose had been tailing him for days, and he hadn't done anything more suspicious than wash his car on a winter day.

The other technicians in the lab? They hadn't really pursued that lead, other than Dolph's background checks.

The sound of the bedroom door opening. Kate came around the corner, still wearing yesterday's slacks and sweater. Billy, in his PJs, was right behind her.

Kate stopped when she saw Skip at the table. She opened her mouth, then closed it again. She knew if he'd had anything to report he would have wakened her, but he shook his head anyway.

She headed for the counter and the coffee maker. Billy got two bowls out of the cabinet, two spoons from the drawer and brought them to the table.

Skip watched him put one bowl and spoon in Kate's normal place at the table. Then he poured cereal into both her bowl and his own.

Since when did my son start looking out for his mother?

Guilt squeezed his chest. Since his father had gotten the boy's older sister kidnapped.

Kate sat down at the table, ignoring the bowl. She held a coffee mug in both hands and brought it to her mouth. Her eyes were haunted, a washed-out gray.

With a jolt, Skip realized they would probably never be their normal sky blue again, if they didn't get Edie back safe and sound.

His stomach churned.

"Rob had a heart attack last night." Kate's voice was flat.

His jaw fell and his own heart stuttered in his chest.

"He's okay. It was relatively mild."

She dropped her gaze to her cereal bowl.

He blinked, his tired brain trying to regroup.

"The guy I suspected…" His voice was ragged from being up all night. He cleared his throat. "The guy I thought might've taken them, we searched his property. No sign of the girls, but we did find some evidence that he's the spy at Strategic."

Her eyes went wide. "There's a connection to that case?"

Damn! He'd forgotten that he hadn't passed along the details of the ransom call. At the time, his guilt wouldn't let him get the words out.

He hesitated, wondering how much he should say in front of Billy, who was slowly and methodically making his way to the bottom of his cereal bowl.

The boy paused, picked up the milk cartoon and poured some on Kate's cereal. She gave him a feeble smile and picked up her spoon.

Skip shook his head slightly. His son was growing up. Time to stop treating him like a kid.

He told them both about the ransom call, what they'd found in the alley, and what they hadn't found at the Allens' house.

"Why would a *kid* be involved in the kidnapping?" Billy asked, a bit wide-eyed.

"His parents would have pressured him, most likely," Skip said.

"And out of fear," Kate added. "He'd be afraid of what would happen to his parents. That might override his conscience."

Billy shook his head. "I'd be too scared to get the words out."

Skip paused. The kid's voice on the phone had sounded pretty scared. Maybe Rose was right about the Allen boy. She was the one who'd interviewed him.

But maybe they should go back today and ask him again. He was the weakest link. Assuming Paul Allen was the kidnapper.

The land line rang, sending adrenaline through Skip's body. He was on his feet in an instant.

But Kate was even faster. She already had the portable phone against her ear. A big smile spread across her face.

Hope surged through his body.

She turned to him with bright eyes. "It's Liz. Rob's doing much better this morning."

He slumped back into his chair but managed a weak smile. Of course he was worried about Rob, but that worry was overshadowed by the other—the gnawing anxiety of knowing his daughter was in the hands of a kidnapper, and it was his fault.

"Shit," he muttered under his breath. "I never should've taken that case."

Billy shot him a startled glance.

"What? You've never heard that word before?" Skip snapped, then instantly regretted it.

But Billy shot right back. "Yeah. Just not from you in front of Mom."

A spurt of pride in his chest, despite the circumstances. His son was learning the rules of being a gentleman. Rules that were perhaps a bit antiquated today, but nonetheless his dad had taught them to him, and he was trying to pass them along. And was apparently succeeding.

Skip was also secretly pleased that Billy had talked back.

Now there's an irony.

But it showed that the boy was learning to stand up for himself.

The distraction of the interchange had allowed his insides to settle down. He took a bite of soggy cereal, chewed and swallowed. His stomach actually felt a little better with something more solid in it. He took another bite.

Kate had ended her conversation and resumed her seat. Ignoring her mostly untouched cereal, she said, "Liz is hoping she can convince Rob to retire from the law firm and just teach."

It was too good an opening to let slide. "Maybe you should consider the same thing."

"What?" Kate tilted her head.

"Son, are you finished?" The boy may be growing up, but he still didn't need to witness a possible argument between his parents. "Go get dressed and brush your teeth."

Billy looked from one to the other of them, then rose from the table and left the room.

Skip said to Kate, "Maybe you should stop doing therapy and just teach."

"I don't even know if I'll like teaching yet. And it doesn't pay as well."

"We'll manage financially." He'd get a second job if he had to. "You keep getting sucked into your clients' messes." His tone was angrier than he'd intended. Indeed, angrier than he thought he was.

Kate narrowed her eyes at him. "This current mess happens to be related to one of *your* cases."

He ran a hand through his hair, grabbed a hunk and pulled. "I was talking about the mess with Murdock. You lose your perspective when your clients get in trouble."

She folded her arms across her chest. Never a good sign. "If Hal had been accused of any other crime, I would have asked Rob to consider representing him and that would have been it. Turns out he was accused of shooting Manny and the whole thing was tangled up in one of *your* cases." She paused, glaring. "And now our daughter…" She trailed off and let out a sob.

Skip was around the table in a second. He tried to lift her from her chair, but she batted his hands away.

He dropped to his knees beside her. "I'm sorry, darlin'. I didn't mean to pick a fight."

"Sure sounded that way to me," she said through her tears.

He wrapped his arms around her. "I'm sorry," he said again.

She gave a slight shake of her head. "We're both wound tight." She grabbed a napkin and wiped her cheeks. "Speaking of Manny, I should call and check on him. Oh, that reminds me of something else."

She shooed her hands at him. He rose, knees cracking, and stepped back.

She went into the living room and was back in less than a minute with a big manila envelope in her hand. "Dolph dropped this off last night. He said not to worry about it until Edie's home safe, but he thought you'd want to see whatever it is before Monday."

He took the envelope.

Kate picked up the phone from the counter and punched in a number.

While she talked to Manny, Skip's mind returned to the current mess. He absently pulled a clump of papers out of the manila envelope.

The caller had said forty-eight hours. That had to mean they were buying time so they could get away.

There'd been no signs of packing at the Allens' house. Maybe Paul was going to take off himself, leave his wife and boy behind.

Skip had trouble imagining a man doing that, but then he wouldn't sell his company's secrets either. Criminals weren't cut from the same cloth as decent people.

But Allen didn't strike him as the criminal type, more a man made desperate by a gambling addiction.

Beatrice Cooper. He could believe *that* young woman was up to something. And it was way too big a coincidence that they'd both left the gambling joint yesterday at the same time.

His gaze dropped to the papers in his hand—the background

checks he'd requested. He shuffled through them, found the one on Cooper.

She was pretty clean. No criminal record at all, except for a few speeding tickets. Dolph had highlighted in yellow one of the paragraphs in the financial section. She lived slightly above her means and had deposited three hefty lump sums in her savings account at erratic intervals over the last year.

Dolph had typed below that paragraph: *Could be from speaking engagements; she's presented at several universities and conferences. Or could be bonuses for the secrets she's stolen from Strategic?*

Skip dropped the reports on the table. They scattered a little, one landing with its corner in a drop of milk on the tabletop. He grabbed it before the liquid could wick farther onto the page and moved it to the top of the stack.

Beatrice Cooper. That's who they needed to track down this morning.

Kate had hung up from her call with Manny. "He's doing okay. The physical therapist has him doing exercises, to get his strength back."

Skip was already headed for the door, digging his phone out of his pocket. "I've got another thread to pull on. I'll call you as soon as I know anything."

CHAPTER TWENTY-EIGHT

Edie's arms felt like lead from holding the heavy vase. She'd long since lowered it to her side.

How long had they been standing here, tense, ready to spring into action? She checked her watch. Nine-fifteen. It wasn't her imagination that it had been over an hour.

Her stomach rumbled. She felt lightheaded.

"I don't think Zac's coming," she said.

"I'm hungry," Connie whined.

Edie shot her a glare, and her gaze landed on the small silver purse, hanging from a long strap across Connie's torso.

Her purse was long gone and she doubted Connie's phone was still inside hers.

"Lemme see your purse."

Connie pulled the strap over her head and handed it to her.

As Edie had suspected, no phone, but she found a credit card. "I'm gonna try something."

She'd seen somebody pop a lock with a credit card during a family night video awhile back. She'd asked Daddy if that really worked. He'd said yes, but it wasn't as easy as they'd made it look.

She took out Connie's card and started sticking it between the doorjamb and door in various places. She could barely get it in there in some spots, but she kept trying, wiggling it around as best she could at each spot.

She wished she'd asked Daddy more about how to do this.

~~~~~~~~~

Damn it, he's doing it again. Closing her out, not telling her what's going on.

Kate grabbed the top page from the stack of reports, the one that had apparently given Skip a "new thread to pull on." The name at the top meant nothing to her, but she recognized the highlighted one near the bottom of the page. It was one of the suspects in the Strategic case.

And right under that name was an address.

Under that was: *One son, Zachary, thirteen.*

Her heart raced. The ransom call was from a teenaged boy. And she'd overheard the girls discussing a boy named Zac at Connie's birthday party. He was apparently interested in Connie.

Her feet were moving toward the kitchen doorway before her brain had time to catch up with her emotions. She'd had enough of sitting and waiting.

Billy pounded down the stairs, now wearing jeans and a long-sleeved tee shirt.

She grabbed her purse from the end of the counter and gestured for him to follow her to the front door. "Lock the door behind me, son, and don't answer it for anyone but Maria or Aunt Rose."

Kate bolted out of the house.

In her car, she struggled one-handed with her seatbelt as she made a K turn. Once headed in the right direction, she instructed her Bluetooth to call Maria.

"*Hola.*" The voice was shaky.

"Skip thinks he has a lead on the girls. I left Billy at the house. Can you go get him, take him back to your place?"

"*¡Dios mio!* Of course. I go now."

Kate tried Rose next, but got a busy signal.

She turned right onto York Road and hit the accelerator.

~~~~~~~~~

Skip's call to Rose had gone straight to voicemail. He didn't bother with a message. Trying to resist the urge to speed—he had no desire to run afoul of the law this morning—he called Mac.

"Where's Rose?"

"At the hospital. Her *madre*'s got pneumonia."

Normally Skip would feel sympathy for the elderly woman, but today there was no room for any emotion but fear for his daughter.

"Look, I've got a hunch about where Edie and Connie may be." He filled Mac in.

"Why would this woman take the girls?" Mac said.

That gave Skip pause. Maybe his tired brain wasn't processing all this accurately? But it was still his best lead.

"I don't know. But I'm sure she's involved in the spying at Strategic."

Mac let out a deep "Humph." Then, "I'll meet ya. Don't go in 'til I get there."

Skip disconnected without answering.

Call the police or not?

The kidnapper might be watching him somehow, to see if he called in the police. But then how would they know who he was calling? He glanced down at the console between the seats, his gaze landing on the earpiece of Hal Murdock's listening device. Or maybe they'd planted a bug in his truck.

His chest tightened as he reviewed what he'd just said to Mac. If Beatrice Cooper was the kidnapper and had bugged his truck, she now knew they were on the way.

The kidnapper had said forty-eight hours to buy time to get away. He was sure of it. Which might mean they were already gone, and the girls were…

He blinked away tears, swallowed hard. He couldn't let his mind go there.

If he was right about Beatrice Cooper, then she had killed Cochlin and maybe Latey, or had been a party to murder.

Driving one-handed again, he dug in his wallet for the business card he'd placed there. At the next traffic light, he hit the button that turned off his Bluetooth, then punched the detective's cell number into his phone and texted, *Think I know who killer is. Too complicated to explain.* He added Cooper's name and address. *My daughter in jeopardy. No sirens, approach with caution.*

He hit send and, too late, realized that the daughter part wouldn't make much sense to Russell.

A horn blared behind him. The light had changed. He took off.

Could Beatrice Cooper be Manny's shooter? A nine millimeter wasn't a woman's first choice in handguns. And how would she have gotten into Strategic's lab that night?

She could have easily lured Cochlin and Latey to those hotel rooms though, and poison *was* a woman's weapon.

Still, his money was on Paul Allen as Manny's shooter, and as the spy. He'd used Cochlin to get the specs that had been changed by the test lab technicians.

Maybe calling in the detective had been premature. Beatrice Cooper might very well be Allen's accomplice in industrial espionage, but it was unlikely she'd played a part in kidnapping the girls.

She might know about it though and could possibly tell him where they were being held.

He floored it, racing through a yellow light.

~~~~~~~~~

Edie stuck the credit card into the crack, next to the knob. She wiggled it and tilted it up and down. Wiggled some more.

She felt something give. She wiggled the card again and twisted the knob. It didn't turn, but the door drifted open.

Air whooshed out of her lungs. Connie, behind her, clapped her hands.

"Shh." Edie eased the door farther open. It was very heavy. She peeked around the doorjamb.

A cement floor, unfinished walls, a big metal door at the other end of a large space. The room they were in was at the back of a garage.

A blue minivan sat in one of the spaces, its side door hanging open. It was half full of cardboard boxes.

Edie waved a hand to Connie to follow her. They stepped out into the garage. Edie started to nudge the door closed again. If Zac and his pervert buddy came out here, she didn't want them realizing right away that their prisoners had escaped.

No wonder the door was so heavy. It had shelves on the back of it, with stuff on them—some small tools and cans of screws and such. She had to put some effort into getting it closed. The door blended in with the other shelves along the back wall of the garage, almost invisible.

The click of a knob turning. She and Connie scrambled to the far side of the van.

Edie looked under the van. Sneakers shuffled across the floor.

"Careful. It's fragile," a high-pitched voice screeched.

Edie revised her mental image of the pervert—a greasy hulk of a man, with a high, squeaky voice. A bubble of hysterical laughter rose in her throat. She clamped a hand over her mouth.

A soft thud, the tinkle of glass items clinking together. "Crap," Zac's voice, muttering, "if any of them are broken, I'm dead."

The sneakers shuffled back across the floor. The snick of a door closing.

Edie peeked around the front of the van. The garage was empty again. She gestured to Connie. They tiptoed across the cement floor to the big metal roll-up door.

But even with both of them tugging on it, it wouldn't go up.

Connie pointed to the ceiling. "It's got an automatic opener," she whispered. "Look for a button somewhere." She walked toward the door to the house.

Edie searched the walls near the garage door. She spotted what looked like a button back in a corner, cobwebs obscuring it.

She extended her hand toward it.

Shoes scuffling against cement behind her. Edie whirled around.

A woman stood behind her, a big gun in one hand. Several fur coats lay in a heap at her feet.

Her other arm was wrapped around Connie's neck.

CHAPTER TWENTY-NINE

Kate turned left off of York Road. A loud bleep. She jumped, bumping her head on the ceiling of the car.

In her rearview mirror, a blue light circled on the roof of the dark sedan behind her. The sun silhouetted the man in the driver's seat.

Great, I'm being pulled over for speeding.

She considered not stopping. Let the cop in the unmarked car follow her to her destination.

The siren bleeped again, a little longer this time.

No, no! A siren announcing their approach would be disastrous.

Kate pulled over to the curb. Should she try to explain or just let the cop give her a ticket? The latter might end up being quicker.

The dark sedan did not pull into the space behind her. Instead, it pulled up beside her car, blocking her in.

Panic sent Kate's heart bouncing around in her chest. She opened her door and jumped out. "Nooo," she yelled. Her knees wobbled, threatened to give out on her. She hung onto the door.

A man stepped out of the sedan and turned to look over his roof at her.

Her jaw dropped and her stomach clenched.

The smile on Detective Russell's face was not a friendly one. "Where are you going in such a hurry, Mrs. Huntington?"

While her brain was still trying to figure out what to do, her mouth blurted out, "Someone's kidnapped our daughter, to keep Skip from investigating the Strategic case."

The smile faded. Was that actual concern in the man's eyes?

"Skip thinks he knows who it is," she rushed on. "He's gone there. I've got the address."

Russell had circled his hood. He reached for her arm with one hand, his passenger door handle with the other.

No, he can't arrest me! She jumped back to avoid his grasp. "I'm not going anywhere with you." Her voice rose to an hysterical pitch. "I haven't done anything."

He grabbed her arm. "Get in."

Adrenaline shot through her. "No." She twisted her elbow, trying to pull loose, desperate to get away, to find her baby girl. Tears streamed down her cheeks. "Let go of me."

He held on, squeezing her arm. "I can get us there faster than you can."

She deflated. "Wha-?"

"I got a cryptic text from your husband. Now it makes more sense. Come on."

Her insides a wreck of jumbled emotions, she reached into her car, grabbed her purse and phone. Not bothering with the keys still in the ignition, she clambered into Russell's passenger seat.

He took off, his light flashing.

"No siren or they might kill–" She choked on the words and then was sobbing.

Russell ignored her as he maneuvered around the cars in front of him, some of which slowed and pulled over, some of which didn't.

Kate pulled the sheet of paper out of her purse and read off the address to him.

"Wait. That's not the address your husband gave me." He pulled over to the curb.

"What are you doing?" Kate heard the hysteria in her voice and tried to take a deep breath. The vise around her chest wouldn't let her.

He took the paper from her hands. "And that's not the suspect he named."

"But that's the one that was on top of the pile, the one Dolph said was a connection between the rumors and the Strategic case." Realizing that likely made no sense to the detective, she leaned over and pointed to the highlighted name at the bottom. "That's the suspect."

He shook his head. "That's not the woman he mentioned either."

He put his car in park. "Call your husband."

My baby, we've got to find my baby, her mind kept repeating as she punched the speed dial for Skip's cell. "Skip, I'm with Detective Russell–"

"Why'd he pick you up?"

"Never mind. Who are you going to see?"

"Beatrice Cooper. I think she's Paul Allen's accomplice. Why?"

"Oh." Her chest felt hollow. "I picked up the report you'd been reading and I thought it was somebody else."

The detective impatiently reached for her phone. Reluctantly, she let him take it.

"Russell here. Your wife had a completely different suspect in mind." He read off the names on the report. "So what are you two trying to pull with this circus?"

He listened for a few seconds, glanced at Kate, then listened again. "Okay, I'll meet you there. ETA thirteen minutes. *Don't* go in." He tossed the phone to Kate.

She wasn't expecting that and almost dropped it.

Russell flipped on his siren and pulled out into the street. "Don't worry I'll turn it off when we get close," he yelled.

Not sure whether Skip had disconnected, Kate put the phone to her ear, sticking a finger in her other one to block out the siren.

"You've got the right suspect, darlin'," Skip shouted. "The pieces all fit. It's one coincidence too many, who she used to be married to. I'll bet she started the rumors too."

Kate wasn't sure what all that meant but before she could ask any questions, he continued, "Call Mac and give him that address."

"Okay."

"I'm on that side of town, ten minutes from there at the most. I'll get our little girl back."

Fear for him jolted through her. "Skip!" she yelled into the phone.

But he'd disconnected.

She knew damn well he wouldn't wait for them.

~~~~~~~~

Edie and Connie sat at the kitchen table, their hands clasped in front of them on the table top as they'd been instructed.

"Go get the strips of cloth," the woman told Zac.

He froze for a moment, his wide eyes staring at the woman. "Why? What are you going to do?"

A strategy was forming in Edie's mind. "Why strips of cloth?" she said, her voice harsh. "So they're no rope marks on our corpses? You got some kind of accident planned for us?"

Zac's mouth dropped open. He rounded on the woman.

She laughed. "You've been watching too much TV, Edie. We're not going to hurt you, as long as you behave. Zac, go get the strips."

Dragging his feet, Zac headed for the door to the garage.

"*¡Corre si puedes!*" Edie whispered. She knew her pronunciation sucked but she hoped they were the right words for *run if you can.*

Connie's eyes went wide. Then the light in them changed. She blinked. "*Sí.*"

"Stop that chatter." The woman's face had morphed into a twisted mask. "You stupid fools."

Edie's empty stomach heaved. She glanced at Connie. Her friend's eyes were now huge in her pale face.

"If you'd stayed put in the storage room," the woman spat out, "I would've called your folks once we were gone, but now you've seen me."

Zac came back into the kitchen. His hands, full of clumps of white cloth, were shaking.

"You can't hurt them, Mom."

Mom?

The woman turned to him, her face relaxing. She was really pretty when she wasn't angry. "I'm not going to hurt them, Zac," she said in a calm voice. "Just tie their hands and feet to the chairs."

"The hell she isn't," Edie said. "She as much as said she's gonna kill us, while you were out of the room."

~~~~~~~~

Skip had parked so his truck was partially hidden behind the leafless skeleton of a big bush. From this spot, he could watch the house without being too obvious.

He called Mac. "Did Kate call you?"

"Yeah. One minute away," Mac growled in his ear.

Skip disconnected, and then he sent another text.

The man deserved to know what was going on.

Less than thirty seconds later, Mac's Hummer pulled up in front of the house three doors down. Mac jumped out and darted in his direction.

I'm not waiting for the police. The only thing that was stopping him from racing up to that house and tearing the hinges off the front door with his bare hands was the thought that getting himself killed would not save Edie.

Mac opened the passenger door and climbed in. "What's the plan?"

"You go around back. I'm going to the front door."

Mac pursed his lips, a sign that he didn't completely approve of that plan. But he didn't say anything.

Skip decided he was glad that Rose was tied up. She would've been much more resistant to such a crappy plan.

Mac got out of the car and slipped along the property line between the houses, using tree trunks and bushes as cover whenever he could. The outline of his pistol was silhouetted against the white of the neighbor's fence. He disappeared around the side of the house.

Skip got out and slowly approached the front, his own gun in his right hand, down behind his thigh.

~~~~~~~~~

"Please don't hurt them," Zac begged his mother. "That'll make me an accessory and I'll never get to come back and see Dad."

Edie glanced at a pair of men's sneakers, too big for Zac's feet, next to the kitchen door. She had a bad feeling. "Where is your dad, Zac?"

"He doesn't live here." Then he followed her line of vision. "Those are my stepdad's." He turned back to his mother. "What about Jason? You gonna leave dead bodies in the house for him to come home to." His voice was growing angry.

"Jason's a jerk," his mother said.

"Then why were you hanging all over him, all lovey-dovey yesterday morning?" Zac's voice rose in pitch. "Telling him to bring you something pretty to make up for him going hunting all weekend."

"Shut up, Zac. I'm trying to think."

"We could take them with us." His tone shifted to wheedling. "Let them go after we're out of the country."

"She's not gonna let us go," Edie said. "And she's not gonna let you come back to see your dad either."

Tears filled Zac's eyes. "You're not, are you, Mom? I'll never see Dad again."

The woman turned on him. "I said shut up and let me think!"

Connie bolted toward the door to the garage. Edie went the other way.

~~~~~~~~~

Skip tested the doorknob. It was locked, of course.

There was a panel of glass on one side of the door but not the other. He sidled over toward that blind side, then reached out with his left hand to knock.

His knuckles hadn't quite made contact when the door was wrenched open from within.

His daughter flew out and ran right into him.

CHAPTER THIRTY

Skip's hand instinctively grabbed for the porch railing to keep from falling. Edie clung to his waist. Somehow he managed not to drop the gun.

Yanking it up in front of him, his finger firm against the trigger, he froze.

Standing in the entrance hall was an older, grimmer version of the boy he'd seen in the photo on Kitt Kitterling's desk.

"Drop your gun." A woman's voice from behind the kid. "Or I'll kill you and your daughter right where you stand."

The woman stepped around the boy, a Glock in her hand.

"Hello, Elaine." He dropped his gun on a table by the door, while his other hand peeled Edie loose and maneuvered her behind him. Not that his body would necessarily protect her from a nine millimeter bullet from a Glock.

Elaine Patterson shook her head in mock sadness. "Skip Canfield, I thought I told you to leave things alone."

"I've never been real good at taking orders."

"Get in here and close the door."

His mind raced, considering options. If he yelled for Edie to run, Elaine might very well shoot her.

He moved forward a couple of steps, one hand on Edie's arm, keeping her behind him. With his other hand, he nudged the door most of the way closed, praying Elaine wouldn't notice that it hadn't latched.

Stalling, he said, "You missed your calling, Elaine. Should have gone into acting. I actually believed you and John Cochlin were lovers."

Her upper lip curled. "That little wimp. Zac, find Connie," she said to the boy.

Zac didn't move.

"Go," she yelled without taking her eyes off of Skip.

The kid headed down the hall, throwing a frightened look over his shoulder. He turned into an open doorway.

Skip called out, "Connie, did you take your medicine?" To Elaine he said, in a voice loud enough to carry, "She's diabetic." He hoped Connie would catch on to why he was lying and answer appropriately.

Not that he expected Elaine to care about the girl's health, since she probably planned to kill them all anyway. He was trying to distract her, and determine where Connie was.

A beat of silence. "She doesn't have it with her." Zac's voice from around a corner, most likely the kitchen.

Where the hell's Connie?

"Zac, tie her up," Elaine yelled. "To the chair, like I told you."

No answer.

"Zac, Mr. Canfield's just trying to upset you. She's *not* a diabetic."

Skip waited, his gaze locked on Elaine's face, his mind calculating the minimum number of steps needed to reach her.

"Zac?" She glanced toward the kitchen doorway.

Skip lunged, arms outstretched, grabbing for her gun hand. His weight took them both down. His hands clamped around hers, holding the Glock well away from them and Edie.

The gun went off, a roaring blast that kicked it up in the air. Glass shattered somewhere in the back of the house.

Praying the bullet hadn't hit Mac, Skip wrenched the pistol away from her. She bit into his flesh. Pain shot up his arm.

He resisted the urge to backhand her with the gun. Instead, he planted the heel of his hand on her forehead and forced her away from him. Her teeth let go.

His forearm stung like crazy.

One hand wrapped firmly around her arm, he struggled to his feet, bringing her up with him.

He glanced toward Edie. The front door crashed open, slamming into her and sending her flying.

Detective Russell stood in the doorway, his service revolver pointed at Skip's heart.

Skip's racing heart ratcheted up another notch. "It's her gun," he said quickly. "I just disarmed her." He raised his gun hand high in the air, the pistol's barrel pointed toward the ceiling, but he didn't dare drop it. If Elaine got away from him and got it... "Mine's on the table beside you."

Russell's gaze shifted to the table, but his gun stayed aimed at Skip. Then he stepped forward, took the pistol from Skip's hand and stuffed it in his waistband. He holstered his own gun and grabbed Elaine's other arm. "Elaine Patterson, you're under arrest for the murders of John Cochlin and Frederick Latey, and the kidnapping of...."

Skip tuned out the droning voice as Russell slapped handcuffs on Elaine's wrists. He darted over to where Edie sat on the floor, her legs sprawled out to either side, a stunned look on her face.

Suddenly, Mac was beside him, his gun nowhere to be seen.

"How'd you get in?" Skip whispered.

"Through the hole that cannon made in a back window. You okay, Edie?"

She nodded, then lifted her arms toward Skip, like she had as a little girl.

Skip picked her up, ignoring the protest from his back. She threw her arms around his neck, clinging to him and sobbing.

His chest swelled until he thought it might burst. Kissing the curls on the side of her head, he whispered, "You're okay now, Pumkin. Sh, sh, you're okay." Tears flowed down his own cheeks.

A large man suddenly filled the doorway, silhouetted against the light from outside.

Skip tensed, twisted to put himself between Edie and this new threat. Mac's gun appeared in his hand.

"Zachary?" the silhouette yelled.

Kitt. Skip flung out a hand in front of Mac. "Don't shoot."

"Zac, where are you?" Kitterling called out.

"In the yard, Dad," came faintly from behind him. "We're out here."

The man bolted from the porch.

Ellie, Kitt called his wife Ellie. That's why he hadn't made the connection.

Skip glanced at Elaine, then away as hot rage shot through him.

He put Edie, still snuffling, down on her feet and herded her toward the doorway.

Kitt was on his knees in the middle of the front yard, his arms around the boy, hugging him and crying.

Connie stood beside them. Kate was stooped down in front of her, hands on the girl's shoulders. Connie shook her head.

"Mommy!" Edie took off for her mother.

Kate's head jerked up. She was on her feet, running, then dropped to one knee and opened her arms.

CHAPTER THIRTY-ONE

Kate knocked gently on her daughter's bedroom door.

"Come in." Edie's voice sounded normal.

So far, so good. Kate nudged the door open and stuck her head in.

Edie was sitting cross-legged on her bed, bent over her sketch pad. From what Kate could see of her face, she wasn't as pale as she'd been yesterday when they'd brought her home, after several grueling hours at the police station.

Edie hadn't felt up to going to church this morning so Kate had stayed home with her. Skip had taken Billy to Sunday school. "I'll convey your gratitude to the Lord," he'd whispered as his lips brushed hers in a goodbye kiss.

"I assure you," Kate whispered back, "I've already expressed my thanks, multiple times."

Connie and Joe Pérez had been grounded by their father. "Until I calm down," Eduardo had said. Kate suspected that might take a few months.

But they'd gone easier on Edie, figuring she had learned the lesson of not going along with another kid's crazy idea. They'd restricted her phone use, however. She would take it to school for emergencies but no texting or calling her friends, except in the evenings after homework was done. And they would check the phone each evening, then it would be turned off and left in the kitchen, plugged in to charge, at bedtime.

Edie had protested this invasion of her privacy, until her father sternly pointed out that they could make the punishment much worse if she preferred.

Kate hadn't told her daughter about the tracking gizmo. She'd almost thrown it away, but had tossed it into a drawer instead. Just in case.

Kate walked to the end of the bed. "How are you doing, sweetie?"

"I'm fine," Edie mumbled without looking up.

Oh goody, we're back to surly preteen already.

"May I see what you're drawing?" she asked.

Edie's head came up. "Sure." Her voice sounded tentative.

Kate moved around the side of the bed. "May I sit down?"

Edie nodded, her eyes a tad wary.

Kate perched on the edge of the bed and leaned over to look at the drawing. With a jolt, she realized the face staring back at her was Maria's. The new, more sophisticated Maria.

Kate's throat tightened. "That's a very good likeness." She heard the strain in her own voice.

Edie turned her head and stared at her. "Do you miss her?"

Kate's eyes stung. "Every day."

Her little girl's face crumpled. Kate wrapped her arms around her.

Edie sobbed on her shoulder. "I miss her so much."

Kate rocked gently back and forth, comforting them both. "Me too, sweetie," she pushed past the tense muscles in her throat. "Me too."

Her chest constricted with guilt. How had she missed the signs? Edie wasn't just rebelling against her, she was grieving.

And part of grief was anger, but Edie couldn't direct that at her beloved Maria. The child was the essence of fairness, always had been. Kate was convinced she would someday be a diplomat, or maybe a judge. Edie knew Maria deserved to have her own life, to be married, to be happy.

Kate's throat closed completely. She struggled to swallow a sob. Eyes stinging, she stroked her daughter's hair.

The child's anger at Maria for abandoning her had been

shifted to her mother. Perhaps she was a safer target because Edie trusted that she wouldn't reject her. That thought warmed Kate's heart some.

She hugged her daughter close. "I love you," she whispered.

"I love you too, Mommy."

Oh my God! Help me remember this moment.

For surely the teenage angst was not done, but Kate now agreed with Skip and Liz. Somehow they would survive it.

Heat flooded her body, flushed her cheeks.

Damn, great time for a hot flash.

She caught herself in mid head shake. Edie might misinterpret the gesture.

Welcome to your new normal, Kate.

She pulled back slightly to look down into her daughter's face. "I was thinking about going to the hospital to see Uncle Rob. Do you want to go with me or stay here?"

Edie's eyes widened with surprise. "By myself?"

"Sweetie, not being comfortable with you being alone has nothing to do with not trusting *you*. It's about the reality that there are some not-so-nice people in the world who might hurt you, when Dad and I aren't around to protect you."

"Like Zac's mom."

"Yes, exactly. And there's the issue of your brother. We don't want you to be responsible for him, when he can be a bit impulsive."

Edie flashed a quick grin, then laid her head on her mother's shoulder again.

Kate's heart melted.

Edie leaned back, tilted her head to one side. "I'd like to go. I wanna see that Uncle Rob is really okay."

They arrived as the empty lunch trays were being gathered from the rooms. Not sure what the rules were about children, Kate used the chaos to slip past the nurses' station and shoo Edie down the hall to Rob's room.

A man in a business suit stood outside the door. When he turned toward her, Kate was surprised to see it was Detective Russell.

"Mrs. Huntington. Miss Huntington-Canfield." He gave Edie a salute and an indulgent smile. She had reminded him repeatedly yesterday of her full and correct name.

"Hi," Kate said. "What are you doing here?" It sounded rude, which hadn't been her intention, but Russell didn't seem to take offense.

"I was here anyway." He gestured toward the elevators. "Taking a stabbing victim's statement. I thought I'd stop by and tell Mr. Franklin in person that his client has been cleared of all charges."

Kate's muscles relaxed completely for the first time in weeks. "Thank you."

"After you, ladies." Russell gestured toward the door.

Rob's eyes lit up as they paraded single-file into his room. Oversized hospital gown was not his best look, but he seemed much improved since the last time Kate had seen him.

"Hey, Edie," he said, "how're you doing?"

"Everybody keeps asking me that. I'm fine."

"Edie!" Kate said. "Don't be rude. People are concerned because they care about you."

"Sorry." Edie sidled up to the side of Rob's bed. "Are you okay, Uncle Rob?"

Rob's eyes met Kate's and they both laughed.

"What? What's so funny?"

Kate shook her head. "Nothing, sweetie."

Rob reached out an arm and encircled Edie's waist. "I'm good now, but Aunt Liz says I have to retire."

Her eyes went wide. "Are you *that* old?"

He chuckled. "Well, I'm not sure what *that* old is, but I've gotta cut back on the stress so I don't have another heart attack." He looked at Kate. "Liz and I compromised. I'll keep my corporate clients, but no more new cases. Eventually, I'll only be teaching part-time."

Kate nodded. "Our careers seem to be following similar paths these days."

As well they should, said a voice inside her head that sounded an awful lot like Skip and Liz ganging up on her. With Maria gone from their household, she needed to cut back on her work hours, spend more time with the kids, quality time, not just supervising homework and their bedtime routine.

And also take better care of her aging body. It had been weeks since she'd been to an *aikido* class.

Her next thought was *I hope I like teaching.* And with that, the decision was made, she would let her private practice fade away by attrition and teach part-time until the kids were older, even if it meant skimming some of the dividends off of the brokerage account for a while.

The sense of relief that flooded her body took her by surprise, and validated the decision.

A throat clearing behind her. Russell stepped forward from where he'd been standing by the door of the private room.

"Good afternoon, Detective," Rob said. "Didn't know you made hospital calls."

"I was here on another matter, but I wanted to make sure you were okay. And let you know all charges have been dropped regarding your client."

"Thanks."

"How's your husband doing?" Russell asked Kate.

"Why?" Rob said in a worried voice. "What happened to Skip?"

"Mrs. Patterson bit him," Edie said, "when Daddy took her gun away from her."

Rob's face registered horror. He put his hand over his chest.

Kate sucked in her breath, then realized he was kidding when he smiled at Edie.

"Good thing I didn't know about all this until it was over," Rob said.

Edie giggled.

"What's happening with the case against Patterson?" Kate said to Russell. "Will you have enough evidence to convict her of the murders?"

Russell looked at Edie, then back at her, one eyebrow raised.

"If she's old enough to live through it," Kate said, "she's old enough to hear about the outcome." If only he knew some of the things her kids had survived. Then again, probably better he didn't.

Russell sighed. "I should give you the can't-comment-on-an-ongoing-investigation line, but I guess I owe you." He looked again at Edie.

"She knows the meaning of confidential," Kate said.

The detective nodded. "Mrs. Patterson isn't talking but Mr. Patterson had some interesting things to say. Seems his wife likes pretty things, the more expensive the better. Two years ago, he cut her off. Took away her credit cards and her checkbook, even took her name off the bank accounts. He started doling out a weekly allowance, a generous one, but one within their means. And he made her go to Debtors Anonymous. Then a few months ago, stuff started appearing around the house. A new sofa, for one."

Russell scratched his head. "He figured she'd somehow gotten a new credit card, and this time he was debating between another confrontation or filing for divorce."

He glanced at Edie again. "Your friend Zachary filled in some of the blanks too. He said his mom told him Thursday that he needed to help her get away or she'd go to jail."

"He's Connie's friend, not mine," Edie said in a sharp voice.

"Well, don't think too badly of him," the detective said. "His mom had promised him you two wouldn't be hurt. She just needed some leverage to get your dad to back off. When Zac realized she probably wasn't going to keep that promise and then your dad came in, he went out through the garage, like Connie had. We found them huddled behind a big bush."

"Daddy said he went along with his gambit about Connie

having diabetes too," Kate said. "That was quick thinking on his part. And it helped distract his mother so Daddy could get her gun."

Edie still had her face screwed up as if she'd tasted something sour.

Kate took a step over to the bedside and put a hand gently on her shoulder. "He's lost his mom, for all intents and purposes. You might try being friendly to him."

Edie looked up at her, and to Kate's amazement, she actually gave a small nod.

"Ironically," Russell said, "his mom's love of fancy things is what tripped her up. She could've taken off Friday, while we were chasing other leads. But she wasn't willing to leave without all her stuff."

"So you've dropped charges against Murdock," Rob said. "Does that mean you think Mrs. Patterson killed both men?"

It'll be a relief, Kate thought, *to only worry about Hal's social skills again, instead of trying to keep him out of jail.*

"Yes," Russell was saying, "but we might only be able to prove that she killed Cochlin. He hadn't closed that mailbox your husband told us about, Mrs. Huntington. He'd mailed a letter to himself there, to the false name he'd used to open the box. The letter was directed to his wife. An 'in the event of my death' type note.

"Patterson was paying him to help her get the details on the project. The night Ortiz was shot, Cochlin had gone to the lab, under Patterson's instructions, to get the last piece of info they needed from Murdock's computer. Something about a design problem that Murdock had fixed. He was also supposed to put some of his own data on Murdock's computer, to frame him for the spying. That's the part that had gotten to his conscience.

"He was copying files when he thought somebody had entered the lab, so he turned off the computer and lit out of there. He was halfway down the fire stairs when he heard two shots. He'd dropped the flash drive with the data on it somewhere along the way, so he'd been surprised when later that week, the payoff he'd been promised was in the maildrop."

"He didn't know who fired the shots?" Kate asked.

"Apparently not, but my guess is Patterson knew he was getting cold feet. Considering that she had a gun with her, she might've been planning to kill him there and claim she caught him stealing secrets. But then he took off and Ortiz arrived. She shot him, maybe hoping one or the other of the men would be blamed. She'd already planted seeds of doubt about Murdock, according to your husband and his partner."

Rob snorted. "Those fire stairs were awfully crowded that night."

Russell's mouth twitched up at the ends. "Yeah. For about five or ten minutes, that building was teeming with people who didn't know most of the others were there. I suspect Patterson had barely gotten out of there when the janitor came down. He was on the seventh floor when he heard the shots."

"And Elaine Patterson's probably the one who started the rumors about Skip's agency," Rob said. "The friend that Latey was doing a favor for, delivering that money."

Russell nodded. "I'm not a hundred percent positive Latey's death was murder. He had lost that contract, which probably meant his career was over. And he was having an affair—wait for it..." He looked at Rob, then Kate, "...with Elaine Patterson. Mrs. Latey said she'd known about it for several weeks but hadn't gotten up the nerve to confront her husband yet. She'd found a receipt for an expensive ring in his papers, and thought he'd bought it as a present for her. But then at the office Christmas party, she saw Patterson wearing a ring that matched the description on the receipt."

Kate wasn't all that surprised that Elaine and Latey were lovers. A woman as calculating as that would have seen him as an inside track to information, and she'd no doubt manipulated him to fire Skip's agency prematurely.

"So you may not be able to convict Patterson for that death,"

Rob said.

"No, but we've got forensic stuff to tie her to Cochlin's, including an envelope of money we found in her purse, with Cochlin's fingerprints on it."

Kate sucked in her breath. "She stole the money back that she'd paid him. That's why no one could find it." Her heart ached for poor Mrs. Cochlin.

Russell nodded again. "Either Patterson got smarter about cleaning up after herself with Latey, or his death really was a suicide. But with one murder charge, the industrial spying, attempted murder of Ortiz, and two counts of kidnapping a minor, we'll be putting her away for a very long time.

"Oh, and tell your husband Vice said thanks for the tip about that bar. They raided it last night. Got quite the haul of gamblers and crooks."

"Was Paul Allen there?" Kate actually felt bad for the guy, for anyone really, who was caught in the grip of an addiction.

"Yes, but if it's his first offense, he'll probably get a slap on the hand. Hawthorne, the CEO of Strategic told me they don't think he was involved in the spying. But he'll be on probation with them for a while, and required to attend Gamblers Anonymous."

"What about that woman, Beatrice Cooper?" Kate said. "Was she at the bar when they raided it?"

"No, but we've talked to her," Russell said. "I'm pretty sure it was purely accidental that her date took her to that joint the first time. But she recognized Allen and came back a few times to 'observe him'" He made air quotes.

Rob nodded. "So maybe she was trying to figure out if she *could* bribe him to reveal Strategic's secrets?"

Kate had been fighting the urge to say something totally flip. Her mature self lost the battle to the imp inside of her. "'Purely accidental,' Detective? In other words, it was a coincidence."

Russell winced. "Somehow I knew you weren't going to let that slide."

He turned to Rob and offered his hand. "You take care,

Counselor."

Then he reached across the bed and stuck his hand out toward Edie. With some hesitation, she put her much smaller one against his palm.

He held it gently and gave it a shake. "You gonna be up to testifying, Miss Huntington-Canfield?"

Edie's face lit up. "You bet."

Kate prayed she was as enthusiastic about that adult responsibility when the time came.

"Uh, Mr. Russell…," Edie said.

"Yes?"

"It might be easier if you called me Edie."

"Okay." He grinned. "And I'm Andy."

"Really?" Edie grinned back.

"Sure, first-name basis is first-name basis."

Russell turned to Kate. "Could I speak to you alone for a moment, Mrs. Huntington?"

"Sure," she smirked at him, "if you call me Kate."

He gave her a lopsided smile and gestured toward the door to the hall. Once out there, he said in a low voice, "You think she'll be okay testifying?"

"Yes, I do. She's a tough kid."

Russell chuckled. "Of course, she is. She's your kid. The defense probably won't be too hard on her. Doesn't look good to a judge and jury to pick on a child." He paused. "Uh, I wanted to ask you about something else."

"What?" Kate leaned a shoulder against the wall of the hallway.

"Is the task force meeting Tuesday night?"

"As far as I know."

"Could you get me on the agenda?"

She straightened. "Your point about political pressures was well taken, but we haven't been able to figure out a way to address that."

He shook his head. "I want to talk to them about something

else. I, uh…" He looked away, stared down the hall. "This case made me realize how close to burn out I am. The job makes you cynical. After a while, everybody's up to something, holding out on you, trying to obstruct justice, and that's the victims and witnesses. The people who are actually committing crimes, they're all scum bags. Even if all they did was shoplift a candy bar."

He turned his head back and met Kate's eyes. "That negativity, that's the biggest stressor of doing police work, in my opinion."

Again, she had underestimated this man. He was far more astute than she'd assumed.

And the task force needed to hear what he had to say. "I'll tell you what, Andy. You can have my slot on the agenda."

He smiled and extended his hand. Kate shook it with enthusiasm.

~~~◇~~~

AUTHOR'S NOTES

If you enjoyed this book, please take a moment to leave a short review on your favorite online ebook retailer. Reviews help to sell books and sales help me keep the series going! You can readily find the links to these retailers at the *misterio press* bookstore.

We at *misterio press* take pride in producing top quality books for our readers. All manuscripts are proofread several times, but proofreaders are human. If you noticed any errors in this book, please e-mail me at lambkassandra3@gmail.com and let me know about them. Thank you!

Please bear with me as I pass around some much deserved gratitude, ramble a bit about the topics in this story, and then I'll give you a hint about the next book in the series.

I am eternally grateful to all those people who help fine-tune and polish my stories. A big thank you to my beta readers, this time including Marilyn Hiliau, whose comments were so encouraging and helpful. And much gratitude as well to my partner in crime at *misterio press*, Shannon Esposito, who read and critiqued this book first, to my wonderful editor, Marcy Kennedy, who helped me unkink and tighten up several places in its rather complicated plot, and to sister *misterio* author, K.B. Owen, who made sure the whole thing still made sense with a final critique and initial proofread. And as always, love and kisses to my patient husband who gave it the final proofread (after I'd messed with it some more).

And a special debt of gratitude to my brother for this one. He always beta-reads and gives feedback on guy stuff and guns, but this time, his input was even more valuable, since he worked for a government contractor that made drones for the Army, in their test laboratory. He provided the information on security, both electronic and physical, at such a contractor's facility. I have fudged a few things for the sake of the story. It would be unlikely, for example, that a contractor would frisk his own employees on their way out. Also, compartmentalization of a project, while not unheard of, is rare. (Any other mistakes regarding this aspect of the story are strictly mine.)

I'd originally intended for the drone issue to play a bigger part in the story, but that never quite panned out. And it's probably just as well, since there were already several subplots going on.

My apologies to Shawn Mendes for appropriating his tour schedule. He was in Baltimore this past August. Hopefully he will come to that fair city again in the future, so Edie can actually get to see her idol.

The Baltimore Arena has a long history. It was built on the same site where the Continental Congress once met in 1776. It opened when I was ten years old and for most of my childhood and adolescence it was called the Baltimore Civic Center. It's gone through several name changes, the most recent in 2014 to Royal Farms Arena. In addition to sports events, it has hosted concerts by many musicians, including the Beatles, Led Zeppelin, Elvis Presley, the Grateful Dead and Bruce Springsteen.

Also apologies to the Baltimore City police chief for giving him more work to do, in addition to his already busy schedule, by placing him on a fictitious task force.

I plan to explore the whole issue of PTSD in police officers and the tensions in many communities between police and citizens of color in the next book, tentatively titled *Police Protection*. I hope to show that there are many facets to this complicated issue, while also entertaining you, the reader, with another Kate Huntington mystery.

That book, #10, may very well be the last in the series. That is my intention at this time, but then I'd intended to make *Anxiety Attack* the last one, until a new story idea popped into my head.

So there is always hope that we will be checking in again with Kate and the gang later on down the road.

Part of this decision comes from the stresses of juggling two series, Kate and my newer one, the Marcia Banks and Buddy cozy mysteries.

I don't have *Police Protection* far enough along to even give you a synopsis just yet, but below is one for Book 3 in the Marcia and Buddy series.

The Call Of The Woof, A Marcia Banks and Buddy Mystery

Combat veteran Jake Black has always had a wild streak that marriage and raising a child have done little to tame, especially since his wife shares his passion for motorcycles. But when he came back from the Middle East with a traumatic brain injury and PTSD, it looked like he would be sidelined... until Marcia Banks trained his service dog Felix to ride in a sidecar.

Being able to ride his beloved bike has given Jake the will to live again and to heal from his injuries, physical and emotional. But now his freedom and even his life are on the line once more. He and his wife have been accused of robbing a local pawn shop. Their rather distinctive motorcycles were seen roaring away from the crime scene.

Marcia Banks and her mentor dog, Buddy—who are at loose ends while their house is being fumigated for termites—jump in to help clear them. But myths and misconceptions about bikers, TBI, and PTSD complicate the investigation. And Marcia's sheriff boyfriend is not happy that she's once again putting herself at risk, and taking him along on her wild ride.

ABOUT THE AUTHOR

Kassandra Lamb has never been able to decide which she loves more, psychology or writing. In college, she realized that writers need a day job in order to eat, so she studied psychology. After a career as a psychotherapist and college professor, she is now retired and can pursue her passion for writing. She spends most of her time in an alternate universe with her characters. The portal to this universe, aka her computer, is located in Florida, where her husband and dog catch occasional glimpses of her. She and her husband spend part of each summer in her native Maryland, where her Kate Huntington series is based.

Kass is currently working on Book 10 of the Kate Huntington mystery series and Book 3 of the Marcia Banks and Buddy cozy mysteries. She also has four novellas out in the Kate on Vacation series (lighter reads along the lines of cozy mysteries but with the same main characters as the Kate Huntington series).

To read and see more about Kassandra and her characters you can go to http://kassandralamb.com. Be sure to sign up for the newsletter there to get a heads up about new releases, plus special offers and bonuses for subscribers. (New subscribers get a free e-copy of the first Kate on Vacation novella.)

Kass's e-mail is lambkassandra3@gmail.com and she loves hearing from readers! She's also on Facebook (https://www.facebook.com/kassandralambauthor) and hangs out some on Twitter @KassandraLamb. She blogs about psychological topics and other random things at http://misteriopress.com.

Please check out these other great *misterio press* series:

Karma's A Bitch
(Pet Psychic Mysteries)
by Shannon Esposito

To Kill A Labrador
(Marcia Banks and Buddy Mysteries)
by Kassandra Lamb

Maui Widow Waltz
(Islands of Aloha Mysteries)
by JoAnn Bassett

The Metaphysical Detective
(Riga Hayworth Mysteries)
by Kirsten Weiss

Dangerous and Unseemly
(Concordia Wells Mysteries)
by K.B. Owen

Murder, Honey
(Carol Sabala Mysteries)
by Vinnie Hansen

Steam and Sensibility
(Sensibility Grey Steampunk Mysteries)
by Kirsten Weiss

Bound
(The Witches of Doyle Trilogy)
by Kirsten Weiss

Plus even more great mysteries/thrillers at
http://misteriopress.com/misterio-press-bookstore/